Shantuu

Raymond
Lozada-Negron

<u>Shantuu</u>
<u>Raymond Lozada-Negron</u>
<u>Copyright 2022</u>

Raymond Lozada-Negron
<u>Website:</u>
www.amazon.com/author/ray_loz_neg

Other novels & theatrical plays by
Raymond Lozada-Negron

Novels

Durango the Bounty Hunter Trilogy

#1. Bounty Hunter from Mars

#2. Starman

#3. Savior of the Universe

Note: Although there is a continuous storyline from Book #1 to Book #2 to Book #3 of the Durango the Bounty Hunter Trilogy, the novels do not need to be read in sequential order, the novels were written where they can be read individually in any order.

Planet X

Shantuu

Theatrical Plays

The Stupidvisor

The Stupidvisor goes Nuclear

The Werewolf from Another Planet

The Monkeyhouse

Never Trust a Junky

I'm going to kill you

My Land is No Land

Monsters (A Short Play)

Shantuu

Raymond Lozada-Negron

Preface

These once untold tales
told yonder
may not be
as
fictional
as
imagined.

Shantuu
Raymond Lozada-Negron

PROLOGUE

Long ago, where the buffalo roamed freely, where edible fruits and other vegetations sprouted as wild as wild, how near and how far, from the breasts of Mother Earth, where the eagle flew high in the clear blue skies, across the prairie plains, over the vast mountaintops, lonesome canyons, raging rivers, feral forests, and dusty deserts, long ago, hundreds of years long ago, thousands of years long ago, millions of years long ago, nobody remembers exactly how long ago, where only the native tribes at the dawn of civilization and the forever few scattered others of the first of the Citizenry to walk the Earth - who learned to speak in the tongues of the first of the first languages - Chaktutu and Teetak were hiding inside a cave dwelling hiding from a pride of lions and lionesses and their cubs - baby lions and baby lionesses.

This was a new, unknown cave dwelling Chaktutu and Teetak had run off to and found, due to the necessity of not wanting to be eaten by so many unruly and hungry lions and lionesses. Chaktutu and Teetak, are, what will be known in the far future as - Bigfoots, Sasquatches, and Yetis. This new, unknown cave dwelling went only so far into the ridge of the small canyon they had run off to, as far enough to hold maybe only four or five of their kind and then there was nothing. It was more so a hovel than a cave dwelling. Chaktutu and Teetak found a few boulders to make the small opening they had crawled through even smaller. They were temporarily safe from being eaten by the lions and lionesses, but for how long? The lions and lionesses remained outside the mouth of the cave opening waiting. The ferocious predators had all the time in the world while Chaktutu and Teetak had only a few fruits and a few strips of meat to keep them nourished for a day, no more. They had no water. Every once and a while one or two of the lions and lionesses would claw away at the boulders at the opening of the cave which was keeping them from their prey – their prey being Chaktutu and Teetak.

"What are we going to do?" Teetak asked Chaktutu.

Chaktutu had always been deferred to by default as the leader of whatever pack he had become part of that had come to be banded together - most of the time – and other packs, or miscellaneous groupings, which were early unofficial formations of a haphazard form of what would become to be known in the future as a Citizenry, or Citizenries. Everyone, after a while, would eventually come to respect Chaktutu's opinion and would go to him for advice and counseling. Many arguments were settled by whatever Chaktutu proclaimed to be just and unjust.

"I do not know, Teetak. It looks as if we have been cornered."

"Will they ever leave?" Meaning the lions and lionesses.

Chaktutu was uncertain. "There are too many of them. Some of the other of them can go away and come back while some of the other of them can remain, guarding us, watching us, waiting, until we starve to death and then they will be able to push away, unhindered, the few boulders we have erected to block them from coming in and devouring us."

"But they are too big to fit through the small opening even if they pushed away the few small boulders we have piled upon the opening."

"Yes, many are too big, but not all of them. Their cubs will be able to fit through the small opening and either devour us inside, at their leisure, bit by bit, or tear us into smaller pieces and bring out the smaller pieces to share with the others."

While Chaktutu and Teetak were nearly over eight-foot (2.44 meter) tall themselves, the adult lions and lionesses were almost twice their size; being fourteen-foot (4.27 meter) to sixteen-foot (4.88 meter) from nose to buttocks; you could add a few foots (meters) more for their tails.

After waiting patiently until the sun began sinking below the horizon Chaktutu and Teetak, for the hundredth time, peeked through the cracks in the pile of boulders blocking the entrance to their cave hideaway/trap/prison – the lions and lionesses where still there, also waiting patiently.

"Do they not have other tasks better to attend to?" Teetak asked Chaktutu who did not answer. They took turns sleeping that night with Chaktutu keeping one arm resting against the pile of boulders blocking the entrance to the cave in case Teetak inadvertently fell asleep and the lions and lionesses happened to dislodge enough of the pile of boulders to break through into the cave – the sudden movements of the boulders would immediately awaken Chaktutu.

That morning the lions and lionesses where still out there patiently waiting and Chaktutu and Teetak were still inside their cave hideaway/trap/prison.

And then suddenly the world went black! The splinters of light seeping through the cracks on the pile of boulders at the cave entrance turned dark. Chaktutu and Teetak struggled to peek through the cracks to no avail. Outside the world had gone from day to night in an instant followed by a deafening roar and an immense rattling of not only the pile of boulders blocking the cave entrance but also everything else inside and outside the cave and the surrounding areas around and beyond the ridge of the small canyon Chaktutu and Teetak had run off to and become entrapped.

The world exploded! It was as if the earth, moon, and all the stars in the sky had collided! The boulders at the cave entrance were flung to and fro as if they were weightless pebbles, several of which had smashed against Chaktutu and Teetak, but not fatally.

"The lions and lionesses!" Chaktutu heard Teetak shouting out, but only barely; the fury of the wind and the shaking of the ground were like thousands of banshees shrieking, whining, crying!

Chaktutu and Teetak were engulfed by a whirling cloud of dust swirling around inside and outside the cave. The dust felt like fire in their eyes and fire on their eyelids after they had instinctively closed their eyes; but the burning sensation continued, burning their faces, necks, chests, backs, and arms and legs.

For more than a few moments Chaktutu and Teetak imagined their flesh being ripped from their bones. Teetak awoke later. He did not know how long later. It could have been minutes, or hours, or days later. Teetak was still unsure as the fog was slowly clearing from his cluttered mind. The dust from the whirling cloud had left a sludge-like residue wedged inside the cracks and crevices of Teetak's eyes, ears, mouth, and in every other exposed orifice of his body. After Teetak had wiped away enough of the muck from his eyes he saw through the small opening at the entrance of the cave – Chaktutu – standing motionlessly, outside the cave entrance, as if he were frozen, staring at the horizon.

"What is it, Chaktutu?"

Teetak was saying as he was walking towards the small opening at the entrance of the cave to make his way to where Chaktutu was standing. Teetak was no longer worried about the lions and lionesses that had been stalking them. If Chaktutu was standing outside the cave entrance without having been devoured by the lions and lionesses, it was clearly evident that the lions and lionesses had run off because of what had just occurred - it was in their nature – the Kings and Queens of the deserts, wildernesses, forests, and jungles of the world were as fickle as they were ferocious.

"So, our unfriendly new friends have scattered and gone their own separate ways to pursue other more meaningful endeavors." Teetak was saying as he was stepping out through the small cave opening to stand beside Chaktutu.

"I do not think so." Chaktutu said as he was pointing to what Teetak had seen him staring at from inside the cave.

There was a gigantic hole in the ground, where before there had been none, as big as the melancholy moon in the darkest of the darkest night sky. It was a massive crater as deep as it was wide. The opposite end of the crater extended further than the naked eye can see. At the center of the crater was a giant rock as big as the broken off tip of a mountain or an iceberg floating in the oceans of the Artic and Antarctic.

Curiouser and curiouser – the giant rock was illuminated, glowing, giving off light like a beacon - sapphire blue, emerald green, diamond white, ruby red. Chaktutu gestured to the walls of the cliffs behind them. There where what appeared to be a few lion furs spread out hanging randomly on the sides of the cliff. Teetak looked closer. The lion furs appeared to have red stains interspersed between the gold, yellow, and brown, of the lion furs. Teetak looked even closer. The lion furs where not randomly detached furs hanging on the sides of the cliffs as if a furrier had purposely put the furs there to allow the furs to naturally dry in the heat of the daylight sun. The lion furs were the carcasses of the lions and lionesses who had been hunting Chaktutu and Teetak the day before and for all of the night the day after. The lions and lionesses were more so splattered against the cliffs walls, unintentionally, as if by some reckless, relentless, unforgiving force.

Chaktutu was watching Teetak as Teetak was looking back and forth from the walls of the cliffs to the giant glowing rock down below at the center of the massive crater.

"The giant rock had fallen from the sky."
Teetak was saying as Chaktutu was nodding in agreement.

"The force from the giant rock was as powerful as the most powerful of storms."
Chaktutu continued nodding.

"The lions and lionesses had been picked up, spun, tossed, and turned to mush."

"And we would have been, too, also, had it not been for the cave that had protected us from the mighty forces of the gigantic rock falling from the sky."
The packs and miscellaneous groupings of Bigfoots, Sasquatches, and Yetis, which would eventually become to be known in the future as Citizenries, had no word for meteor – sky rock – is what the meteor had become to be referred to as.

Chaktutu and Teetak made their way down the slanted slope of the crater the sky rock had made after it had collided with a stubborn, remorseless, taciturn, Earth, falling and stumbling one too many times until they reached the bottom and stood at the edge of the sky rock, which was not as big as a mountain, but as big as a small hill. There were broken off bits and pieces of the sky rock scattered everywhere, some as small as apples and oranges, and even as smaller as berries and grapes, others as big as cantaloupes and melons, and even bigger, as big as Chaktutu and Teetak, and even bigger than that. The sky rock was hot, but not too hot for Chaktutu and Teetak to touch with their bare hands, but as hot as if Chaktutu and Teetak had been standing too close to a cave fire. They were instantly sweating. Their furs were moistened in a matter of minutes from the sweat pouring out of their pores from the heat of the sky rock.

Chaktutu picked up a small piece of the sky rock about the size of an apple and an orange and was examining the small piece in his hand all the while thinking that it was too hot and that he wished he was on top of a snowy mountain ridge breathing in the cool mountain air with the cool mountain wind brushing against his face and back. Chaktutu stepped forward to touch the enormous, bigger, gigantic sky rock with the smaller piece of the sky rock still in his hand.

In one moment Chaktutu was standing there beside Teetak at the bottom of the massive crater and then the next moment Chaktutu was standing on a snowy mountain ridge just like he had been imagining, all alone, by himself. Chaktutu, in a panic, immediately dropped the small piece of the sky rock he was holding in his hand.

"Teetak! Teetak! Where are you! Teetak! What happened?" Chaktutu kept shouting out, but Teetak was nowhere to be found.

"Teetak!" Chaktutu kept shouting out louder and louder.

14

Teetak did not answer him back. The only sound Chaktutu heard was the whistling of the cool mountain wind.

Chaktutu gazed down at the palm sized piece of the sky rock he had been holding in his hand. There had to be a connection there. What was it about the enormous, bigger, gigantic sky rock that had fallen from the sky and the smaller piece of the sky rock he had been holding in his hand? Chaktutu gingerly picked up the smaller piece of the sky rock, holding the smaller piece of the sky rock between his thumb and pointer finger as he was still trying to imagine what had happened to Teetak.

In one moment Chaktutu was there standing on the snowy mountain ridge and then the next moment he was back at the bottom of the crater standing beside Teetak who stumbled backwards and fell over in shock after seeing Chaktutu suddenly disappearing and reappearing.

"Chak-Chak-Chak-tu-tu! What happened to you! Where did you go? Teetak asked Chaktutu.

Chaktutu's mind was exploding like a volcano erupting. He was looking back and forth from the smaller piece of the sky rock in his hand to the enormous, bigger, gigantic sky rock.

Was it because of what he was imagining? That what had occurred - had occurred? Chaktutu was thinking and thinking and thinking. Dare I try again? Chaktutu was thinking and thinking and thinking. Yes, no, yes, no, yes, no, yes, no, and then, why not?

Teetak was watching as Chaktutu held up the broken off smaller piece of the sky rock he was holding in the palm of his hand as he was stepping back and nonchalantly resting his other hand on the side of the enormous, bigger, gigantic sky rock.

Teetak watched in amazement as Chaktutu disappeared into thin air right before his very eyes.

"Chaktutu!" Teetak cried out, but not very loudly. Teetak knew deep down in the bottom of his heart that it was futile to call out to Chaktutu. Chaktutu was no longer there. How? Why? By what means? Teetak was not sure. Then several minutes later Chaktutu reappeared, standing before Teetak, standing where he had been standing only moments before.

"Chaktutu." Teetak repeated, but very quietly this time, so quietly it was as if Teetak was whispering. "Come!"

Chaktutu said to Teetak as he was tossing the smaller broken off piece of the sky rock to Teetak who reluctantly caught the smaller broken off piece of the sky rock in his hand.

"Do you remember?"

Chaktutu was saying to Teetak as he was bending down to pick up another palm size broken off piece of the sky rock.

"Do you remember Teetak when we were further away way over the many mountains and valleys we have traveled and many other mountains and many other valleys we have traveled? Do you remember the cool, fresh waters of the stream where there were more trout, salmon, catfish, and tuna than we were able to eat?"

"Where there were even as many more fruits and vegetables." Teetak added. "Hanging from as many more trees and as many more growing from the ground, so many, too many, for us to carry or store for the winter."

"Do you remember Teetak? Remember Teetak! Remember!"

Teetak's eyes were closed as he was remembering, envisioning, remembering, envisioning, the cool, fresh waters, of the most plentiful stream and woodlands they had come across in so many long hot summers and so many long cold winters.

"Are you remembering Teetak?" Chaktutu asked Teetak."

"I am remembering." Teetak said to Chaktutu.

"Touch the enormous, bigger, gigantic sky rock with your other hand." Chaktutu said to Teetak as he was about to do so himself standing still with his own other hand inches away from the enormous, bigger, gigantic sky rock.

Teetak did as he was told and touched the enormous, bigger, gigantic sky rock with his other hand. With his eyes still closed he felt the ground below his feet change and the wind brushing against his face and back change. Where before it was hot and he was sweating, he was now cool and there was an even cooler wind whipping around his chest, face, back, and between his legs.

Teetak opened his eyes.

He was no longer standing at the bottom of the crater by the enormous, bigger, gigantic sky rock. He was standing by the stream he was remembering, envisioning, remembering, envisioning.

What?

How?

What had happened?

And then in another instant Chaktutu was standing beside Teetak standing beside the cool, fresh stream they had left behind so long ago.

What?

How?

What had happened?

Chaktutu answered Teetak as if he were reading Teetak's mind.

"The sky rock is magic!"

Teetak remained speechless as Chaktutu was making his way to the stream to scoop up a trout or two to fill his belly.

"It is magic! Magic! There can be no other explanation!"

You could hear the splash, splash, splash of Chaktutu stepping into the stream and then standing still to keep from frightening away any unlucky fish swimming by close enough for him to swoop down and grab up with one quick lightning-fast thrust.

"There!"

Chactutu had found one. It was a salmon. Chactutu bit off the head of the salmon and then proceeded to swallow the other half of the salmon all the while as he was licking his lips and smacking his gums in ravenous delight.

"Ah!" Chaktutu had caught another fish, another salmon, which he tossed to Teetak, who ignored Chaktutu's gift, allowing the salmon to bounce off of his chest and fall to the ground by his feet, flopping up and down and up and down and up and down; even though Teetak was practically starving after having been trapped inside the cave for far too long without enough sustenance to replenish his depleted natural energy reserves.

Teetak was still in shock.

"Can we travel back, just as we had come?" Teetak asked Chaktutu.

"I assume so. There and back, and there and back again, and to anywhere, we imagine!"

Teetak was staring at the broken off smaller piece of the sky rock in the palm of his hand.

After a few more moments Teetak said to Chaktutu as he was bending down to pick up the salmon Chaktutu had offered him.

"We will be like Gods!"

"We will be that and more! All of us! All of our kind!"

And so that was how the Citizenry was born thousands of years ago.

CHAPTER ONE

It was a beautiful morning out here in the wilderness of the Colorado Rockies. Professor Robert Salinas was enjoying a day of hiking and picnicking with his wife Anna and their nine-year-old daughter Mira. Robert Salinas was a Professor of Anthropology at Colorado State University, and his wife Anna was a heart surgeon at Saint Joseph Hospital in Denver. They had taken a canoe several miles downriver and where presently walking along a trail beside a rocky hilltop.

Professor Salinas was squinting at something faraway in the nearby horizon. He pointed with his finger.

"Look there! That ridge higher up! That looks like a nice place to stop for lunch!"

His wife Anna had to agree. "The view from up there must be subliminal!"

"Can we roast some marshmallows?" Their daughter Mira inquired.

"Of course, Sweet pea." Professor Salinas said to his daughter. "Be careful now as you're walking along. We don't want you to trip and fall and hurt yourself."

"Like the other day when I scraped my knee."

That made Professor Salinas chuckle. "Yes, like the other day when you scraped your knee."

They laid out a picnic blanket that day on a clifftop ledge and enjoyed a meal together overlooking the valleys and streams of the Colorado Rockies.

Mira remembered that day as the best and worst day of her life.

If her father wasn't too busy teaching and lecturing, or her mother wasn't running back and forth all the time between one trauma center or hospital emergency room, when they were at home, they were always still always too busy studying and working. Mira understood. What her parents were doing was important. Her mother was saving lives and her father was unlocking the mysteries of the evolution of the human race and species known and unknown, and in particular of the species unknown were that of the Bigfoot, Sasquatch, and Yeti. Many times, while Mira was home alone, she would ruffle through her father's study examining the artifacts and papers he always had lying about. One day she asked her father, why did he have so many drawings and statues of big gorillas scattered all around his study. He even had a statue of a gorilla's hand, which he sometimes used as a paper weight. They're not gorillas, he told Mira, they are Bigfoots, or Sasquatches, or in the north and south poles they are called Yetis, and their fur is supposed to be white instead of brown, black, or gray. Mira remembered playing with the big, heavy, plaster rendition of a Bigfoots hand. It was then that she also became interested in Bigfoots, sasquatches, and Yetis. Are they real? Or are they just a legend? A myth? Told around campfires, along with other scary stories of ghosts, ghouls, and goblins?

As they continued walking along the ridge making their way to the bottom where Mira's parents had parked the range rover, there was suddenly the sound of a rumble coming from up above, along the side the cliff, a rumble like a giant burping. Professor Salinas looked up for a moment. There was another rumbling sound coming from up above followed by a click, crack, click sound which echoed along the deep void of the canyon they had come to explore on their hike. The click sound reverberated like the screeching of an eagle or the howling of a wolf.

Click-click-click, ca-click, ca-click, ca-click, click-click-click, ca-click, ca-click, ca-click, click-click-click-click-click-click.

For a few moments more there was nothing. A shocked expression came over Professor Salinas's face. Mira's mothers seemed even more concerned.

"Quickly! But quietly! As Quietly as possible begin heading down and do not stop, not even for a moment!" Professor Salinas said to them, but before they had taken no more than a few steps more, there was another rumble, this time the rumble was followed by what seemed like a long-drawn-out yarn – then all hell broke loose!

The first few rocks that fell downward from up above the cliff where small, fist size, then three to four boulders, the size of a full-grown man or woman came crashing down. Mira would always relive the living nightmare in her mind as it had happened in slow motion. One of the three to four boulders struck her mother, squashing her, and then sending her somersaulting over the ridge, down the side of the cliff. Her father shouted out to Mira. Run! Run back the other way! Another oversized boulder struck Mira's father on the shoulder, almost sending him falling over the ridge, but he seemed to roll and bounce and roll and bounce backward. It was then that Mira was blinded by smaller falling debris. She slipped and fell over the edge. There was a branch sticking out from the side of the cliff. Mira quickly reached out and grabbed hold of the branch. The rest of the falling debris fell over her head to disappear in the canyon down below. The landslide had stopped Just as quickly as it had started. Professor Salinas was frantically crying out to his wife and daughter.

"Mira!" "Anna!" "Anna!" "Mira!" "Please God! No! Please God! Nooooo! No!" "Please spare Anna and Mira!" "Anna!" "Mira!" "Anna!" "Mira!"

Mira could hear footsteps coming from up above.

"Oh no! Oh my God! Don't move Mira! Hold on! Hold on tight!"

Mira saw her father's head peeking over the ridge from up above.

"Hold on tight! Hold on tight! I'll be right there! I'll be right there!"

He was saying to her.

Mira had only fallen maybe fifteen feet (4.57 meters) over the ridge before she had, luckily, come across the branch sticking out from the side of the cliff.

"Don't' look down! Mira! Don't look down!"

There was something there in her father's eyes as he was looking at her and at something else, something that had frightened and shocked him.

Her father began sobbing.

"Don't look down, my dear, don't look down."

This time her father's tone was fragile, less brusque, more regretful.

Melancholy.

Mira's father was begging her not to look down with an intense, sincere, profound, sadness, the like of which Mira will never, ever, experience ever again in the course of her whole entire lifetime.

"Don't look down, baby, please, don't look down."

There were tears in her father's eyes, yet she obeyed him, still.

She did not look down.

Mira's father began a slow crawl down the side of the ridge, crawling, climbing, descending, towards his daughter hanging onto the fragile branch limb sticking out from out of the side of the cliff. As he was crawling, climbing, descending, down the side of the ridge, they both heard the slight cracking sounds of the branch limb slowly being stretched beyond the limits of its ability to sustain the weight of the poor child dangling helplessly from its unforgiving grasp.

"Hold on, baby, hold on!"

Professor Salinas kept saying to his frightened daughter. He made the fifteen-foot (4.57 meters) jaunt down to where his daughter was hanging on for her life on the branch limb, but only to where the bottom of his boots came into contact with the top of Mira's head. He could climb down no further. There was nothing there for him to hang onto, or to use to descend further.

"Grab on to my boot, Mira, grab on to my boot and then hold on with every ounce of energy you have!" Professor Salinas was saying to his daughter as he was simultaneously reaching down with one hand to grab onto her the moment she was able to climb up to as far as his ankle.

"You can do it, Mira! You can do it!"

Mira managed to get a toe hold on a crack in the ridge and in one quick push, she let go of the branch limb and grabbed onto the top of her father's boot and in another quick push, she lifted herself up and was able to grab hold of her father's boot with both hands, just in a miracle, once in a lifetime, nick of time. The moment Mira let go of the branch limb was the moment the branch limb could no longer sustain the weight of its unwanted visitor. The branch limb broke off from the side of the cliff and was sent tumbling all the way down below to the bottom of the canyon.

"Climb up my leg, just a little, Mira, just a little, and then I'll be able to grab hold of you! Just a little Mira! Just a little!"

Mira did as she was told. The second she was far enough up the side of her father's leg he did as he had promised. He grabbed hold of his daughter and gently lifted her up to where she could grab hold of his shoulders.

"Careful now, Mira, careful! Wrap your arms around my neck! You can do it Mira! You can do it!" She did do it. She wrapped her arms around her father's neck and held on for dear life.

"Hold on baby! Don't let go! I'm going to start climbing to the top! Hold on baby! Don't let go!"

Professor Salinas was breathing extra hard. Mira could feel the lungs inside her father's chest expanding and contracting, expanding and contracting, expanding and contracting, in syncopation with his heaving, rasping, scratching, breath.

Professor Salinas began slowly climbing upwards towards the top to the ridge nearby up ahead.

"Hold on baby! Don't let go! Hold on baby! Don't let go! Hold on baby! Don't let go!" Professor Salinas kept repeating to his daughter. He made it twelve feet (3.66 meters) up the ridge, three feet (0.91 meters) short of where he would be able to lean one arm over and grab hold of the flat, topside of the ridge, where he will be able to hoist himself up with his daughter, up and over the ridges edge to safety. All of a sudden they both heard it. That unsettling sound of the snapping and crackling of the rocks and muck that made up the cliffs edge. They both knew it was going to happen in an instant. The rocks and muck they were hanging onto, holding onto with their lives, was going to break and fall apart at any moment.

"There's no time to think! Mira! Just do as I say! I'm going to lift you up off my back and I want you to grab hold of whatever you can grab hold of and flip over onto the flat side of the ridge! Just do it! Don't think! And remember! Remember what your Mother and I taught you about survival! Remember! Survival! Survival comes first before crying and worrying and feeling sorry for yourself! Survival! Survival first! Everything else is second!"

Mira could feel her father taking one more deep breath before he shouted out at the top of his lungs – "Now Mira!" Professor Salinas in one quick lunge, hoisted his daughter up, or more so, flung his daughter up and over the cliffs, rickety, ridge, edge, and then, when the snapping and crunching was overcome by one, quick, long, whoosh! Professor Salinas, Mira's father, fell over the side of the cliff, all the way down to the bottom of the canyon, bumping and twirling, and twirling and spinning, a few times, and bumping against the rocky side of the cliff a few times more, until Mira, up on top, heard a shallow, distant, thud.

"Daddy! Daddy!" For a moment Mira was afraid to look. She knew what had happened. She didn't need to look.

Mira's father was lying, twisted and bent, motionless, without making one, single, solitary sound, at the bottom of the canyon, over the boulders and rocks that had crushed her Mother to death only moments before.

"Daddy!" Mira kept whimpering.
There was nothing she could do. In the back of her mind, she knew that to be true, but her heart was struggling to except that.

"Daddy! Mommy! Please don't go! Please don't go!"

It was a rhetorical lamentation. The broken bodies of Mira's father and mother were lying there at the bottom of the canyon. Their souls had moved on, gone to wherever souls may go, after they did not need their bodies, or their bodies could no longer sustain their souls, or when they have been called up to Heaven by God.

"Survival…"

It was as if a voice from beyond this world, a voice from another world, was speaking to Mira inside her mind or whispering in her ear.

"Survival…"

Mira was simultaneously hearing her father and mother's voices speaking to her, from her memory, or were the voices actually, only coming from her memory? Just as they were locking up the range rover just before heading out on their hike, earlier that day, Mira remembered her father stopping and turning to look down at her with a quizzical smirk on his face. Mira's mother was standing behind her father, also smiling whimsically. Yes, Mira remembered, yes… She looked from where the sun was rising and then from the opposite side and the side of the side of the opposite side and the other side of the side.

Mira smiled back at her mother and father. Where the sun was rising was east, and where the sun would be sinking, disappearing, later that night, into the horizon, was west. Facing the rising sun, Mira said to her father and mother, "That way is east, behind is west, and to the left is north, and to the right of where we are standing is south." Professor Salinas embraced his daughter and lifted her up, holding her firmly, but at the same time, gently in his arms.

"That's my girl! Remember! No matter what may happen, survival is always first on the agenda! We can always cry and lick our wounds afterwards, after we are safe."

"Yes, Daddy." Mira kissed her father while her mother was snuggling behind her, kissing her on the back of her head and tenderly caressing her cheek.

There was that ominous rumble coming from up above, again, higher up on the cliff. A few pebbles came tumbling down the side of the cliff. Before she allowed herself to be buried under a pile of rocks or knocked over the edge of the ridge by another landslide, Mira quickly grabbed her father's discarded backpack before running away to safety, but her father's backpack was too heavy. She could barely lift the backpack up all the way, so instead, she half carried, half dragged the backpack along the ridge as far down, and as far away, from the side of the cliff as possible. After a while, Mira was so far away from the side of the cliff, if there was another landslide, she was out of harm's way, and as the saying goes, be careful what you wish for, it may come true, Mira did not wish for it, there was another landslide. Mira watched as the small edge of the ridge they had used to hike up the side of the cliff was now completely buried under big and small rocks and twisted and bent tree limbs and uprooted bushes and muck and dry soil.

Thank you God - and God - why did my Daddy and Mommy have to die? Mira was thinking as she was uncontrollably crying, again, survival, Mira, survival, Mira remembered, survival. She was immediately rummaging through her father's backpack, searching first, for the keys to the range rover and her father's cellphone. Even though Mira did not know how to drive, at ten years old, she was too young, she could still use the vehicle for shelter and protection, if she should be discovered by a bear, or mountain lion, or God forbid, a pack of hungry, ravenous,

28

wolves. The keys to the range rover was there, but the cellphone was not, also the one compass they had brought along on their trip was not there. Her father must have had his cellphone in his pocket and the compass could have been anywhere, in her mother's backpack, or they could have left the compass back at the car. There was a radio in the range rover. To call for help in case of an emergency. Mira had to get to the range rover. There was a sandwich and a couple of bananas and an apple in her father's backpack, but that was it. His canteen of water was always hanging from his belt. Hopefully, she wasn't going to be stranded out in the wilderness by herself for too long, Mira was thinking. Which way was the range rover? Mira was staring back and forth at the unfamiliar clump of trees on the left, and the unfamiliar clump of trees on the right. Didn't they come up through here on the left, or there on the right? What about over that big boulder further to the right? Didn't they walk around that big boulder further to the right? Didn't they or did they? Mira wasn't sure. She was supposed to remember... but she never imagined what happened would ever happen.

"Daddy! Mommy! Mommy! Daddy!"
Mira began crying uncontrollably, again.

"Mommy! Mommy! Daddy! Daddy! Mommy! Mommy... Daddy!"

Her eyes were like clouds that had burst – the rains of Heaven were falling like the oceans turned upside down.

But the nightmare, unforgivably, was only just beginning...

CHAPTER TWO

The tea kettle began to whistle. Tea, if you liked to drink tea, which was okay for Colorado State Park Ranger Lucy McGill, but for her partner Park Ranger Timothy Spencer, the hot water from the tea kettle was only good for making a cup of instant coffee, or hot cocoa; whatever Ranger Spencer happened to be in the mood for at whatever moment.

At the moment that would most definitely be a steaming, hot, cup of instant coffee.

Park Ranger McGill heard mumbled voices outside speaking to each other, then the slight roar of a car engine, then a little louder, "Goodnight! Drive safely!" Park Ranger Spencer, or Tim, as Park Ranger McGill would call Park Ranger Spencer when they were behind closed doors, or off-duty, and vice versa, Tim would call Park Ranger McGill – Lucy, or Luce, when nobody was around, or when they were able to relax and act casually.

"Who was that?" Park Ranger McGill asked Park Ranger Spencer.

"That was the Henderson family. All there and accounted for."

"Hmm." Park Ranger McGill crinkled her nose as she was concentrating for a moment as she checked off the Henderson family from the visitors list.

"That should be all of them for the night." Park Ranger Spencer was saying as he was walking over to the steaming, hot, tea kettle to make his preferred cup of instant coffee.

"No!" Park Ranger McGill shouted back to Park Ranger Spencer. "The Salinas family hasn't come back yet!"

"The Salinas family? Maybe they were going to camp out overnight, but they forgot to check in at the Rangers station?"

"No! Tim! They didn't forget to check in. I saw them when they were coming in this morning. Professor Salinas said he was only going out camping for the day with his wife and daughter!"

"Are you sure, Luce?"

"I'm sure! I'm looking at the visitors list right now!"

"Are you sure you didn't forget to check them off the visitors list?"

"I'm sure! I didn't forget to check them off the visitors list!"

Park Ranger McGill and Park Ranger Spencer were looking back and forth at each other. Park Ranger McGill was bent over a desk examining the list of campers, hikers, hunters, fishermen, fisherwomen, outdoorsmen, and outdoorswomen who had checked in at the Rangers station earlier that day. Park Ranger Spencer took a sip from the cup of freshly brewed instant coffee he had in his hand as he looked on watching Park Ranger McGill perusing the visitors list, logbook at the Rangers station, and any other relevant document relating to the matter at hand.

"They should've been back by now." Park Ranger McGill said to Park Ranger Spencer. "I know the Salinas family. I know them personally, or I've gotten to know them as well as any of us can get to know anyone coming to visit the park." Park Ranger McGill continued whether Park Ranger Spencer was interested or not. "That would be the Salinas family of Professor Robert Salinas of Colorado State University, Dr. Anna Salinas, she's a fancy schmanzy heart surgeon or something like that, and their elementary school age daughter Mira Salinas."

"Oh yeah! That's right!" Park Ranger Spencer was nodding, contemplatively. "I remember him now! Professor Salinas! Our local Bigfoot expert and his wife and daughter!"

"Yeah!" Park Ranger McGill fired back at Park Ranger Spencer. "He said he was just taking the family out for a picnic!"

Park Rangers Spencer's lips were pursed in consternation. "See if you can get them on the radio." Park Ranger McGill tried the best that she could. There was no answer coming back from any of the members of the Salinas family. They tried calling the two cellphone numbers listed on file for Professor Robert Salinas and Doctor Anna Salinas. No one was answering any of the cellphones from the two cellphone numbers they had. Park Ranger McGill left messages on the automated answering services of the two cellphone numbers listed.

"They're running late." Park Ranger McGill was saying to Park Ranger Spencer as she was finishing off the last few drops from her delicious honey and lemon-flavored cup of tea. Park Ranger McGill always liked a few spoonfuls of honey and lemon extract in her tea. They were both looking out of the window of the Rangers station staring at the setting sun as the setting sun was slowly being replaced by a rising crescent moon.

"They should be okay." Park Ranger McGill was wishfully thinking out loud, not at all as unreassuringly as she was feeling.

"I hope so." Park Ranger Spencer replied.

CHAPTER THREE

Mira had come upon a large open grassy plain. It did not look familiar. She had been sure that her parents had hiked in this direction from where they had parked the range rover. She backtracked trying to literally trace back her own steps to where she had originally taken a wrong turn. All the trees and bushes all looked alike. Was she heading southeast? Or did she accidently walk all the way around without noticing and was now heading northwest instead of southeast? She could barely see the position of the sun through the tops of the many tree branches covering the sky up above. Are the shadows of the branches of the trees pointing east and the opposite direction is west? Or vice versa? Mira was becoming confused. The images of her parents kept overtaking her thought processes. She had collapsed to the ground many times curling up into a fetal position crying her eyes out. The steps she had traced backwards led to more unfamiliar places in the forest, places so unfamiliar Mira was often times feeling like she had entered into another world.

"Mommy! Daddy!" Mira kept whimpering as she continued trying to find her way back to the range rover or any kind of semblance of civilization.

The sun had set. The forest was engulfed in darkness. Mira's world had gone black in more ways than she could ever have imagined. She had lost track of the position of the setting sun. There was no light anywhere to be found; no campfires burning in the distance, no lamp lights, no beaming flashlights helping nighttime wanderers find their way.

I'm lost! Mira whispered to herself. Lost! It was what she had been thinking for a while now. By saying it to herself, out loud, she was subconsciously reaffirming the reality of her situation. She ruffled through her father's backpack again, which was lighter to carry after she had discarded any unnecessary items she didn't need to survive until she would, hopefully, be rescued. There still was no compass to be found in her father's backpack. She just thought if she looked one more time, again, a compass might pop out, hidden in the folds of the backpack, or wedged in between something or another of the few supplies contained therein. What difference would a compass have made? The sun rises in the east and sets in the west. The best compass available was there... up above in the sky. Mira looked up at the crescent moon through the cracks of the many branches of the many trees. She was tired and she was hungry, maybe even a little dehydrated. She had half of a canteen of water. That should be enough to keep her alive until tomorrow. She'll probably be rescued tomorrow, or she'll bump into a few hikers, or campers, or hunters, or fishermen... she hoped so.

Maybe it was time for her to get down on her knees and do a little praying. She still could not fully accept the fact that her father and mother were gone, even though she had experienced the cold, hard, reality with her own heart, mind, and soul.

Mira was afraid to light a campfire, afraid the light from the fire might attract any wild animals lurking nearby. Wild animals like a mountain lion, or bear, or rattlesnake, or God forbid... a hungry pack of wolves! She found a small cliff with a small rock outcropping which wasn't too difficult to climb. She nestled there for the night, curled in a ball, with a thin blanket wrapped around her, which she had found in her father's backpack. For as hot as it was during the day, the night was an exact opposite – cold, relentlessly frigid, unforgiving, and cruel. She awoke in the morning by the light of the rising sun. Find the range rover! Mira kept telling herself. Find the range rover! Or any campers, or hikers, she might happen to come across. By the late, late, afternoon, after spending a little more than half the day searching for the range rover, or other hikers, or campers, there still was no range rover, or campers, or hikers, anywhere to be found; there was not even any hunters hunting, or fishermen fishing… and then she heard the tatta-tat-tatta-tat-tatta-tat-tat of a helicopter propeller up in the sky. There! Faraway in the distance! She saw a helicopter flying nearby, but not nearby enough, and the helicopter was flying away, in the opposite direction, into the horizon. Mira knew she could never yell loud enough to attract the attention of the helicopters crew. She would never be overheard over the roar of the helicopter's propellers and the helicopters powerful engine. Mira didn't need to look through her father's backpack to search for a flare gun and flares. If she had seen a flare gun and flares, she definitely would have remembered. Oh God! How she desperately needed a flare gun and flares at this moment. She ran towards the helicopter, or in the direction the helicopter was flying, hoping that the helicopter will circle back and that she could find an open space in the dense tangle of trees and bushes where she would be able to jump up and down and wave her arms in the air to attract the attention of the helicopters crew. The helicopter was already too far away for Mira to light a fire and attract the attention of the helicopters crew with the smoke from a fire. I'm coming! I'm coming! I'm coming! She kept whimpering to herself as she was running in the direction the helicopter was flying. I'm coming! I'm coming! I'm coming! Mira came across a river the helicopter had flown over. The helicopter had flown over the river and disappeared, somewhere, faraway, on the other side of the forest. Mira had to wade across the river to keep following the helicopter, or she hoped she could wade across the river and keep following the helicopter. She leaned down by the river's edge and stuck her arm in the water. The river at this end was only about twelve to fourteen inches (3.66 meters to 4.27 meters) deep. I have to follow the helicopter! Mira stepped into the river and began walking to the other side. As the river was getting deeper and deeper, the water was rising higher and higher, first up to her hips, then up to her chest, then up to her chin. Mira kept thinking the river was not going to get any deeper, or that the water was not going to rise any higher. The river, unfortunately, did indeed, get deeper, and deeper, and deeper, and the water, did indeed, rise higher, and higher, and higher, and the currents of the river had become stronger, and stronger, and stronger. It was too late for Mira to circle back to the safety of the land by the river's edge. The rivers strong currents lifted Mira up, off of her feet, and sent her bobbing, up and down, and up and down, and up and down, the river, all the while, swallowing and spitting out, too much of the river's waters, she kept continuously, uncontrollably, accidently swallowing. The rivers currents were too strong, too powerful, for Mira to be able to stay afloat on top, or to swim to the other side of the river. Mira knew that she was eventually going to drown until she felt something big brushing up against her back. In an instant Mira noticed that the strange object brushing up against her back was a large tree branch that had broken off from a large tree, somewhere along the river's edge, bouncing, up and down, and up and down, and up and down, on the strong and powerful river currents, much the same way that Mira was bouncing, up and down, and up and down, and up and down, on the strong and powerful river currents, but the large tree branch was bouncing, less than more, up and down, on the strong and powerful river currents, due to the fact that the many large limbs from the large tree branch was functioning as a sort of natural floating device. Mira held onto the large tree branch, for dear life, and her life did indeed, depend on her holding onto the large tree branch. If Mira should happen to become disengaged from the large tree branch, she will definitely drown and die. If was a hard task, indeed, holding onto the large tree branch, even after coming across, more than a few mini-waterfalls that she had barely survived, almost losing her grip or being tossed off the large tree branch by the strong and powerful river currents. After so much time, bouncing, up and down, and up and down, and up and down, on the strong and powerful currents of the river, for so long, for so far away down the river, the strong and powerful currents of the river, after a while, became less strong and less powerful. Eventually, the large tree branch had bounced, up and down, and up and down, and up and down, for so long enough to come to a lower elevation of the river and closer to land, eventually, to a lower enough elevation of the river and closer enough to the land for Mira to be able to release her life-or-death grasp on the large tree branch and wade back to dry land. Mira collapsed on the moist, mud, by the river's edge, and heaved, and coughed, and spat out, almost nearly enough, but not nearly enough, as much of the rivers, waters, that she had swallowed. Her father's backpack was gone. The backpack had fallen off her back in all the excitement. The helicopter was also gone. The helicopter had disappeared into the horizon as if it had been an illusion, or something that she had seen in her dreams and couldn't tell the difference between what she had seen in her dreams while she was sleeping or what she was seeing while she was awake.

Where was she now? Even further away from civilization than she had been before? She hoped not, but hope is an emotion, an aspiration, a wishful thought that sometimes came true and sometimes did not

Mira began crying again.

Mommy! Daddy! Mommy! Daddy! Mommy! Daddy! Mommy! Daddy!

CHAPTER FOUR

A few overnight campers had seen the landslide from a distance where they had pitched their tents on a nearby plateau which overlooked the small canyon on the opposite side of the cliff Mira and her parents had chosen for a hike and a picnic that day.

That morning the campers had decided to hike to the other side of the canyon to take a closer look at the landslide from the day before. En route they had also encountered another group of overnight campers who had also seen the landslide from the day before.

To their shock and horror, they had discovered the lifeless bodies of Professor Salinas and his wife, Doctor Salinas, or a leg and a hand of Doctor Salinas; as she had been almost entirely completely covered by the rocks and debris of the landslide.

All kinds of panic and mayhem had ensued after the frightening discovery, especially when the Parks Rangers on-duty that morning had learned that the deceased college Professor and his wife had gone out hiking for the day with their young adolescent daughter; who was nowhere to be found.

It was as if a large-scale military operation was put into motion by the end of the second day. Besides the Colorado State Park Rangers, several local Fire Dept. and Police Search & Rescue Teams, and a whole platoon of United States Army National Guardsmen, there were also over a hundred civilian volunteers helping to find the missing child.

The landslide had occurred in a deep hillside basin at northwest of where the Colorado State Blue Valley Ranger Station was located in the Colorado Rockies. The child had either hiked southeast towards where many campers and hikers parked their vehicles before venturing out into the wilderness, and where the Salinas family had parked their vehicles; which happened to be an oversized, clunky, sun-bleached range rover.

The range rover was there, but the child was not.

CHAPTER FIVE

Her father's backpack was gone, lost somewhere on the river, washed away downstream. Mira could no longer make a fire and use smoke to alert anyone nearby, or any rescuers who might be searching for her, or if a random helicopter, or plane, should be flying by. All the matches and lighters where in her father's backpack and Mira had never been any good at lighting a fire – the old-fashioned way – by rubbing twigs together. How did anybody ever do that in the first place? Mira had wondered, even though she had seen it done, with her very own eyes, a few times – lighting a fire – by rubbing twigs together. She was never able to do that. She was not able to do that now, even though her life depended on it.

Survival!

Always concentrate on surviving!

No matter what may happen!

Her parents' words came back to her, all that her parents had taught her, if she should ever be stranded out in the wilderness by herself or if whomever she may have been stranded out in the wilderness with, if they should ever be injured or come to some harm – do what you have to do to survive.

Never give up!

Never! Never! Never! Never give up!

Feeling sorry for yourself will never do you any good. It was counter-productive. Mira was having a hard time refraining from feeling sorry for herself. She had nothing now. She had thought that she had nothing before, with what little supplies were in her father's backpack, but to be completely devoid of even those few, little, supplies, she was only now beginning to despair. Do not despair! Do not despair! Do not despair! Her parents would have been telling Mira, if her parents were here, alive, instead of gone forever, on the other side of the river at the bottom of a canyon covered by the merciless rubble of a landslide.

Mira knew she was further away from where any Search & Rescue Teams, professional and volunteer, would be looking to find her. They will never think she was as far away as she was now – from her original point of origin. As she was trying to make her way back, or the way back she imagined would take her closer to where any Search & Rescue Teams, professional and volunteer, may be searching, she was overcome with the immense feeling of dread that somebody... or something was watching her, somewhere out there in the shadows.

Somebody... or something... was following her.

At certain times the birds would stop chirping, the frogs would stop croaking, the rabbits would stop ruffling through the brush.

Everything would become silent.

The only sound for several minutes would be from the swaying branches of the trees swaying in the wind. And then the birds would go back to chirping, the frogs would go back to croaking, the rabbits would go back to ruffling through the brush.

It was off and on again, and off and on again, and off and on again, and off and on again...
Mira was too frightened to cry out, too frightened to scream, at whoever... or whatever... may be out there... hiding... unwilling, for whatever reason, to show themselves... or itself?

Mommy... Daddy... Mommy... Daddy... Mira had become too frightened to cry.

As Mira was looking up and around at all four points of the horizons, east, west, north, south, she

42

realized she was now surrounded by three unfamiliar mountain ranges faraway in the distance.

Had she been swept away that faraway down river?

Mommy... Daddy... Mommy... Daddy... she continued quietly whimpering.

I have to find my way back - back to where? She was not sure. She no longer had any semblance of an idea or notion about which direction she should go. There were several planes flying by faraway, but those were commercial planes from commercial airliners. Those planes were flying too far up in the sky and too far away in the distance to even be able to spot Mira, or to notice that Mira was a child, lost and stranded in the hostile wilderness, alone, by herself; with no one to help her, with no one to guide her. Once and a while she heard the tatta-tat-tatta-tat-tatta-tat-tat of helicopters flying in the sky, but the helicopters were too far away. The helicopters were searching for her, further upstream, on the other side of the river.

Go in that direction, Mira told herself, go in the direction of where she was hearing the occasional helicopter flying.

That's where she will find and re-encounter the civilized world, or hikers, or campers, or hunters, or fishermen going out fishing for the day; who will help her, who will rescue her.

In that direction, in that direction, in that direction, after so much time had gone by, and after Mira had been hiking for so long, the sun began to sink, once again, one more time, behind the horizon.

It was the beginning of Mira's second night lost out in the wilderness of the Colorado Rockies.

She was becoming dehydrated. She did not find any edible nuts and berries during her travels that day that could sustain her and keep her strong.

CHAPTER SIX

The rescue teams and volunteers were becoming weary, but they were still not ready to give up hope.
It was still too soon.

In the back of some of their minds they were fearing that the lost child had already been taking away and being made a meal of by some wild animal or wild animals.

Park Ranger Lucy McGill and Park Ranger Timothy Spencer were watching as one of the two helicopters that had joined the search & rescue operation was landing on an area of the Blue Valley Rangers station parking lot which was partitioned off specifically for helicopter traffic. One helicopter belonged to a local TV news station and the other was a city police helicopter.

"That isn't...?" Park Ranger McGill did not finish the sentence.

The helicopter crew were removing two stretchers from the helicopter and loading the stretchers onto a nearby ambulance.

Park Ranger Spencer finished the sentence for Park Ranger McGill. "The bodies killed in the landslide."

"We've never had that happen before."

"Death by landslide. That hasn't happened since about eighty years ago. That's the last recording of that on record."

"What a shame." Park Ranger McGill was becoming teary-eyed. "What a terrible shame."

"Let's hope that that is the only dead bodies, or body parts, we find this week, and next week, and every week for the rest of the year, and the next year, and the next year, and the next year, and every year thereafter."

"What bad luck... and their baby... what had become of their young child?"

"Let's hope she's still out there, wandering around."

"What is she supposed to be? Ten-years-old?"

Park Ranger Spencer was nodding his head. "Yup. She won't survive alone out there too much longer."

CHAPTER SEVEN

Was that a wolf howling in the faraway distance? Mira was wondering... She had found another rocky ledge to sleep on for the night. She heard the occasional buzz-buzz-buzz of helicopters and r-r-r-r-r-roar of planes flying even further away in the distance. In the back of Mira's mind, she knew that the helicopters and planes were searching for her, but whatever Rescue & Search Teams, professional and volunteer, who had come to help did not imagine that Mira could have been accidently washed away downstream to a whole other world of the many worlds of the primeval forest.

Mommy... Daddy... Mommy... Daddy... Why did this happen? Why have you been taken away from me? Why have I been left alone to... God forbid... perish... out here in the wilderness.

Survival!

Survival!

Survival!

Survival!

Mira had to survive! At whatever the cost! But at the moment her belly was hurting. She was thirsty. Oh my God how she was thirsty. She could drink a whole river. Never mind sterilizing the water... first. She was so thirsty; she did not care anymore. All that she knew, all that she was feeling, is that if she had some water that maybe her belly will stop hurting.

Mommy... Daddy... Mommy... Daddy...

Was that another wolf howling in the faraway distance? Or the same wolf? There was another wolf howling further away on the opposite side of where the first wolf or wolves were howling. Mira was listening, intently, her head was craned to one side. There was nothing... now. No more howling, or at least, no more howling for the moment. There were a few hoot-hoot-hoots. There was definitely an owl, or two, or three, somewhere, around, nearby. It was better to be hearing owls hoot-hoot-hooting, than to be hearing wolves howling however far away or nearby.

And then it happened... suddenly... again... all the noises in the forest were immediately silenced, as if all the noises in the forest had been turned off, or switched off, by the flick of a switch. Mira could feel the hair on the back of her neck twitching. There was something out there. There was something out there stalking Mira, other than any howling wolves, or hooting owls. The howling wolves and the hooting owls must have been feeling the same sensation, too, as well as all the other nocturnal creatures lurking in the brush, at this moment, at this time, under the ominous glow of the crescent moon.

And then Mira heard the slightest, very slightest sound of a twig snapping, nearby, down below, from where she was stretched out on top of a large boulder. From behind, Through the several small openings between the leaves of a bush where she had heard the slightest, very slightest sound of a twig snapping, she saw reflected by the faint glow of the moon, two luminescent eyes staring back at her... but only for a quick moment... and then the two luminescent eyes disappeared, intentionally or unintentionally, before Mira could ascertain which was which, intentionally or unintentionally, Mira heard the low rumble of a faint growl, up above, from where she was stretched out on top of the large boulder.

Two wolves? One stalking her from up above and the other stalking her from down below?
Her question was answered even quicker than she had imagined.

The wolf crouching down below sprang out from the darkness of the bush down below and grabbed hold of Mira by biting into her ankle with its powerful jaws and razor-sharp fangs as the wolf stalking her from up above dived down to grab hold of Mira by biting onto her neck, to snap her neck, or to rip her throat open, so that she would instantly bleed out and become an easy and quick meal for the wolves to stuff their bellies.

But not just the two attacking wolves, there was a whole pack of ten to fifteen other wolves surrounding the alpha and beta wolves as they began to make mincemeat of the soon to be fresh kill.

That was not to be so!

In an instant a large furry arm appeared, as if from out of nowhere, and swatted away the wolf lunging forward from up above. Powerfully smashing would've been a more appropriate word to explain the blow given to the wolf lunging from up above, which was only, merely, one-tenth of a second away from ripping open Mira's throat and jugular vein.

Just as quickly, another large furry arm grabbed hold of the neck of the wolf that had attacked Mira from down below, and in a few more bites would've bitten off Mira's foot. The large furry arm, instantly snapped in two, the neck of the wolf biting into Mira's ankle. The lifeless jaws of the wolf biting into Mira's ankle unclamped itself from Mira's ankle. The large furry arm tossed the lifeless corpse of the wolf that had almost, nearly, bitten off Mira's ankle at the other wolves waiting down below. Several of the other wolves in the pack lunged forward, continuing with their attack, while several of the other wolves, maybe not as brave, or maybe not as hungry, casually circled back away. The two large furry arms, which were connected to a large furry head, a large furry chest, and two large furry legs belonged a Bigfoot – a Bigfoot standing at least eight-foot (2.44 meters) tall.

After fighting off the few remaining wolves, when the Bigfoot felt that the attack was ending and he could safely relax for a moment, but not exactly relax, the Bigfoot quickly tied a cloth around Mira's profusely bleeding ankle, wrapping the cloth around Mira's ankle several times. Mira might still not survive. The one wolf who had attacked from down below had almost, nearly, completely bitten off Mira's foot. She had fainted in shock. The Bigfoot, gently, as gently as possible, cradled Mira in his arms and began running, or fast walking, as fast as possible, away from the site of the near total carnage. By the morning, the Bigfoot with Mira still cradled in his arms had reached the entrance to an underground labyrinthian cave dwelling of the Citizenry of the Heseetu, one of several many hidden locations spread-out throughout the forests and woodlands of the Colorado Rockies.

Mimi, a young female Bigfoot, who at the moment was tasked with the duty of minding the entranceway of the cave dwelling, was the first to encounter the hitherto unnamed Bigfoot who had saved Mira.

"Shantuu!" Mimi cried out. "Have you lost your mind?" She was staring in shock at the human child cradled in the arms of the now identified Bigfoot – Shantuu - was the name given to him by the Citizenry of the Heseetu.

"The human child is badly injured! There is very little time. We must act quickly!"

"I cannot allow this!" Mimi said defiantly to Shantuu.

"You will and you must! We cannot allow the child to die! Find Threnatta immediately and send her here!" Threnatta was a Healer. She should be able to help mend the wounds of the injured human child.

"I... I... I...!"

"Go now! Find Threnatta!"

Mimi hesitated for a moment, then turned and disappeared into the shadows of the many passageways, pathways, cave tunnels, and cave enclaves of the labyrinthian City of Caves.

There was a small fire burning around the corner of the entranceway to a smaller separate rocky cave enclave with several furs spread out on the floor. Shantuu laid the injured human child on one of the furs by the small fire. After a short while several more Bigfoots appeared. Mimi had done as she was told to do.

"Shantuu!" Threnatta shouted as she entered the small separate rocky cave enclave. "You have indeed lost your mind!"

"I told you so! I was unable to stop him!" Mimi added as she appeared behind the others.

"This is an abomination!" Threnatta's assistant and student – Tantoon – cried out. "We must return the human child to wherever the human child was found!"

"I cannot allow the human child to die!" Shantuu fired back at them. "Her parents were killed in a landslide! She has been lost, wandering around for the past two days! lost! She was almost made a meal of by a pack of hungry wolves!"

Tantoon's fur was an even lighter shade of brown to appear as close to blond as any Bigfoots, Sasquatches, or Yetis, have ever been, or been known to have been. Shantuu's fur was also a lighter shade of brown, but still brown. You could have easily mistaken Tantoon for being an albino; which he most definitely was not. Tantoon's mother had been slain by human bigfoot hunters when Tantoon was barely a few years old. Tantoon was being

51

trained to be a Healer. It was hoped that by helping to heal others that Tantoon himself would also be healed.

Mira had been going in and out of consciousness ever since the first wolf had nearly bitten off her leg. She had seen from the corner of her eye as a Bigfoot had appeared as if from out of nowhere and swatted away another wolf attacking her from up above. She was no longer freezing and there was a bright light from a fire reflecting the shadows of other Bigfoots who seemed to be talking to each other. Mira was not afraid. She felt deep down inside her heart that the Bigfoots were trying to help her; that she had nothing to fear from them. They were speaking to each other, but not in English, or in any other language Mira did not immediately identify. In her dreams, she finally imagined that they were speaking to each other in certain Native-American dialects. Dialects that she was aware of because of her father's fascination with archeology, history, folklore, and ancient civilizations. The Bigfoots were speaking in the Native-American dialects of Chemehuevi, Mohave, Hopi, and Navajo. They seemed to be extremely adept, proficient, and scholarly in there command of the ancient languages.

"Mommy... Daddy... Mommy... Daddy..." Mira kept repeating has she was going in and out of consciousness; falling asleep, and awakening, falling asleep, and awakening, falling asleep, and awakening.

Threnatta was heartbroken as she was listening to Mira crying out for her forever gone father and mother.

"As you wish." Threnatta conceded. "Give the child a few droplets of the dreamsleep elixir."

Tantoon hesitated but did as he was told. Tantoon was Threnatta's most passionate, agile, and adept student.

After Threnatta had carefully unwrapped the cloth Shantuu had tied around Mira's ankle, she couldn't help but to grimace in disgust.

"We may have to amputate the human child's foot."

"Please! Do whatever you have to do to save the human child." Shantuu pleaded.

"The bones have been broken in several different places. The main artery has not been severed. We will have to set the bones the best that we can and stitch her ankle back together."

"Yes! Please! Threnatta! Please! Do not let her die!" Shantuu pleaded.

After so long a while Threnatta began negatively shaking her head. "I cannot stop the bleeding! The bones are not set properly! We are going to lose the human child!"

"No!" Shantuu roared. "No! Do something! Do anything!"

Threnatta was still negatively shaking her head. She gestured for Tantoon to bring her one of the other pouches she had brought along.

"Take three wandererstones! Return to your former home of the Citizenry of the Cororuru! Go find your former mentor and teacher - Morgana - and bring him here! Immediately!"

Tantoon was saying to Threnatta as he was fumbling through the pouch picking out three wandererstones out of a batch of seven wandererstones. "Morgana is many, many, many, sunsets, sunrises, and moons away. He is too far away. It is not worth the time and the effort to waste on a human child or any human for that matter!"

53

"Morgana is only as far away from the lands the humans call state Washington. He is not on the other side of the big waters east and west." (Big waters meaning - east - the Pacific Ocean, and west - the Atlantic Ocean.) "Put the three wandererstones on the palms of both of your hands." Threnatta ordered Tantoon. "Concentrate on the lands of state Washington." Threnatta said to Tantoon as she also grabbed onto the three wandererstones on the palms of Tantoon's hands. "Concentrate Tantoon! Concentrate!"

"I am Threnatta! I am!"

Threnatta let go of Tantoon's hands as the three wandererstones began flashing like strobe lights in a human nightclub or discotheque - bright blue, bright green, bright red. Tantoon seemed to fade in, fade out, fade in, fade out, fade in, fade out, fade in, fade out, and then he faded out one last time and was gone. Maybe ten to fifteen minutes later, Tantoon and another of the Citizenry faded in, faded out, faded in, faded out, again and again and again and again, until they both faded in again one last time. Standing in the cave enclave, beside Threnatta, the wounded human child, Mimi and Shantuu, were Tantoon and Morgana.

"What is all the ballyhoo about? I was resting! I'm getting too old for all of these fatal tragedies and last moment catastrophes! What is wrong here now? Let me see! Let me see!" Morgana was immediately bent over Mira examining her wounds."

"She was attacked by a pack of wolves. Her leg has almost been completely bitten off." Threnatta said to Morgana as she was stepping to the side so that Morgana could have a better look.

"This is bad! This is very bad! But I have seen worse!"

54

Morgana's fur was spotted with many flecks of gray, or white, which only appeared gray, because of being mixed together with his usual, younger, brown fur. There were more wrinkles around his eyes and more creases on his forehead, cheeks, and chin.

"Where did you learn to stitch like that? This is living flesh! This is not a bed of furs or a rucksack!"

"I will still always refer to you, Morgana! You are the Master of Masters."

Morgana merely grunted as he took over the mending of the wounded human child's leg.

"Tantoon! Come here! Watch!" Threnatta gestured for her student to come closer and study Morgana at work. "This is a once in a lifetime opportunity."

Shantuu was overcome with emotion. "Thank you... Threnatta... thank you Morgana... thank you Tantoon..."

"Do not thank me yet." Morgana only looked up at Shantuu for a quick moment before returning to mending the human child's leg the best that he was able too. Shantuu felt guilty.

He should have done more to help the lost human child as he was following her, watching her, for those two days. He should have reacted sooner before any one of the wolves in the pack had a chance to take a bite out of the human child...

But just as Shantuu had been watching the human child - the pack of wolves had been watching them both - Shantuu and the human child.

The pack of wolves had known better to stay downwind.

CHAPTER EIGHT

Three days had gone by, and then four days, and then five days, and then six days, seven days, eight days, nine days, ten days... and then on the eleventh day the hound dogs found dried blood on the side of a boulder far down on the other side of a nearby river. There was a bloodied swath of cloth by the dried blood on the boulder. There were other splashes and small puddles of blood further away from the boulder, and also bits of dried flesh and bone bits; which turned out to be the blood, dried flesh and bone bits from several different wolves. DNA from the dried blood on the boulder and the bloodied swath of cloth matched the DNA of the parents of Mira Salinas – Professor Robert Salinas and Doctor Anna Salinas.

The Search & Rescue Teams, professional and volunteer, were beginning to fear that Mira Salinas had been eaten by a pack of wolves. There should have been more blood by the boulder, or a blood trail, and maybe a few more bloodied and torn strips of clothing lying about, nearby, or further away. It seemed that the pack of wolves that had attacked Mira had attacked a few wolves from its own wolf pack? Why would a pack of wolves attack and eat other wolves from their own pack when they had the fresh meat of a human child to satiate their hunger? It did not make any sense.

Later that week, Park Ranger Lucy McGill and Park Ranger Timothy Spencer returned to the area where the dried blood and bloodied swath of cloth had been found which belonged to Mira Salinas.

"God forbid! I hope she didn't get eaten by a pack of hungry wolves! Poor thing!" Park Ranger McGill was saying with tears in her eyes.

"Maybe... maybe not." Park Ranger Spencer answered Park Ranger McGill from further away down a slope. He was brushing aside some branches from a thick bushel of leaves by a large tree. "Take a look at this, Lucy!"

"You found something?"

"How did we miss this?"

After making her way down the slope Park Ranger McGill was looking over Park Ranger Spencer's shoulder at what he had discovered. There at the foot of the tree was an imprint in the mud of the ball of a bare foot – half of the front of a foot with five toe marks indented into the mud, that was more so dried than moist, after being exposed to the dry weather the past week. The only difference between the imprint of the ball of a foot and the five toe marks from a regular human foot imprint was that this foot imprint was at least three to four times larger than the imprint that a normal, regular, human foot would have made.

Park Ranger Spencer, was scanning the horizon, perusing the landscape with his naked eyes, his own gut feelings, and his natural senses.

"Something tells me that the pack of wolves didn't intentionally kill a few of its own from its own pack." Park Ranger McGill was following Park Ranger Spencer's train of thought; emotionally, as well as intellectually.

"The wolf pack didn't attack and kill a few of its own."

Park Ranger Spencer was nodding. They both looked down at the oversized footprint in the mud.

"Maybe... that's why there is only a small amount of the lost child's blood on the boulder."

"The wolf pack would've torn her to shreds within seconds."

"Her blood would've sprayed out from the many bite marks and have been splattered all over the place." Park Ranger Spencer and Park Ranger McGill locked eyes for a moment.

"Are you thinking what I'm thinking?" Park Ranger Spencer asked Park Ranger McGill.

"I've never heard of Sasquatches' eating small children." Park Ranger McGill answered Park Ranger Spencer.

"Me neither."

"Either way... I certainly hope not."

They both turned to stare back down at the oversized footprint in the mud.

CHAPTER NINE

Morgana was resting by the fire. Shantuu couldn't help but notice that the wrinkles and cracks under and on the side of Morgana's eyes seemed to be more numerous and pronounced – or was Shantuu just imagining that.

"I'm getting too old to teleport from one side of the world to another side of the world and back."

"Is that what it is called that the wandererstones do? Teleporlort?"

"Teleport." Morgana corrected Shantuu. "Teleport. The word is teleport, not teleporlort. It is a human word."

"Thank you for your help." Shantuu said to Morgana.

"Why does the life of this human child mean so much to you?" Morgana asked Shantuu.

"I don't know... I cannot explain it."

Morgana seemed to smile. Shantuu did not know Morgana well enough to fathom what he might be thinking and feeling or whether he was appeased or dissatisfied.

"You were following your heart. Our hearts can sometimes take us to places we would normally never go." Morgana and Shantuu suddenly noticed the injured human child had awakened and was staring at them, wide eyed, from where she was lying on the bed of furs by the fire.

Shantuu switched from speaking in the Native-American dialects of Chemehuevi, Mohave, Hopi, and Navajo to speaking in contemporary English. Shantuu tenderly stroked Mira's forehead and cheek and said to her, "Rest now child. We will not harm you. Your wounds need to heal. You are not well enough to travel. When you are well enough to travel, I will, personally, return you to your people. We will take care of you until then. We will protect you and keep you safe until then."

Mira dozed off again. She was still experiencing the effects of the dreamsleep elixir.

"She will now know of the existence of the Citizenry." Morgana said to Shantuu.

"I sincerely apologize for my transgressions, but I could not allow the human child to die. Besides…" Shantuu looked back and forth from the injured human child to Morgana. "There have been others in the past."

"Yes, there have been others in the past, and there will be others in the future, just as we have this poor, injured, human child, here, now. The secret of our existence has been kept, more or less, for centuries past, and hopefully for centuries into the future. We must, whether we desire to, or not. As you know, my dear friend, we have always been outnumbered."

"Why have we been cursed to where there have always been so many of them and so few of us."

"There have only ever been several thousands of us, spread-out, throughout the world, throughout history, at any time, and billions of them, everywhere, all of the time." Morgana mournfully decried. "It is a sad reality. The Citizenries have always propagated, sparingly, while the human race have reproduced like fungus, like mold, like vines and weeds, engulfing whole mountain ranges, and the vast and many plains, stretching further, beyond, than where the eagle and hawk can fly."

Morgana sighed once more.

"We are handfuls of sand, and they are entire deserts. We are droplets of water, and they are oceans and seas."

Morgana looked back at the injured human child lying by the fire on a bed of furs.

"She will need much attending."

"She is already becoming stronger. She was strong from the very beginning."

It was then that Tantoon reentered the small separate rocky cave enclave of the section of the cave dwelling which had now been set aside as sort of a recovery area for the injured human child.

"Why did we not succumb and idly stand back allowing the human child to die?"

Shantuu looked back in shock and horror at Tantoon standing in the opening of the small separate rocky cave enclave..

"How can you say that, or even think, such a thing as that?"

"She will expose us! The human child!"

"Then we will be exposed! She is not the first and she will not be the last."

"Why do we persist in groveling at the feet of these puny and weak humans? They are more animal than animal. They are more savage than savage. They only have love for their possessions, gadgets, and frivolous adornments. They make war with each other and kill for other than food or survival."

Tantoon pointed at the sleeping human child.

"They are vain, conceited, and deceitful."

"This human child is not! She is neither! She is innocent!"

"Enough!" Morgana raised his hand in the air.

"What's done is done!"

"I am only saying..."

Morgana angrily cut off Tantoon. "What you are saying will make us no better than the humans you are chastising."

"But… but… but…"

"But nothing! Have I not taught you better than that?"

"Say what you may say!" Tantoon fired back at Morgana. "I can snap the human child's neck in two and be done with it. We can all go our separate ways and forget any of this has ever happened."

Morgana knew better than to engage Tantoon any further.

Morgana knew that Shantuu was going to step in and give Tantoon a piece of his mind – which he was in the process of doing as he was slowly standing and slowly turning to stand face to face an inch (0.03 meters) away from where Tantoon was standing.

"If you so much as attempt to lay one finger on this human child!" Tantoon could feel Shantuu's moist, warm, breath, brushing against his face as if Shantuu was physically licking Tantoon with his moist, wet, tongue. "It will be your neck, that will be snapped in two, not the human child"

Morgana allowed the two to stare back at each other for a few more moments.

"Back away now! Back away!"

Shantuu and Tantoon did not say anything further after that. They remained silent, staring back at each other in anger, as if one or the other was about to strike the other down dead.

"Back away!" Morgana repeated.

Shantuu and Tantoon reluctantly did as Morgana requested.

As Shantuu and Tantoon were begrudgingly backing away from each other Morgana added –

"There is more to being civilized than rhyming poetically and building monuments."

It was Morgana's turn to stand face to face with Tantoon.

"You have much to learn, Tantoon." Morgana turned away from Tantoon. "Go away now. I have nothing more to say to you now. We will talk more… later."

As Tantoon was walking away his final words were.

"Threnatta also agrees!" And Tantoon was gone. Shantuu and Morgana were staring back and forth at each other in silence.

They were pondering what had just occurred, or what might have, regrettably, have happened, but did not happen.

They were pondering what Tantoon had said. After a while Morgana said as if to himself only. "We will never become that."

Several nights later, Mimi, rushed to awaken Shantuu, where Shantuu was sleeping in a, separate, cave enclave, which was, side by side, but separate, from the cave enclave where the human child was recuperating and healing from her wounds. The two, separate, cave enclaves were far enough away from each other, where the human child would not notice Shantuu sleeping, a far enough distance away, but still close enough, for Shantuu to be able to keep an eye on the human child. Mimi was gently nudging Shantuu to awaken him, but Shantuu was already awakened.

"Why have the furs and food supplies been set on fire?" Mimi immediately inquired.

"So that is what has been filling my nostrils and awakened me."

"You did not do this?"

"Burning where?"

"In our supply storage area in the next upper level."

63

"Why would I ever do anything as insane as that?" Shantuu was already rising from his bed of furs and rushing down the hollow passageways and rocky cave tunnels to where the fire was burning. By the time Shantuu had reached the cave enclave where the furs and food supplies were burning, others living in the cave dwelling had already arrived there and responded by extinguishing the still slightly smoldering fire.

"What happened?" Shantuu asked the others there.

"We do not know." The others there were just as confused and perplexed as Shantuu and Mimi.

Just as quickly, they all heard the flap-flap-flapping of feet stomping on the ground coming towards them. It was Threnatta. She was out of breath. "Come quickly!" She was heaving heavily. "The fire is a ruse! Set by Tantoon! Tantoon is on his way to kill the human child! We may be too late already!"

Shantuu did not hesitate. He was off and running like a wild beast lusting for blood.

Tantoon was leaning over Mira with a boneknife in his hand, raised and ready, to strike down and cut the human child in two, just as Shantuu was turning the corner to the cave enclave.

"Tantoon!" Shantuu immediately shouted at the top of his lungs.

The sudden shock of being discovered before Tantoon had a chance to finish the vile deed he had come to do, was just enough of a distraction to cause Tantoon to hesitate for a moment, for a moment long enough for Shantuu to spring forward and simultaneously block and topple Tantoon to the ground. Tantoon was quick to respond, immediately regaining his senses and equilibrium. He lashed out at Shantuu with the boneknife, slashing back and forth many times, many times just barely missing Shantuu as Shantuu dodged each successive attempt of Tantoon to cut him and stab him. Tantoon eventually came around to where Shantuu had been standing at the enclave entrance and knocked over Mimi who was standing there at the entrance. Before Shantuu could jump on Tantoon's back Threnatta had caught up to them and was standing outside the cave enclave entrance huffing and puffing trying to regain her exasperated waning breath. Tantoon grabbed Threnatta and brusquely pushed Threnatta in front of him, using Threnatta as a shield to block Shantuu from tackling him to the ground. Shantuu stopped dead in his tracks. Tantoon had the boneknife raised and tightly pressed against Threnatta's throat.

"Stand down!" Tantoon shouted to Shantuu. "Stand down or I will split Threnatta's throat open!"

"How can You? Tantoon!" Shantuu said to Tantoon. "What are you doing? Have you lost your mind?"

"I have not lost my mind any more than you have by bringing a human child into our cave dwelling and exposing us, exposing our world to the dregs we have been groveling at the feet of when we should be worshipped as Gods and not dismissed as if we were vermin!"

"Release me... release..." Threnatta could barely speak as Tantoon was choking her by the throat with his other hand.

"Step back! Step back! Now!" Tantoon screamed, ordering Shantuu and Mimi to step back away from him as he was holding Threnatta as a hostage. "Step back and keep stepping back! Step back! Now!" Tantoon screamed even louder as he pressed the boneknife harder against

Threnatta's throat. A trickle of blood seeped down, drop by drop, down from Threnatta's neck where Tantoon had the boneknife tightly pressed.

"Okay! Okay Tantoon! We are stepping back! We are stepping back!" Shantuu said to Tantoon trying to calm him.

Shantuu and Mimi carefully stepped back away from Tantoon. Step by step, back away.

"Step further back!" Tantoon screamed at them again. "Step even further back than that!"

They did. They stepped, further and further, back away, from Tantoon with Tantoon still holding the boneknife still tightly pressed against Threnatta's neck.

"Further back! Further back!"

Tantoon in an exasperated fit of passion angrily bared his tainted, stench, stained teeth, at Shantuu and Mimi. "How dare you deny my right to defend 'our' people!"

Shantuu was shaking his head in disgust. "You are defending no one! You are only bringing to fruition the paranoid delusions of your imagination. You are no longer of 'our' people, because of your deeds, wants, and desires!"

"There is 'us' and then there is 'them.' I cannot shed my fur and become, bare skinned and hairless, by the scraping of a knife! I will only, ever, still be 'one of us,' bare skinned and hairless, but still 'one of us.'"

"That may well be. It is time for you to refrain from your misguided predilections. Lay down the boneknife and go in peace." Shantuu passionately repeated. "Go in peace! Tantoon! Go in peace!"

"I will go, but not in peace! I will never be in 'peace' until we are all 'one'! However good or bad, right or wrong, just or unjust!"

Tantoon growled and bared his tainted, stench, stained teeth at Shantuu and Mimi once more. "So, it will be! A life for a life!"

And then, much to the shock and horror of what Shantuu and Mimi will always regret, for the rest of their lives, that they were unable to stop, Tantoon slashed open Threnatta's throat and tossed his soon to be former mentor and master, forward, as he ran backed away to the end of the cave tunnel. Shantuu turned and made eye contact with Tantoon as Tantoon was lifting up his arm and turning the palm of his hand upward to face the ceiling of the cave tunnel. There was something glowing in the palm of Tantoon's hand. It was as if Tantoon was holding a greenish, blue, purplish, red, strobe light in his hand.

It was a wandererstone.

One moment Tantoon was there standing at the end of the cave tunnel – the next moment he was gone. Shantuu and Mimi tried their best to prevent Threnatta from bleeding to death right before their very eyes. No matter how hard they pressed and how thoroughly between the both of them they had covered the open wound at Threnatta's neck with their bare hands, the blood pumping threw Threnatta's heart, arteries, veins, and blood vessels, kept gushing out around the sides of their bare hands and threw the cracks of their stubby fingers.

Only a miracle could have saved Threnatta. There were no such miracles happening today.

Threnatta kept bleeding out, all the while gasping, violently, as she continued struggling to breathe until she could struggle no more.

Her eyes went blank.

Her heaving chest stopped heaving.

Shantuu gently and tenderly shut Threnatta's eyes as Mimi looked on.

"She's gone." Shantuu said to Mimi.

"Why?" Mimi was mournfully shaking her head.

"Why did Tantoon do what he has done?"

Shantuu sighed before answering Mimi's question.

"Tantoon's mother had been killed by human hunters when Tantoon was a very young child." Shantuu quietly confessed. "The Elders had thought that by becoming a Healer that it would help to heal the wounds Tantoon has suffered... inside..."

Shantuu looked up to where Tantoon had run off to and vanished.

Mimi compassionately laid her hand on Shantuu's shoulder to comfort him and as if she were reading his mind. She said to Shantuu. "We will never find him. It will be futile to pursue him now."

Shantuu nodded in agreement.

"Maybe now... but not forever..."

Shantuu was angrily proclaiming.

"Not forever..." Shantuu repeated.

"Tantoon's day of reckoning will soon be coming!"

CHAPTER TEN

The next day, after the dreadful incident of the vicious murder of Threnatta and the attempted murder of the human child - Mira – it was decided that the human child was to be moved to a more secluded, more private, area of the cave dwelling where she would be attended to, solely, by Shantuu.

Shantuu was now officially Mira's hero, savior, benefactor, protector, bodyguard, and nursemaid
The plan was that the human child will no longer see, or interact, with any of the others of the Citizenry, other than Shantuu. From here on now, as far as the human child was concerned, there were no other Bigfoots in the wilderness of the Colorado Rockies - other than Shantuu.

Mimi would remain nearby, but out-of-sight, to assist Shantuu, if he should ever need any assistance; until the human child was well enough to be returned to her people.

Morgana had long ago returned to the state of Washington using the ancient magic of the wandererstones to disappear and reappear, teleport, or to enter and exit, from one dimension to another dimension, in space and time.

There still was the possibility that the human child's leg may still have to be amputated, that is if the human child's leg did not heal properly, or if her wounds should become infected, or if gangrene should set in. Naga, a worthy and competent Healer in her own right, had regrettably, stepped in to take over for Threnatta. Naga was going to be sneaking in, back and forth, from time to time, for the next few weeks while the human child is sedated with the dreamsleep elixir and evaluate the status of the human child's condition.

Mira was not afraid of Shantuu. She had seen Shantuu fighting off the pack of wolves. Her ankle had been sewn back together and bandaged and her leg was now, expertly, wrapped in a cast made of sticks, leaves, and twigs. The Bigfoots were like big, furry, Teddy Bears. They seemed to be even more so, as they have been, or so Mira was feeling, as time went on. Naga alleviated the pain from the human child's wounds by sedating the human child with variations of the dreamsleep elixir, which in smaller doses acted as a hallucinogenic, rather than a tranquilizer.

Every time Shantuu noticed that the human child had awakened and was silently staring at him from her bed of furs, Shantuu would comfort the human child. He would keep reassuring the human child that as soon as she was well enough to travel, that being able to walk, or to be able to stand on her own two feet, that he would, personally, return her to her people; not to her home, or to her mother and father. Her mother and father had died. Shantuu had no idea about what kind of home was out there waiting for her.

After a few days, the human child finally spoke to Shantuu. "What's your name?" She asked Shantuu.

"I am Shantuu. What is your name?"

"I am Mira." And then a little later before dozing off again for the night the human child said to Shantuu.

"Thank you."

Later that week Mira awoke to find a stuffed doll lying beside her on her bed of furs. The stuffed doll at first resembled a classic Teddy Bear, but after examining the stuffed doll closer, Mira realized that the stuffed doll was not a stuffed doll of a classic Teddy Bear, but a stuffed doll of a Bigfoot, which another of the Citizenry had acquired and had given to Shantuu to give to the now famous human child. Many tourist stores and souvenir shops in the area had Bigfoot memorabilia, such as stuffed Bigfoot dolls, Bigfoot paperweights, Bigfoot snow globes, Bigfoot posters, Bigfoot pencil erasers, books on Bigfoots, etc., etc. Mira craned her head to the side and spotted Shantuu crouching down in the back of the cave enclave watching her. Mira held up the stuffed Bigfoot doll and said to Shantuu,

"Thank you, Shantuu."

Was that Shantuu smiling?

Were Bigfoots able to smile?

After another few days Mira found a checker and chessboard lying beside her on her bed of furs. Shantuu was sitting beside her, watching her.

"I like chess." Mira said to Shantuu. "Checkers are too easy and boring."

"I thought so." Shantuu said back to Mira.

In the next few weeks Shantuu and Mira had bided their time by playing chess and talking... talking about anything and everything. Shantuu and Mira had become close friends. Shantuu began to feel that he was going to miss Mira even more than he had originally imagined, when he had first met Mira, when the time would come for her to be returned to her people. During her sleeping time, Naga would sneak in and examine the healing process of the human child's wounds. Her bones are healing well. The bite marks are also healing well. The time will soon come for the human child to be returned. How much longer? Shantuu would ask Naga. Not much longer, Naga would answer Shantuu, not much longer, and then one day while Mira was sedated with the dreamsleep elixir, Naga came in and removed the caste of sticks, leaves, and twigs, which were holding the human child's shattered bones in place during the healing process. The human child's threading's, or in human terms, stitches, or sutures, were removed long ago.

Naga noticed Shantuu standing behind her teary-eyed as she was removing the caste of sticks, leaves, and twigs.

Naga remained silent.

She understood the pain and regret Shantuu was feeling.

Naga understood, too, the love Shantuu was feeling for the human child.

Naga, who had also come to know and love the human child, after taking over after Threnatta's unfortunate murder, was also going to miss the human child.

At least the human child had survived and was going to live to grow old.

That was a blessing.

CHAPTER ELEVEN

After so many more days Mira awoke to find Shantuu
sitting beside her with the stuffed Bigfoot doll in his hand.
Was Shantuu crying? Did Bigfoots cry? Mira gingerly
wiggled and wobbled her way to stand beside Shantuu.
She tenderly with her pointer finger touched a teardrop
falling from Shantuu's eye.

> "You are sad because the time has come for me to
> go away."

Shantuu slowly nodded.

> "Why can't I stay here? With you? Why do I have to
> leave?"

> "You belong with your people."

> "My mother and father are gone. I have no one
> else to go back to."

> "You have your grandparents and the sister of your
mother. Remember? You had told me about them. They
will want you back. Even more so after losing your mother
and father."

> "I don't want to go!" Mira angrily replied.

Shantuu tenderly stroked Mira's head with his hand which
was at least five times bigger than Mira's small head. "You
know, yourself, when you look inside your own heart what
must be done."

> "I guess so... I know... it will be too dangerous... for
> you and the others if I were to remain here."

> "Many in the past have been shocked and repulsed
by my kind. Others have embraced us in friendship in the
past, but that was a long time ago. They did not have
machines that can fly or guns that have no other purpose
than to kill."

Mira hugged Shantuu. "I will never tell anyone about you, or about the others. Your secret will always be safe with me."

That seemed to put Shantuu in a better mood. He seemed to chuckle and giggle.

Did Bigfoots chuckle and giggle?

"I don't think anyone would believe you if you did."

"Well, I won't, anyway. I know that you don't want me to."

"I will miss you forever and forever and forever and forever and forever."

"I will miss you, too... forever and forever and forever and forever and forever."

Shantuu hugged Mira back.

"Tomorrow will be the day. In the meantime..."

Mira finished the sentence for Shantuu. "We have enough time to play a few more games of chess."

The next day Shantuu and Mira began their final journey together, not in the early morning, but in the evening as the sun was setting.

"It is better to travel by the dark of night. I will have to take you closer to the populated areas where an eight-foot (2.44 meter) tall Bigfoot is a sight not usually seen on a regular basis."

The others of the Citizenry of the Heseetu, at the cave dwelling, who had remained out-of-sight during Mira's stay at the cave enclave had found, or stolen, or borrowed? From clothing lines, fresh, brand-new clothes for Mira to wear. She had a fresh, brand-new, red and white checkered dress to wear, complete with white ankle length socks and black shoes. Shantuu made sure to bring along a thick sweater to keep the child warm in case the weather should become much chillier than was usually anticipated. The sweater was also red to match Mira's brand new red and white checkered dress. They were coming to the end of summer, which was another reason to return the human child to her people. Better now before the bitter cold and the big snows of winter arrived. The only other possession Mira was taking along, besides her brand-new dress, shoes, socks, and sweater, was the stuffed Bigfoot doll Shantuu had given her.

"We must practice first."

Shantuu said to Mira after carrying her out of one of the many cave entrances/exits back out into the heart of the primeval forest. It was the first time Mira had felt the warmth of the sun on her face, back, and shoulders, for as long as so many weeks? Or months? Mira had lost track of time. It must have been at least three months if they were coming to the end of summer. Mira still needed professional therapy to relearn, more or less, to walk using her still weak and fragile leg.

"I'm going to put you on my shoulders." Shantuu carefully lifted Mira and placed her on his shoulders as if his shoulders and neck were an oversized saddle.

"Wrap your arms around my forehead, or around under my neck, or both, wrap one arm around my forehead and your other arm around under my neck and whatever you do! Be careful not to cover my eyes when you're holding onto my forehead!"

Mira practiced holding onto Shantuu's forehead and neck while he steadied her by wrapping his large Bigfoot hand around Mira's torso to keep her from accidently falling off his shoulders.

"Now we're going to practice walking fast and slow and fast and slow."

Shantuu said to Mira, all the while forewarning her every time he was going to speed up his pace to a fast

75

walking – not running – so that Mira could practice and become comfortable riding along on his shoulders which what was basically going to be a Bigfoot giving a human child a horsey-back ride on its shoulders.

This will be one of those circumstances where the saying 'fact is stranger than fiction' properly applies – if anyone else should ever be, lucky enough or unlucky enough, to witness the phenomenon.

After a while Shantuu was able to successfully trot to a close enough running pace where he didn't have to worry about the Mira accidently falling off his shoulder and, God forbid, hurting herself, or getting hurt, again. Mira loved it. Bouncing up and down on Shantuu's shoulders as he was quickly running up and down slopes and jumping over fallen tree stumps and boulders. Shantuu may have gone on a little longer than he should have. Shantuu was enjoying seeing his new friend, Mira, giggling and laughing after the nightmare events and ordeals she had recently come to suffer.

"Are you ready?" Shantuu asked Mira.

Mira nodded.

"We will be traveling all night until the sun rises and a little longer after that."

"I'm ready." Mira said to Shantuu.

"You are the bravest human I have ever met in my whole entire lifetime."

Mira hugged Shantuu or attempted to hug Shantuu the best that she was able to, being that Mira was barely able to wrap her arms around one of Shantuu's legs, let alone Shantuu's whole, entire, body. Shantuu returned the warmth and love by gently caressing Mira's head and tenderly ruffling her hair.

As the sun was setting, Shantuu with Mira horsey-back riding on his shoulders, made their way, slowly, but not too slowly, back to civilization; slowly because of the long distance they had to travel, no matter how fast walking, or trot running, Shantuu had to do to prevent Mira from accidently being tossed off of his shoulders, the distance was still too long to make their journey any shorter than humanly? Bigfoot? Possible.

By the morning Shantuu with Mira still horsey-back riding on his shoulders were still making their way back to the more populated areas of the Colorado Rockies. On several occasions Mira had accidently lost her hold on the stuffed Bigfoot doll she was carrying. More than a few times Shantuu had to stop and double-back to relocate Mira's stuffed Bigfoot doll. As frustrating as that might be, Shantuu did not ever complain, or let alone ever think about leaving the stuffed Bigfoot doll behind.

There was one occasion when Shantuu with Mira horsey-back riding on his shoulders had almost, accidently, stumbled upon a small group of hikers on a trail. The hikers were downwind. Shantuu had, more so, heard the hikers, instead of picking up their scent.

Shantuu heard a child, or a human woman, shouting out.

"What the hell is that?"

Shantuu immediately dived behind several trees and a thick outcropping of bushes and was gone.

By noon that day Shantuu stopped beside a worn-out dirt road used by humans driving vehicles and riding horses to travel back and forth on a dirt road to a stream in Blue Valley called Little Bear Creek.

This was going to be good-bye.

Mira hugged Shantuu again, and again, and again. Mira didn't want to ever let go. In the last few weeks, Shantuu had come as close, as possible, to being a second mother and father to Mira, or an uncle, or a big, furry, living and breathing, walking and talking, chess and checker playing Teddy Bear.

Shantuu was sniffing the air.

"Yes."

Shantuu nodded.

"Yes."

Shantuu was satisfied with whatever he had identified by using the super-sensitive olfactory nerves in his nose.

Shantuu lifted Mira and stepped out onto the worn-out dirt road. He placed Mira on the stump of a fallen tree.

"Stay here."

Shantuu sniffed the air one more time.

"There are two Guardians of the Forest coming this way from the road up ahead riding on their wheeled mechanized devices."

Shantuu hugged Mira for what will be the very last time.

"They are coming. They are nearby. I hear them." In a flash Shantuu dived back into the thick clump of bushes and was gone.

"Good-bye, Shantuu, good-bye." Mira said keeping her eyes on the road to prevent whoever was coming from spotting Shantuu.

From a nearby distance Mira heard Shantuu whisper to her.

"I am still watching. I will wait until the two Guardians of the Forest have safely taken you away."

There was the light roar of a jeep engine coming from the worn-out dirt road up ahead. The Park Rangers riding in the jeep must have spotted Mira sitting on the stump of the fallen tree down the road. They slowed the jeep to a halt, stopping by the stump where Mira was sitting.

One of the Park Rangers – Lucy McGill – said to the other Park Ranger in the jeep – Timothy Spencer – "It's a little girl."

"Where's her parents?"

As Park Ranger McGill was stepping out of the jeep Park Ranger McGill was saying to Park Ranger Spencer. "Doesn't she look familiar?"

Park Ranger Spencer squinted at the young girl sitting on the tree stump.

"She looks like… the lost girl… Mira Salinas."

"She's been gone for almost four months."

"Impossible!"

Park Ranger McGill stepped closer.

"Young lady… where are your parents?"

"What is your name?"

Mira signed sadly. "My Mommy and Daddy were hurt… in a landslide… a… a… a… while ago. My name is Mira. Mira Salinas."

Park Ranger McGill almost collapsed in shock.

"It's a miracle!" Park Ranger Spencer kept repeating as he took Mira by the hand and escorted her to the jeep.

As they were riding away Mira spotted a big, brown, furry hand waving to her from out of the top of a thick clump of bushes.

Mira waved back.

Park Ranger McGill noticed Mira waving.

"Who are you waving to?" Park Ranger McGill asked Mira.

"Nobody." Mira mournfully answered. "Nobody. I was just saying good-bye to the forest."

CHAPTER TWELVE

Several months later Park Ranger McGill was sipping from a hot cup of freshly brewed tea at the Blue Valley Rangers station she and her co-worker were assigned to when her co-worker Park Ranger Spencer entered the radio room on the top floor of the Rangers station.

A rush of cold air blew in from the frozen forest outside. The first snows of winter had fallen.

"Hey! Shut that door!" Park Ranger McGill yelled back at Park Ranger Spencer as he was shaking the snow off of his hat, jacket, and boots.

"You're letting all the warm air out!"

Park Ranger Spencer strutted up to where Park Ranger McGill was seated and dropped a copy of the NATIONAL ENQUIRER on the desk in front of her.

"Look at that! Do you see that?" Park Ranger Spencer was pointing and tapping with his finger at the front cover of the NATIONAL ENQUIRER for emphasis. Park Ranger McGill carefully placed her cup of hot tea on the side of the desktop far enough away from the copy of the NATIONAL ENQUIRER where she didn't have to worry about accidently knocking over the cup of hot tea and having it accidently spilling onto the copy of the NATIONAL ENQUIRER.

Park Ranger McGill leaned forward over the desk for a moment to take a closer look at the cover of the copy of the NATIONAL ENQUIRER and then she leaned back in her chair.

"A UFO abductee gave birth to an alien-human hybrid."

Park Ranger McGill was sarcastically shaking her head.

"What else is new?"

"No! Not that!" Park Ranger Spencer began tapping his pointed finger again on the front cover of the NATIONAL ENQUIRIER at a photo below the headline of a UFO abductee giving birth to an alien-human hybrid.

"That!" Park Ranger Spencer continued tapping his finger on the photo.

Once again Park Ranger McGill leaned forward to take a better look at the cover.

"It's..." Park Ranger McGill crinkled her nose in shock and dismay. "A photo of a Bigfoot with a young girl riding horsey-back on its shoulder... with a stuffed Bigfoot doll in her hands!"

Park Ranger McGill and Park Ranger Spencer looked back and forth and back and forth again and back and forth again and again a few more times from the photo on the cover of the NATIONAL ENQUIRER to a photo on the wall of the radio room of both of them with the lost child they had miraculously found this summer - Mira Salinas.

In the photo on the wall of the radio room - the young girl Mira Salinas - was also holding a stuffed Bigfoot doll in her hands.

"The lost child, Mira Salinas, had the same, exact, Bigfoot doll when we found her as the child in the photo?" Park Ranger Spencer said to Park Ranger McGill.

"Yes. She did. Yes. She definitely did have a stuffed Bigfoot doll that looks exactly like the stuffed Bigfoot doll in the photo when we found her sitting on that tree stump out in the middle of nowhere."

The photo in the NATIONAL ENQUIRER was slightly blurred and whomever had taken the photo was only able to capture the backs of the Bigfoot and the young girl - that is if the photo was actually authentic and not a hoax -

as so many photos of Bigfoots, Sasquatches, and Yetis have been disproven to be.

The reappearance of the lost child - Mira Salinas – who had been presumed to be dead had become one of the greatest mysteries of the 21st century. The fact that Mira Salinas had been missing for five months from May to October that year and had conveniently reappeared at the end of the summer before the harsh snows of winter had begun to fall, was too, unbelievable, to be believed, and furthermore, the fact that intricate surgery had been performed on the lost child's leg stretched the limits of credulity.

"I don't remember what happened after my Mommy and Daddy died." Was all Mira Salinas ever had to say about the matter. "I don't remember." And that was that.

"Is the photo real?" Park Ranger McGill asked Park Ranger Spencer.

"There are some experts who are saying the photo is real and then there are other experts who are saying the photo has been photoshopped. One expert in particular is saying there is a smudge on the photo by the neck of the Bigfoot where a zipper has been covered up."
Park Ranger McGill was shaking her head, side to side.

"Naaaaa! No way! Its real! It's freakin' real!"

Park Ranger Spencer was slowly nodding his head, up and down, in agreement. "You know it and I know it. We know it now. All of these 'so-called' experts didn't see it with their very own eyes. Like we did. All of these 'so-called' experts didn't stumble across Mira Salinas, out there, in the middle of nowhere, sitting like a bump on a log like we did. We know better."

"Most definitely so..." Park Ranger McGill continued shaking her head, side to side. "We know better... now! Nobody ever believes anything, anyway, about anything we say!"

Park Ranger Spencer was staring at the photo on the front cover of the NATIONAL ENQUIRER with his mouth opened agape in wonder and horror.

"What more is there out there?"

"I would've been afraid to be thinking about it if I haven't already been thinking about it for the longest time."

CHAPTER THIRTEEN

Twelve years later during the summer after her fifth year in college a twenty-one-year-old Mira returned to the tree stump in the Colorado Rockies Blue Valley where the kind and gentle Bigfoot - Shantuu - had taken her, after rescuing her, to be returned to her people; so long ago. Mira had begun attending college at the age of fifteen, when she should have been graduating from Junior High School or begun attending High school. Mira was a prodigy. She didn't like the term 'genius.' Geniuses made breakthroughs in science, medicine, and engineering, that permanently changed the present and the future of humankind and the world. She had merely as many other prodigies like her had done, in the past, present, and will continue to do so in the future, mastered the basic and standard educational curriculums of their present days and times. By the end of her last year in Junior High School, school officials had decided that her time would be better spent attending college. She had received several scholarship offers by that time; but she chose to follow in her Mother and Father's footsteps by remaining in Colorado, attending Colorado State University. Mira graduated in two years with a Master's Degree in Chemistry, and two more years later with a Master's Degree in Biology; after one more year, which was her fifth year altogether, Mira was well on her way to receiving a third Master's Degree in Anthropology – which was one reason why she had returned to the wilds of the Colorado Rocky Mountains. What better research subjects could there ever be than the mysterious an elusive Bigfoots, Sasquatches, and Yetis, of the forests, woodlands, jungles, swamps, snow peaked mountaintops, and wildernesses of the world - and besides - Mira missed Shantuu.

She still had with her as she was sitting there on the tree stump, which she was currently cradling in her arms, the stuffed Bigfoot doll Shantuu had given her when she was still recovering from her wounds, so long ago, back in the cave dwelling – the secret cave dwelling of the Citizenry of the Heseetu – which she had been unsuccessfully trying to locate for the past few days. Mira had never told another living soul about her big, furry, friend and savior – Shantuu – or about any of the other Bigfoots she had encountered, or about the secret cave dwellings which were the homes and hiding places of the community of Bigfoots.

During the past several days as Mira was searching for the entrance to the cave dwelling or the entrance to any cave dwellings, she would tack to the sides of as many trees as possible 8.5x14 inch (0.22x0.36 meter) posters, which she had made with two photos of herself – then and now – holding the stuffed Bigfoot doll in her hands with a short message proclaiming –

I am here – where are you? Your friend Mira.

Mira only had the time and money to spend ten days this year searching for her long-lost friend – the Bigfoot – Shantuu. Today was the last of the ten days she was able to sacrifice pursuing this endeavor. After tonight she will have to return to her personal and professional duties and commitments, until after another year – if she could find the time and money.

Life always takes over no matter what we do. We have only so much time to do the things we want or need to do. We have to pick and choose, sometimes, not always for the better, or for the most fulfilling reasons.

I don't know when I will be able to come back, Mira was mournfully thinking. This is going to be good-bye, without ever having had the chance to say hello – one time once more – for the longest time.

Oh well, oh well, oh well... and then Mira heard a twig snapping from behind where she was sitting on the tree stump.

She turned around.

Standing there behind her was...

Shantuu!

Mira was immediately thinking that she was still unable to tell if Bigfoots were able to smile? Shantuu seemed to be smiling... but she still was not sure.

CHAPTER FOURTEEN

Twenty-two years after Mira had been rescued by Shantuu
and twelve years after Mira and Shantuu had been
reunited way back then so long ago...

Shantuu was hiding behind a thick beechwood tree
as several vehicles were passing by on the gravel road
several feet away. The brown trunk of the beechwood tree
helped to camouflage Shantuu's extra-large nine-foot
(2.74 meter) frame, with a little help from the many leaves
on the many bushes, weeds, vines, and wild brush
interspersed between the many other beechwood, maple
and pinewood trees. He very quickly sprang out from
behind the beechwood tree and very quickly sprinted over
and across the gravel road with the hand-sewn leather
pouch he was carrying slung over one shoulder flopping up
and down as he was running to camouflage himself, again,
behind the many other trees and many other bushes,
weeds, vines and wild brush on the other side of the gravel
road. He looked back for a moment, sniffing the air, and
listening for the slightest of sounds. There was nothing. No
one was following him. No one had noticed him. Not that
anyone would be following him. Any sane human being,
that is; ordinary people were instantly shocked and
repulsed when they accidently came upon or encountered
him and the many others of his kind, out here, in the
wilderness, woodlands, deserts, and forests.

Shantuu - repeating from the previous narrative - is
what is commonly known in folklore, urban legend and in
scientific circles as a Bigfoot, or Sasquatch, or, in the Artic
and Antarctic regions, a Yeti. Others have referred to his
kind as the missing link. He heard the snap, crunch, thump,
snap, of footsteps running away from him further down
the hill. Shantuu was very quickly up on his feet running

towards where he had heard the snap, crunch, thump, snap, sounds coming from.

Whoever was running from Shantuu was trying to hide the fact that they were running from Shantuu as Shantuu, himself, was also, equally, trying to hide the fact that he was chasing after them. All to no avail, as each of them were aware of each other's motivations and intentions.

Shantuu dug into the leather pouch slung over his shoulder and pulled out what appeared to be a hand-carved wooden flute, but only half the length of a regular hand-carved wooden flute with four holes running along on the shaft and two holes at the tip of both ends. Shantuu put one end of the whispererwood in his mouth - whispererwood - being the name the Citizenry had given to the ancient wooden device and Citizenry - being the name of the society of Bigfoots, Sasquatches, and Yetis, Shantuu belonged to and was part of, was born into and raised to become the Shadow-walker, he was presently today. As Shantuu blew into the whispererwood, covering and uncovering the four holes running along the shaft of the whispererwood in sets of several different sequences, producing several different sequences of sounds inaudible to the human ear. A whispererwood was a Citizenry - Bigfoot - version of a dog whistle. The others of the Citizenry who were following behind had received and answered Shantuu's message with whispererwoods of their own.

The Sawtooth, or Rogue, they were chasing after did not speak, did not know, did not understand the strange sounds the whispererwoods were making; he only knew the scent of the three that resembled his kind kept matching his footsteps, matching the paths he was traversing, for whatever reason, his untrained, feeble mind, was unable to discern.

There was a crunch and a snap sound coming from somewhere behind where Shantuu was hiding, crouched down behind in the middle of a row of thick green bushes. Without turning to see what had made those crunch, snap sounds, Shantuu said, "If you were trying to sneak up behind me, I would've already flipped you over on your back, or put a dreamsleep dart in your side."

Cazzii giggled. "I was hoping you would've guessed it was me." Cazzii giggled some more. "I know better than to try to sneak up on you, Shantuu."

"Like Ringru is currently attempting to do so now."

Shantuu was staring straight ahead. Cazzii did not immediately see what Shantuu was seeing, then she saw the bushes up ahead 'not swaying' when the bushes up ahead should have been 'swaying.'

"He sees you." Cazzii said to the 'not swaying bushes.' "You're wasting your time by trying to blend in with the bushes yourself."

There were some more crunch and snap sounds coming from up ahead where Shantuu and Cazzii were facing and then from out of the thick clump of bushes came Ringru.

"¿Como sigues hacienda eso?/How do you keep doing that?" Ringru said to them in Spanish. "Hice todo lo posible para permanecer camuflado."/I did my best to remain camouflaged."

"Patience and practice, Ringru. It takes patience and practice." Shantuu said to Ringru in English.
"A lot of patience and a lot of practice." Cazzii added, also in English.
Ringru did not waste any more time mincing words. He pointed to the southwestern sky. There were several

curved lines of smoke sticking up from out of the horizon disappearing into the clear blue skies. Smoke from several chimneys nearby.

"El va hacia el borde de una ciudad poblada/He is going towards the edge of a populated town." Ringru said to Shantuu and Cazzii still speaking in Spanish.

"We cannot allow that to happen." Shantuu was saying in English as he was sighing. "How have we survived all of these past centuries?"

Ringru was speaking to Shantuu and Cazzii in Spanish and Shantuu and Cazzii was speaking back to Ringru in English. They all understood what each other was saying.

Shantuu was a male, about as large, at nine-foot (2.74 meters) tall, as Bigfoots, Sasquatches, and Yetis, usually grew too. His fur was a lighter shade of brown, but not very light, Ringru was also a male, about eight-foots (2.44 meters) tall, his fur was pitch black, and Cazzii, a female, was a little shorter than Ringru. Cazzii being about seven-and-a-half-foots (2.29 meters) tall, with gray fur, which sometimes seemed to be blue, depending on the dark or light of the day, or the glow of the moon at night.

"The Rogue cannot speak" Ringru was saying to both Shantuu and Cazzii in Spanish. "If we frighten him, he might try to escape through the open streets of the nearby town. All the humans will see him and photograph him with their cameras on their communication devices."

"Cellphones." Shantuu corrected Ringru. "Their dispositivos de communicacion, or communication devices, are called cellphones, in English, and cellular, in Spanish."

"Sell fones." Cazzii clumsily mimicked Shantuu in broken English.

"Sneak around in front and flank the Rogue before he has a chance to enter the human habitat." Although Shantuu was nonchalantly suggesting a course of action as if he were having a casual conversation with Ringru and Cazzii. Shantuu's suggestion was actually an order given to two subordinates. Shantuu was an Elder of the Citizenry of the Heseetu, and Ringru and Cazzii were Underlings.

"We may have to put the Rogue into a foreversleep instead of a dreamsleep." Ringru was saying, meaning that they might have to outright kill the Rogue with a poison dart from a blowstick, instead of a tranquilizer dart. A tranquilizer dart took longer to affect the metabolism of those who have been shot. The Rogue might still make it into a populated area of the human habitat/town and pass out in the middle of a street as hundreds of humans are passing by.

So far, the Citizenry of Bigfoots, Sasquatches, and Yetis, have remained in the background, out of sight, in the shadows. The majority of Humans still believed that Bigfoots, Sasquatches, and Yetis, were a myth, that they were not real, that they did not exist.

The duty and responsibility of the Citizenry was to maintain that disbelief, to keep their existence secret, as they have done so for so many centuries.

Shantuu, Cazzii, and Ringru suddenly craned their heads upward towards the sky. Their highly attuned olfactory senses were picking up the presence of a bear, or bears, or a pack of wolves, or one of their own kind? Nearby... slowly approaching heading towards the Rogue.

"¿Que es eso?/What is that?" Ringru said, still speaking in Spanish.

"I don't know... but we will soon find out." Shantuu answered, still speaking in English.

"Whatever it is... I don't like it." Cazzii added, still speaking in English.

Then from where the Rogue was last spotted, hiding, resting behind a large tree, they heard the sounds, however faint - crunch, crunch, snap, snap, crunch, snap, crunch, snap, crunch.

"The Rogue is making a run for it!" Shantuu half whispered, half shouted. "Go after him! Go after him now!"

Cazzii and Ringru were instantly on their feet disappearing into the thick brush. Shantuu maintained a steady pace following behind to wherever the Rogue was running off to. Bigfoots, sasquatches, and Yetis were able to run as fast as lions, tigers, and bears. Ringru had made it around, ahead, in front of the Rogue with Cazzii doing the same on the opposite side. Ringru jumped out from the brush in front of the Rogue, surprising the Rogue, causing the Rogue to react and run to the side, where Cazzii, also jumped out from the brush, in front of the Rogue, surprising the Rogue, causing the Rogue to react and run backwards to where Shantuu was waiting with his blowstick raised. It happened instantaneously and simultaneously like lightning striking. As the Rogue was breaking out through the brush in front of Shantuu, Shantuu heard the snap, crunch, snap, crunch, of running footsteps coming from his left side as his nostrils were filled with the scent of the other presence they had vaguely detected. Another one of their kind burst through the brush, smacking the blow stick out of Shantuu's hand and brusquely knocking Shantuu to the ground. Shantuu's attacker had disappeared into the brush as quickly as he had appeared grabbing the Rogue by the arm and taking the Rogue with him.

The first thing Ringru and Cazzii had to say as they were breaking through the brush to were Shantuu was presently sprawled out on the ground.

"¿Lo conseguiste?/Did you get him?" Ringru asked Shantuu followed by Cazzii who asked, "What happened?" As Shantuu was stumbling to get back on his feet. "It was another of our kind."

"¿Otro de la Cuidadania?/Another of the Citizenry?" Ringru asked.

"Another Rogue?" Cazzii also asked.

Shantuu was rubbing his shoulder and back. The surprise attacker had hit him hard. If Shantuu had been a human, and not a Bigfoot, the surprise attacker would have broken his back, neck, and skull. Shantuu would have been dead.

"It was not a Rogue or a Sawtooth." (Sawtooth - another word for Rogue with a minimal understanding of language and a rudimentary knowledge of basic educational skills.) "It was one of Tantoon's fanatical followers." or soldiers; as far as anyone was concerned. There was little to no difference between fanatical followers and soldiers when it came to Tantoon's twisted congregation of decrepit worshippers.

Tantoon was once a well-respected member of the Citizenry, apprenticed as a Healer, until he rebelled and became a murderous psychotic thug. He vanished into the wilderness and began recruiting lone Rogues and Sawtooths, wherever he could find them, forming his own, haphazard, disjointed, unconventional, unofficial Citizenry, or Army. Tantoon would only teach the Rogues and Sawtooths enough to function at certain specific duties, to do his bidding, to work for him as barely no better and no more than brainwashed slaves.

An intricate game of cat and mouse ensued, or Bigfoot and Bigfoot, as the Rogue and his newfound companion and savior continued to evade Shantuu, Ringru, and Cazzii's efforts to curtail their descent into the populated areas; where no humans have ever seen or believed the existence of Bigfoots. After so many run-ins and near run-ins, Shantuu, Ringru, and Cazzii had finally cornered the Rogue and the Rogues companion/savior in a small open patch of the dense forest. Shantuu, Ringru, and Cazzii slowly moved in to hopefully subdue the Rogue and the Rogues companion/savior. The Rogue and the Rogues companion/savior were surrounded. Shantuu, Ringru, and Cazzii were now able to see that the Rogue companion/savior had a hand-sewn leather pouch slung over his shoulder much the same as the hand-sewn leather pouch Shantuu had slung over his own shoulder.

"We mean you no harm." Shantuu was saying to the companion/savior. "We only wanted to prevent the Rogue… from making a spectacle of himself. We cannot allow our kind to make spectacles of themselves in the world of humans."

"That is never good." Cazzii added.

"Especially as we have always been outnumbered."

The companion/savior quickly pulled out a dull blue rock from his leather pouch, which fitted perfectly into the palm of his hand. At first the dull blue rock was lifeless, like a switched-off blue light bulb, then the dull blue rock began to flash bright blue, like a switched-on blue light bulb, back to dull blue, back to bright blue, back to dull blue, back to bright blue and then remained bright blue like a blue colored light bulb permanently switched-on. Shantuu knew exactly what was happening, or about to happen. Before he could react, the Rogue's companion/savior said to Shantuu —

"You are Shantuu. We will meet again, soon."

The Rogue's companion/savior grabbed hold of the Rogue, putting his arm around the neck and shoulder of the Rogue, and then in an instant, they were gone, they had disappeared, they had vanished into thin air.

"Did you see that." Shantuu was saying to Ringru and Cazzii.

"¿La roca azul intermitente que el otro picaro tenia en la palma de su mano?/The flashing blue rock the other Rogue had in the palm of his hand?" Ringru said to Shantuu and Cazzii, still speaking in Spanish.

"It was a wandererstone."

Shantuu did not say much afterwards and Ringru and Cazzii also remained silent for a while. Wandererstones were enchanted runes used for millenniums by alchemists and ancient mystics to open the doorways of the many dimensions in space and time. You could say that wandererstones were natural teleportation devices. Merlin, the 'so-called' Magician from ancient folklore and fables, may or may have not been an actual magician - if he had ever actually existed. Merlin may have just possessed and had learned or been taught how to unlock the secrets of the enchanted runes known as wandererstones...

But that was not what Shantuu was thinking. What Shantuu was thinking is that the Rogue's companion/savior had recognized him and that he had recognized the Rogue's companion/savior.

They had recognized each other.

The Rogue's companion/savior was none other than - Orgu - a friend and confidant of Tantoon - who had long ago turned his back upon and rebelled against the world for what many say, is because, Tantoon's mother – Tanara – had been slain by human Bigfoot hunters when Tantoon was a child.

Not all accidents are unintentional.

CHAPTER FIFTEEN

The portable laboratory - which was a black mini-bus about half as long in length as a commercial public transportation bus - was parked in the alleyway behind a five-story building identified with only the numbered street address over the front doorway entrance. Very few people in the surrounding neighborhood were aware that the five-story building, which was located in the city of Denver, Colorado, was actually owned and operated by Rand Biotech; one of the largest research and development conglomerates in the world.

Dr. Mira Salinas was alone in the laboratory/minibus tapping away on her computer when she heard the tap-tap-tap of footsteps walking up the three-step, switch-operated, retractable ramp at the entrance of the van.

A tall hulk of a man was standing at the entrance. He slightly bowed his head and touched the rim of his camouflaged hunter's hat. He was dressed in more or less hunters clothing. His pants and shirt were the same color of brown, as trees, bush branches and ground soil in the forests and woodlands and the vest he was wearing matched the same pattern of fabric as his camouflaged hunter's hat; which was made to resemble the green, brown, and yellow of the leaves on trees, bushes, and clumps of overgrown grass.

"Good day Milady." He said as a salutation to Dr. Salinas. She preferred to be called by her first name – Mira – by her friends, she did not consider Hector Amaro, also officially and unofficially known as Hector the Hunter, a friend; the aforementioned hulk of a man standing at the laboratory/minibus entrance.

"Good day to you, too, Mr. Amaro."

"Hector. Call me Hector."

Mira did not say anything to that, but merely continued typing away at her computer keyboard.

"Did you hear the news?" Hector the Hunter said to her, knowing damn well that she did indeed hear the news. Everyone at this particular job site had heard the news.

"There's going to be hell to pay, one way or another."

Mira stopped typing. "Why would anyone switch the bone sample? For what purpose? If anyone wanted the bone sample, they would've just stolen it, outright, instead of playing games like trying to hide the existence of the bone sample by replacing it with another bone sample."

"It wasn't just the bone sample, they suspect, has been tampered with, they're also saying hair strands found earlier do not match the hair strands they have currently locked away in the vault."

"Why would anyone do that?" Mira turned to Hector the Hunter, giving him her full attention. "What would anyone have to gain by doing that? It doesn't make any sense."

"Corporate espionage!" Hector the Hunter blurted out. "That would make a lot of sense."

"The bone sample and the hair strands cannot be worth much." Mira was shaking her head.

"If the bone sample and the hair strands proved the existence of sasquatches, out here in the wild, they would be priceless!"

Mira did not say anything but returned to typing away at the computer keyboard.

"Anyway, Rand Biotech has some top security specialists checking out everything."

"Happy hunting to them." Mira mumbled inconsequentially. "I hope they find whatever they are looking for. I'm too busy trying to get some work done around here to be worrying about super spies sneaking around."

"Speaking of work, are you all packed and ready to go on our next big trip together?" Hector the Hunter was purposely teasing Mira. He knew she was not looking forward to spending a few days out in the wild with Hector the Hunter and any of the other professional outdoorsmen and wilderness guides Rand Biotech had hired to escort the research team on their next field trip.

Mira waved away Hector the Hunter. He was giggling at that as he was walking out through the doorway of the laboratory/minibus. Mira was nervously staring at his retreating back.

They had just had one of those conversations where what was said was too much and the too much that was said was not enough.

The next morning at the break of dawn the research team and the aforementioned professional outdoorsmen and wilderness guides - who seemed to be more so hired mercenaries and out of work retired soldiers than outdoorsmen and wilderness guides - were loading the last of their supplies onto one of two black minibuses. What kind of professional outdoorsmen and wilderness guides went on hiking trips equipped with assault rifles, tranquilizer pistols, stun grenades, steel mesh nets and metal cages big enough to hold a large bear?

The professional outdoorsmen and wilderness guides had their own separate, personal, black minibus which was not equipped with laboratory and medical facilities. Their black minibus was more so a once empty husk, now filled with camping equipment, a small armament, and a few cages.

The research team consisted of Dr. Mira Salinas, Dr. Kasper Weinberger, who was so old he could have easily passed for being over one-hundred years old, Dr. Lisa Wintergarden, who was a trust fund brat, and Dr. Dobie Doberson, who was born and raised poor and had sacrificed and worked hard to be where he was today. Dr. Salinas, Dr. Weinberger, and Dr. Doberson, were all in their early thirties and had recently graduated with Masters Degrees in several different fields from the most prestigious colleges and universities in the world.
The hunters or professional outdoorsmen/wilderness guides - also worked as security guards for Rand Biotech - consisted of Hector Amaro, also officially and unofficially known as Hector the Hunter, Jason 'Red' Redfield, and Crystal Gains. They were all ex-military and as far as anyone on the research team was concerned – functioning psychopaths. Hector the Hunter was a middle-aged male, while Red, which was what everyone called Jason Redfield, and Crystal, which was what everyone called Crystal Gains, were also in their early thirties. Red was an Irish-American male with pinkish white skin covered with orange freckles and a mop of bushy orange hair on top of his head which matched his bushy orange mustache. Crystal was an African-American female. She liked to keep her hair short and meticulously braided.

Last to come onboard to join the research team and the hunters on their excursion was a Rand security expert by the name of Ulysses Springfield. He was quiet and mostly kept to himself, except for when he was privately conferring with Hector the Hunter. They seemed to have a lot in common? Or they were old friends? Which they were not, friends, however long they may have been acquainted with each other. Conspirators with a secret agenda. That would better describe what was going on there between the two.

They drove for most of the day, until past sundown and then into the night, random volunteers amongst the research team and hunters taking turns behind the wheels of the minibuses. They drove until there were no more highways or paved roads anywhere nearby or faraway. This was the forest primeval, or the closest you can get to it outside the city limits of Denver, Colorado. It was as if they had journeyed to another world.

Mira had fallen asleep. She was awakened by the vehicle suddenly coming to a stop and the rumble of the engine ceasing to silently vibrate along the ceiling, floors, and walls. As she was stepping out of the black minibus she was instantly aware by the position of several of the nearby mountaintops in the horizon that they had detoured, overnight, northwest, towards Blue Valley, instead of continuing southeast, to Pine Valley; as she was told would be their destination. Mira noticed Hector the Hunter and Security Expert Springfield watching her indirectly by glancing at her by slightly twisting their heads to the side.

It was Hector the Hunter who spoke up first.
"Whatsamatter, Milady? Is there something bothering you?"
"I thought we were going southeast to Pine Valley? Why did we detour Northwest to Blue Valley?"
"New orders, Milady."
"Can you please stop calling me – Milady!"
"Yes, Milady, as you wish, or should I say – Madame?"
Mira snorted disgustingly. "That sounds even creepier! Especially coming out of your mouth."

Hector the Hunter merely chuckled at that.

"I thought you knew about the last-minute change of plan." Kasper said to Mira.

"Last-minute change of plan! What last-minute change of plan? Nobody told me anything about a last-minute change of plan."

"It's all there on the updated itinerary. Just pop it up on your computer." Hector the Hunter added

"Updated itinerary! Last-minute change of plan! Who's in charge here?"

"You're supposed to be, deary." Dr. Dobie Doberson said to Mira.

Mira was shaking her head, negatively.

"That's the way Rand Biotech likes to do things." Dobie was shaking his head, too.

"It's another wonderful, glorious, day at Rand Biotech!" Lisa added as she was gently patting Mira on the back. "I am just as surprised as you are."

Mira was not going to allow the matter to be as easily dismissed as the others were so happily permitting. "We were supposed to be investigating Frosberg Park in Pine Valley! Why did we detour northwest to Blue Valley?" Mira crinkled her nose in dismay. "Isn't that the Waywan Cliffs? We weren't supposed to take a field trip to the Waywan Cliffs until a month from now!"

"It's what the big boss at Rand Biotech wants us to do." Hector the Hunter loved rubbing it in. "You can complain when we get back, or you're free to write an angry email." Hector the Hunter was smiling sardonically. "You can write all the angry emails your heart desires!" He chuckled one time before moving on to quickly inventory the equipment and supplies they were going to be taking on their hike.

They were walking down into a canyon in the Waywan Cliffs for an hour or two before Hector the Hunter suddenly stopped on a hillside ledge they were using as a sort of natural trail. He was staring at the branch of a thick bush surrounded by hundreds, if not thousands, of other thick bushes.

Crystal and Red who were further up ahead detoured back to rendezvous with Hector the Hunter with Red immediately saying to Hector the Hunter.

"What's going on? What happened?"

"Didn't you see that." Hector the Hunter turned away from the bush.

"See what?"

"I don't see anything." Crystal added.

"There!" Hector the Hunter was pointing at the aforementioned bush. "There! You don't see that?" Red and Crystal leaned forward to take a closer look. A branch on the bush had been snapped in two. Hector the Hunter was running his finger along the tip where the branch had been broken off snapped in two.

"That had not been done naturally, or accidently, by any forest animals running along. It was done purposely."

Hector the Hunter was looking up and all around while simultaneously sniffing the air like a hound dog. "We are not alone..."

"What do you mean?" Red was quick to say. "We're in the middle of nowhere! There are no other vehicles out here! I don't see any tracks anywhere! No one is out here but us!"

Hector the Hunter crouched down on the ground examining the foliage.

Mira was nervously watching Hector the Hunter as Security Expert Springfield - the Rand Biotech security expert - was nonchalantly watching Mira - watching Hector the Hunter..

"Look there!" Hector the Hunter was pointing to a small branch with several leaves still attached to the branch that had been discarded several feet away which Hector the Hunter had assumed was purposely left there as a marker."

"By whom? And why?" Red was shaking his head.

Mira finally spoke up. "What? Are you seeing ghosts now? Is that why you are taking us all the way out here? To catch the Boogeyman?" It was Mira's turn to chuckle sardonically – touché.

Hector the Hunter stared back at Mira for a moment. Okay! Let's keep moving along!" He ordered the members of the field trip even though no one was particularly in-charge. Mira slowed her pace a bit purposely falling behind the others as they were trotting along.

"Are you okay?" Lisa asked Mira.

"Oh. Don't worry about me. I think I tied my boot laces too tight. Go on. I'll catch up."

You could hear Hector the Hunter shouting back at them from further up ahead. "Don't take too long to retie your boot laces. You might get snatched away by a mountain lion or a hungry pack of wolves might jump out of the bush and tear you to shreds before we can get back to you and shoot off a few rounds at them with our guns."

"Go on! I'm okay! What are you now? A mother hen?"

The others moved on ahead as Mira sat down on the soft foliage to fiddle about with her boot laces. It seemed, as if, as soon as the others were out of sight... someone... or something... tossed a small leather pouch out from the thick bush which landed in front of where

Mira was seated. Mira quickly snatched up the small leather pouch and instantly dropped the small leather pouch into her backpack. Just as quickly, she grabbed an almost identical small leather pouch from her backpack and tossed it back at the area of the thick bush where the first small leather pouch had been tossed from. Mira quickly stood up and continued walking along the rocky canyon ledge to catch up with the others, without untying, and retying, her boot laces. When she turned a corner or two she abruptly came face to face with Hector the Hunter who stood in front of her like an unmovable boulder blocking her from moving further.

He was watching her suspiciously.

"So… you haven't been eaten alive by a carnivorous predator hiding in the shadows."

"I told you I'd be okay."

Security Expert Springfield was further up ahead suspiciously watching Hector the Hunter suspiciously watching Mira.

Mira noticed Security Expert Springfield up ahead watching them.

"Don't you guys have anything better to do!" Mira said to them as she was walking around passed Hector the Hunter simultaneously sneering at Security Expert Springfield as she was also walking around passed him. "What do I need? Cannibal pygmies attacking to get you two off my back!"

"They don't have those out here." Lisa was saying from further up ahead on the rocky canyon ledge.

"If they did." Dobie answered. "Rand Biotech would've sent a bigger research team with a whole platoon of armed mercenaries."

"Rand Biotech wouldn't need a platoon of armed mercenaries as long as they had us!" Crystal was also saying.

"No they wouldn't" Red added to that.

Mira was relieved. For a moment there she had thought that Hector the Hunter had seen her exchanging leather pouches with someone or something in the bush. When Hector the Hunter and Security Expert Springfield did not ask to search her backpack, Mira knew she was more or less free and clear; except for the annoying possibility that Hector the Hunter and Security Expert Springfield seemed to be suspiciously watching her a bit more than she would have preferred.

"Keep moving along!" Hector the Hunter shouted out to everyone. "We want to find a safe place to camp before the sun sets."

They kept moving along until Hector the Hunter told everyone to stop.

"This looks like a good spot. Unpack and set up the tents!"

Surprisingly, after a campfire had been fired up, everyone seemed to relax and begin joking and playfully teasing each other, as if they were all in a good mood, but Mira knew, the teasing wasn't so much harmless bantering than passive-aggressive pent-up anger being gingerly released instead of manifesting itself in all-out, knockdown, drag'em out, fist fighting bouts. Dobie had a ukulele stored somewhere in his backpack and Red pulled out a harmonica he was hiding amongst his camping supplies and portable armaments he was carrying on his back. Together, they weren't as half bad at belting out a few folk songs and classic campfire singalong tunes as they were at stomping about and dancing to their own music.

After so many swigs from a whisky bottle, Hector the Hunter seemed to relax and calm down a bit. Mira sat by the campfire watching them all, joking and laughing, halfway talking shop and halfway, timidly, flirting with each other. Mira wouldn't be surprised if one or two of them detoured into the bush for a private conversation, or a short, long, walk; where conversing and walking were only prerequisites for more intimate personal encounters. They were all fully grown adults. They could do whatever they wanted to do. It would be nobody's business to interrupt, intervene, judge, or reprimand.

Live and let live. Isn't that what life is supposed to be about? In dreams... may all our dreams come true. Now all they needed was a bag of marshmallows, a few chocolate candy bars, and a box of graham crackers to roast up some s'mores over the campfire.

Later that night, after almost everyone, except for a few stragglers, had either gone to their tents, or to lay out, out in the open, on sleeping rolls by the campfire for the night - who went to where was all a matter of preference - some liked the nostalgia of camping outdoors, under the stars, while others just wanted to be safe and warm tucked away inside a tent. As Mira was switching off her netbook heading towards her designated tent, she heard the crunch of a boot snapping a few twigs on the ground behind her. The stench of stale alcohol filled the air. She turned around and standing behind her was a very bloodshot-eyed, and very drunk, Hector the Hunter.

"Want some company for the night?" He said to her.

Mira was immediately thinking... he must be drunk, or out of his mind, and then she said to him, aloud. "You must be drunk, or you've lost your mind, or both!" Then as mean-spirited as possible Mira added. "Your definitely drunk, and you've definitely lost your mind!"

"Meow!" Hector the Hunter giggled and mimicked a cat lashing out trying to scratch Mira with its extended claws.

"Go away before I kick you between the legs with my boot or shoot you with your own gun!"

"Prickly, prickly, you're very prickly, my dear."

Mira sprinted in through the entrance of the tent she was sharing for the night with Lisa and quickly closed the door flap of the tent behind her.

Lisa rolled over on the sleeping roll she was laying on and squinted at Mira standing at the tent entrance.

"What's going on?"

"Nothing." Mira answered Lisa. "Don't worry about it. Go back to counting sheep and dreaming about winning a Noble Prize."

"Was that dirty old man bothering you?"

"He was trying to, but not really."

"He was trying to bother me a few times, too, the other day."

"Somebody should do something about that."

"He'll get his up comings one day, sooner or later."

"Hopefully, sooner, than later."

Lisa rolled back over on the cot and remained silent for the rest of the night.

Mira was watching Hector the Hunter through a peek hole of the tent standing outside staring in the direction of the tent. After a while he seemed to lose interest and walked away.

Mira exhaled sighing in relief.

They were all up, out of bed, and back on the way as the sun was still rising in the horizon. They hiked further and further, deeper and deeper, into the nether regions of the Waywan Cliffs. After hiking for a couple of hours, of course, stopping here and there for the research team to take samples of the flora and fauna and whatever might be out of the ordinary, such as tracks and unnatural structures. The outdoorsmen and wilderness guides were also doing what they do. The outdoorsmen and wilderness guides were also examining anything that seemed out of the ordinary, just as the researchers were doing, but for other reasons.

Eventually, they came upon a small waterfall, or stream, which seemed more like the drizzle from a leaky water pipe or faucet, out here in the middle of nowhere. Only out here in the middle of nowhere there were no water pipes or faucets or plumbing of any kind.

Mira was immediately entranced, as they all were. It was serene, as if they had stumbled upon paradise on Earth. The back of Mira's neck was moist and sticky from sweating from the heat and from hiking non-stop since sunup. She knelt down by the edge of the stream and began pouring handfuls of water from her cupped hands onto her face and the back of her neck. She barely had time to react when she heard the ruffling of the bushes in front of her. A large mountain lion jumped out from the bushes. A split second before the mountain lion would've had Mira's neck clamped tightly in its jaws, there was another ruffling of the bushes coming from behind were Mira was kneeling. It happened so fast, no one could tell exactly what it was? A bear? A gorilla? A hairy eight-foot (2.44 meter) man? There where bears out here, but no gorillas, or hairy eight-foot (2.44 meter) tall men, or woman, of any kind, out here, or anywhere, presently, or in the past, on the planet. It was a bigfoot. It was Ringru. Ringru swatted away the mountain lion before the mountain lion had a chance to grab hold of Mira and disappeared back into the brush as quickly as he had appeared. The mountain lion had literally spun around in midair from the force of Ringru's powerful arm pushing and tossing the mountain lion a safe distance away from Mira. After rolling over a couple of times, the mountain lion was back on its feet and lunging towards Kasper who was standing several feet away from where Mira was kneeling down by the stream. Red, Crystal, and Hector the Hunter were just as quick as the bigfoot Ringru had been. Red, Crystal, and Hector the Hunter were prepared. They had been waiting all along for the possibility of being attacked by wild animals, such as mountain lions, wolves, and bears, out here in the middle of nowhere. Red, Crystal, and Hector the Hunter, were immediately shooting at the mountain lion. The mountain lion jumped back away from Kasper. Either the mountain lion was hit, or the crack and thunder of Red, Crystal, and Hector the Hunter's guns blasting away had sent the mountain lion running back into the dense foliage, trees, bushes, overgrown weeds, and soil clumps.

Hector the Hunter, Lisa, and Dobie were quickly examining Mira and Kasper all the while asking them, "Are you okay? Are you alright?"

"I'm okay. I'm alright. I'm alright. I'm okay." Both Mira and Kasper kept repeating.

"I'm a bit shocked." Kasper continued. "But I'll survive."

"It's nothing." Mira chimed on.

"That mountain lion almost took a bite out of you!" Hector the Hunter was saying to Kasper.

"It's no big deal. I'm not going to be sweating it. I used to be a marine!" Kasper was proudly affirming as he was smiling back at Hector the Hunter. "You know what they say about the marines?"

It was Lisa who answered Kasper's inconsequential question. "That there are more homosexuals in the marines than in any other branch of the military, because marines have no hang ups about their masculinity, because their marines."

Kasper was immediately giving Lisa a confused and quizzical look. "Where did you hear that? I never heard about anything like that before! No! The saying goes, once you become a marine, you will always be a marine for the rest of your life!"

"I know what you mean, amigo." Hector the Hunter said to Kasper. "Once a marine, always a marine."

"Oo-raa!" Kasper tapped himself on the chest with his fist.

Then, as if they were all on cue, on stage, in a pre-rehearsed theatrical production, they all turned to look in the direction where the bear? The gorilla? The hairy eight-foot (2.44 meter) tall man? had run off too.

"Did you see that?" Dobie was saying.

"I did! But I can't believe my eyes!" Lisa added.

"Believe it!" Hector the Hunter snorted. "Quickly everybody! Saddle up! That was a Bigfoot!"

"Let's go get'em!" Red and Crystal were saying as they were reloading their pistols and rifles.

Everyone ran off into the direction of the 'so-called' bigfoot; everyone except for Mira.

"Smart." Mira was thinking. "Very smart."

If the hikers had continued in the direction they were originally traveling, which is the opposite direction the bear? Or the gorilla? Or the hairy eight-foot (2.44 meter) tall man? Or Bigfoot? Had run off too further down the ridge, they would've discovered, not the research team, but Hector the Hunter, Red, and Crystal, with all of their tracking and hunting experience, a large cave opening hidden by a thick wall of bushes and trees; a large cave opening which was the entrance to a labyrinthian structure of natural interlocking passageways, pathways, cave tunnels, and many separate rocky cave enclaves, small and large. Some as small as a hole in a wall where only a few of the Citizenry may gather, others as large as mammoth-size caverns, where hundreds or thousands of the Citizenry may gather; if there were ever that many of the Citizenry gathered together, at all, at one time. The Citizenry of Bigfoots, Sasquatches, and Yetis were always only a few in numbers at any given time throughout history – which was one of the many reasons the Citizenry have chosen to remain elusive and unseen in a world of billions of others not of their kind.

Yes, Hector the Hunter, Red, and Crystal, they would have, definitely, have noticed the cave entrance right away. However careful the inhabitants of the cave dwelling may have been, there was always some misplaced dirt, leaves, rocks, pebbles, and twigs, an ordinary hiker would be completely oblivious of, but the trained and experienced hunters and trackers, or outdoorsmen and wilderness guides, they would've noticed immediately and found the cave opening, the cave opening which led to the cave dwelling of the Citizenry of the Heseetu.

Mira was whispering, barely audibly, under her breath. "The mountain lion was an unforeseen, unplanned, circumstantial event, but the aftermath and outcome was a well-executed example of distraction and deception.

I believe we simple humans call that 'bait and switch,' if we simple humans should ever become aware that we were being 'baited' and 'switched.'

There's a sucker born every day...

CHAPTER SIXTEEN

Shantuu sat by a firepit inside the carve dwelling of the Citizenry of the Heseetu playing with the cool ashes of a long-extinguished fire. It was too hot to light a fire during these hot summer days. For light, the Citizenry of the Heseetu had several small torches burning inside hand carved indentations spread-out along the rocky walls, passageways, and cave tunnels of the cave dwelling. Not that they needed any light of any kind to see in the dark. Bigfoots had natural night vision. They could see in the dark as clearly and well as they could see in the light of day.

Ringru stumbled into the cave dwelling and dropped the leather pouch by where Shantuu was sitting which Ringru had exchanged with Mira out in the forest a day and half a night ago.

Shantuu looked down at the leather pouch. "What took you so long, Ringru?" Shantuu was saying to Ringru in English. "You are the best and most adept Shadow-walker of the Citizenry of the Heseetu. Have you lost your edge? Are you becoming too old already?"

A Shadow-walker in the world of the Citizenry was sort of a *'formally trained'* Foot Soldier/Messenger/Spy/Surveillance and Reconnaissance Expert - they were tasked with the duties of going out into the world, unseen and unheard, to do the work, the average, ordinary, others of the Citizenry were unable to do, due to the danger, or the difficulty, or severity, of a certain, specific, designated, task at hand.

"Tu mascota favorita y su sequito se habian ido al oeste, en lugar de al este/Your pet and her entourage had gone west, instead of east." Ringru answered Shantuu in Spanish.

Shantuu did not react to Ringru's snide remark about Mira being Shantuu's favorite pet. Mira was more so an adopted daughter or sister to Shantuu. Shantuu knew that Ringru did not mean any harm. Ringru's attempts at humor were often not as wistful or complementary as he imagines; most of the time.

Shantuu picked up the leather pouch and was holding it in the palm of his hand as if he were trying to mentally guess the contents of the pouch for whatever strange reason.

"We have struggled for so long..." Shantuu sadly reminisced. "To no avail. We are struggling still."

Ringru remained silent for a moment, watching Shantuu, until Ringru finally had to confess, or more so explain the reason for his tardiness.

Ringru switched to English, fearing that he might have upset Shantuu with his, what he now realized, tasteless remark about Shantuu's human friend. Ringer did not want to anger Shantuu any further, if he did, indeed, anger Shantuu; even in the slightest way. English was Shantuu's preferred language, or the language Shantuu has always been most commonly known to converse by.

"As I was maneuvering for a proper place to exchange the packages (meaning the leather pouches) with your human friend (This time Ringru did not refer to Mira by a snide remark) I sensed the presence of a big cat who was stalking the group your human friend was traveling with." (Big cat meaning a mountain lion). "I was unable to successfully shoo away the big cat." Ringru had picked up the scent of the big cat/mountain lion while he was waiting to exchange leather pouches with Mira. Shantuu cocked his head to the side giving Ringru his full attention. He was completely absorbed by Ringru's harrowing narrative of the encounter with the big cat/mountain lion.

"I was too late. The big cat almost snatched away your human friend. I had to expose myself to save your human friend."

"Did the humans take photographs or videos of you?"

"I did as I have been trained to do. If anything, I could have been no more than a blur in their eyes; but there were those amongst the humans who could have been no other than Shadow-walkers themselves."

"They followed you?"

"Unbelievably so, being that they were humans. I doubled back in the opposite direction and lost them in the dark of night."

"Well done, Ringru, well done." Shantuu placed the leather pouch on top of a small boulder which was being used as much as the same way as a bedside table or coffee table was used in a human domicile. "Leave me now to my own devices. I have much to do."

Ringru turned and exited the cave enclave, leaving Shantuu to remain alone, by himself. After Ringru was gone, Shantuu carefully untied the leather straps binding together the contents of the leather pouch. Shantuu began examining the contents of the leather pouch. There were several glass vials the size of a human finger, some filled with a clear liquid, others were empty. There was also a bundle of syringes, carefully taped together and a letter. Shantuu raised the letter over by the light of the fire to better peruse whatever was written on the letter. Shantuu silently read whatever was written on the letter. When he was done, Shantuu tossed the letter into the campfire and solemnly watched as the letter was engulfed by the flames. Shantuu rubbed his tired, weary eyes, over and over again, like most humans will do, silently contemplating the past, present, and future, or whatever possible future lay ahead for his kind, the Citizenry; not just the Citizenry of the Heseetu, there, in the Colorado Rocky Mountains, but also elsewhere, around the world – in the north and south, over the large water masses of the Pacific and Atlantic oceans, in other continents, in the Amazonian rain forest, or whatever was left of the Amazonian rain forest. He was thinking about the others of his kind in the Artic and Antarctic regions, in the jungles of Africa – Shantuu was thinking and contemplating and thinking and contemplating and thinking and contemplating and thinking and contemplating.

CHAPTER SEVENTEEN

Ulysses Springfield was recruited by Rand Biotech as his tenure with the C.I.A. - (Central Intelligence Agency) - was coming to an end. He had been recruited by the C.I.A. much the same way when his military career in the United States Army Special Forces was winding down. He was between middle-age and old-age. He still had many years left ahead of him to plunder, wreak havoc, raise hell, and stomp the beaten paths.

He was a young recruit who had only just recently graduated from the Training and Doctrine Command U.S. Training Infantry School at Fort Benning, Georgia, as a Lieutenant at the start of Desert Storm – the gulf war waged by the United States led coalition of 35 nations against Iraq in response to the Iraqi invasion and annexation of Kuwait in August/02/1991.

During the combat phase of Desert storm from January/17/1991 to February/28/1991 Lieutenant Springfield had acquired 21 confirmed kills as a sniper along with Sargent Amaro (Hector the Hunter) who himself had also acquired 18 confirmed kills as a sniper. Ulysses Springfield and Hector the Hunter had met way back then and had become friends, although Hector the Hunter, who would never publicly admit, was always somewhat put off by the cold and dispassionate nature of Lieutenant Springfield's attitude when it came to killing in combat. Hector the Hunter considered killing in combat a soldier's duty, while his unforgiving fellow unbrotherly Brother-in-Arms, Lieutenant Springfield, relished the idea of taking a human life. Lieutenant Springfield looked forward to killing each day as if it were a hobby, or a video game, or as if he were shooting lifeless cardboard cut-outs at a rifle range.

Lieutenant Springfield never expressed any regret or remorse when it came to taking a human life, even when on two separate occasions he had shot and killed children, who were tricked by adult enemy combatants into walking towards groups of soldiers carrying what might or might not have been a grenade or an I.E.D. (Improvised explosive device). On one of two separate occasions when the suspected grenade or I.E.D. turned out not to be a grenade or I.E.D., Lieutenant Springfield coldly shrugged off the fact that he had taken the life of an adolescent child. He did not seem to even lose any sleep over the nightmare tragedies; Sargent Amaro/Hector the Hunter had noticed the many times he had been watching Lieutenant Springfield while he was sleeping peacefully on his bunk back at the fort, as if he did not have a care in the world, the night after. Lieutenant Springfield had a bunk in the same tent as Sargent Amaro/Hector the Hunter way back then, so long ago, when they were both younger than young.

Their paths had crossed again, many years later, when they both had been recruited by an underground, covert, privatized version of official, legitimate, legal, espionage, and counter-intelligence espionage agencies of the world – which was a separate, unofficial, off-the-books, branch of Rand Biotech.

Hector the Hunter was crouched down on the ground examining the foliage. He was gently brushing aside the soil on the ground and a few twigs and discarded leaflets with Security Expert Springfield standing over him looking down over his shoulder.

"Don't tell me we've lost the whatever." (Meaning Bigfoot).

"We've lost the whatever, but we've learned a lot."

"How so?" Security Expert Springfield asked Hector the Hunter.

"We've learned a lot, a lot, a lot!"

Red and Crystal were nodding their heads in agreement with Hector the Hunter.

"Indeed we have." Red spoke out.

"A lot, a lot, a lot!" Crystal spoke out, also.

"I'll have to take your word about whatever the hell you're talking about." Security Expert Springfield bemusedly replied.

Hector the Hunter, still crouched down on the ground was sniffing a leaflet he had picked up. "The whatever had manipulated us just like as if we had been a pack of dogs being led along by ropes strapped around our necks."

"Like puppets on strings." Security Expert Springfield did not mean that as a compliment.

"Marionettes." Red added mimicking an English-speaking person speaking with an Italian accent.

"Where do we go now? What do we do?" Security Expert Springfield asked Hector the Hunter.

"You're asking me?"

"You're the tracker/guide."

"And you're the hunter/killer."

Security Expert Springfield was taken aback by Hector the Hunter's unprovoked, misplaced, unwarranted comment; referring to an incident which had occurred the first year they had both been reluctantly reunited after being hired by their present off-the-books, unnamed, under-the-radar employers.

"You're not still breaking my balls about Kuwait and Iraq." Security Expert Springfield said to Hector the Hunter.

"Forget I said anything. Never mind."

"You're still pissed-off about Columbia!"
"Never mind. Don't worry about it. I told you to
forget about it."
Security Expert Springfield hesitated for a moment before
replying.
"You are! You're still pissed-off about Columbia!"
They were both staring off into space for more
than a few moments, without realizing that they were
both staring off into space for more than a few moments
and then for more than a few moments more and then for
more than a few moments more.
Hector the Hunter and Security Expert Springfield
were remembering, remembering, remembering of a time
long ago, but not too long ago.
It seemed as if it had only just happened yesterday
and at the same time as if an eternity had passed...

>>>>><<<<<

Emilio Rodrigo was in charge. He was the operations
contact in the city of Agua Azul in the southeast region of
Columbia. The city was more so a ramshackle bamboo hut
village in the middle of the Amazonian rainforest than an
actual city.
It was a joint operation - officially and unofficially -
between the Columbian Government, the Central
Intelligence Agency, and Rand Biotech. The Drug Lord
Humberto Camarera, also infamously known as La Culebra,
in Spanish, or the Snake, in English, had hired biologist and
chemist Hienrich Von Lichtenstein, at first to develop a
system where cocaine could be divided into several
different elements where they could be transported legally
into every country of the world and then recombined later
in secret laboratories and sold wholesale to local criminal

organizations, but as the hostilities between the Colombian government and the Rebel forces intensified, becoming worse and worse every day, rebel forces which were financed by the drug trade, went from standard military skirmishes to outright blood feuds and retaliatory strikes which were becoming more so massacres than military operations. La Culebra began delving into chemical and biological warfare with a little help from his friends – that being Hienrich Von Lichtenstein and his associates in the illicit and underground world of fringe science for hire.

It was supposed to be your basic, simple, high tech, super espionage, counter terrorism, smash and grab job, and the terminations with extreme prejudice of as many of the high target, high profile fugitives and bad guys on the Topmost Wanted Lists and any combatants aiding and assisting the targets.

Deep in the jungle and separated from any of the secret, hidden, cocoa, opium, and marijuana plantations and processing plants was a secret, hidden, underground biological and chemical warfare laboratory; which was constructed in secret to specifically developed and store lethal manmade germs, viruses, toxins, and poisons – all under the supervision of biologist and chemist Heidrich Von Lichtenstein and financed by El Culebra, Drug Lord Humberto Camarera.

Emilio Rodrigo was in the rented warehouse that was being used as a temporary base for the operation, with several of the other members of the capture and extraction team, or assassination and sabotage team, if they were unable to extract anything of substance or value; whatever was going to be easier and more convenient to accomplish. There were tables with assembled and unassembled arms and munitions and maps and diagrams on the walls with photos of many of the targets they were hoping to capture or kill.

Hector Amaro/Hector the Hunter had never met up, or had ever seen ever again, his former fellow soldier, Ulysses Springfield, after their time together in Afghanistan and Iraq. Either of the two had no idea if any of the other of them was even still alive.

"Uno cerveza?" Emilio said to Hector the Hunter as he held out an ice-cold bottle of Presidente - Colombia's most popular imported beer – imported from the Dominican Republic.

"Don't mind if I do." Hector the Hunter said, smiling, as he gratefully accepted the beer.

"A fellow Americano will be arriving today to join the team."

Which will be another added American member to the team, as there were already at least five Americans out of the twenty or so members in the team that Hector the Hunter had met or been introduced to, formally and informally. As team leader, Emilio wasn't always as forthcoming with information and exact details, as any team leader of a dangerous, covert, operation was supposed to be. Of the other twenty, or so, team members, half were Colombian or of Latin descent and the other half were a mix of German and Russian.

"Oh?" Was all Hector the Hunter had to say. He knew better than to ask for exact details. In their line-of-business it was never good to ask too many questions. Less was more. You only needed to know what you needed to know – was always the status quo.

"I hope he, or she…" Hector the Hunter hesitated for a moment, smiling back at Emilio, before continuing, "That he, or she, knows what they are doing."

"He." Emilio answered Hector the Hunter. "Has a very good reputation. He is highly regarded amongst his peers, or so I have been told."

"That's good. We're not going to have the time to babysit amateurs still wet behind the ears."

"Amado and Cecilia are picking him up at the Aeroporto right now... as we are speaking... and drinking."

Emilio held up his bottle of beer.

Hector the Hunter clinked beer bottles with Emilio.

"Salud!' They both respectfully saluted each other.

The other, added, American team member finally arrived at the warehouse after being picked up by the dirt road at the edge of town that was used as an airstrip.

They recognized each other immediately. When they were out of hearing range of the other team members in the warehouse, Ulysses Springfield said to Hector the Hunter.

"Sargent Amaro."

"Lieutenant Springfield. What a surprise."

"It's Captain Springfield, retired, I was promoted after you shipped out."

"A lot can happen after two wars."

"A lot did."

Ulysses Springfield cocked the pupils of his eyes to the side, using the pupils of his eyes, for emphasis, to point to Emilio Rodrigo and the other team members gathered in the warehouse.

Ulysses Springfield whispered to Hector the Hunter. "I got your back, old buddy."

Hector the Hunter did not want to comment to Ulysses Springfield that he was not his 'old buddy.' Hector the Hunter did not want to start a conflict, unnecessarily, especially considering the danger of the mission they were soon going to be embarking upon.

Hector the Hunter merely nodded, slightly, very slightly, he did not want to attract the attention of the other team members in the room. It was more so that Hector the Hunter was going to be watching his own 'back' even more cautiously now that his former unbrotherly Brother-in-Arms and sometimes unofficial nemesis had joined the operation.

It was a standard rule of the mission that all team members were to maintain a low profile as they were organizing and planning the operation during their stay at the town of Aqua Azul. There were to be no drunken late-night parties or consorting with any of the local, professional, ladies of the night. They were all getting paid well enough to take a temporary break from partying and revel rousing. It was very much to the dismay of team leader Emilio Rodrigo that two of the team members have been doing exactly that, what they were supposed to not be doing - sneaking around at night, drinking all night in public, and sampling all the ladies of the night they could find working in the local bars, street corners, and back alleys.

Hector the Hunter noticed Emilio having a close, personal, conversation with Ulysses Springfield, who nodded to Hector the Hunter when he noticed Hector the hunter noticing him and Emilio talking together in private. Afterwards, Emilio had his own close, personal, conversation with Hector the Hunter.

"It is no secret to our employers that the new Gringo team member and you have worked together before."

"Oh. I suppose. I guess there's no use in denying it." Was all Hector the Hunter had to say. He was not surprised.

"There are those amongst us who have broken the rules knowing the consequences of breaking the rules." Emilio did not offer Hector the Hunter an ice cold cerveza this time. "I have asked your compadre, Ulysses to take care of the matter and he has asked if you were available to assist him. He has great confidence in your abilities. He has told me that you are the most reliable professional he has ever had the honor to work with."

"Honor?" Hector the Hunter, with raised eyebrows, repeated what Emilio had just told him.

"That is what your Gringo compadre said." Emilio grimaced. "Could you kindly volunteer to assist your Gringo friend."

Emilio was not asking. It was an order.

"We are not friends." Hector the Hunter said to Emilio. "We have worked together in the past. Take that however you want."

"Se Señor, se. I understand. It is the way it is. It is the way things are done. It is the way things have to be done."

Emilio's last words at that moment were that they were going to be assisted by two other volunteers, that night, and that Hector the Hunter should go back to his hotel room and get some rest.

Hector the Hunter went back to his hotel room and slept for as long as he needed to. He awoke and dressed. As he was finishing his supper or breakfast, whatever applied, he heard a very light tapping on his hotel room door. He knew who it was that was knocking at the door. As he was stepping out into the hallway Ulysses Springfield was there at the end of the hallway by the stairs... waiting.

The first thing Hector the Hunter said to Ulysses Springfield, "So, we are taking on some extra-curricular activities?"

"In for a penny – in for a pound."

"Do me a favor, old buddy." Hector the Hunter was being sarcastic by calling Ulysses Springfield 'old buddy.' "In the future, don't ever volunteer me for any extra assignments on any job we are working together on."

"Ouch! Ooh!" Ulysses Springfield answered, also being sarcastic. "Don't be so sensitive! You're the only swinging dick around here I can trust."

"You trust me?"

"To get a job done right."

"You know I don't like to kill."

"But you do it so well when you have to."

"I wouldn't be having to, right now, if you didn't volunteer me."

"Calm down, amigo, Emilio was going to volunteer you anyway."

Their conversation was interrupted by the crunch of footsteps on the ground coming towards them where they were hiding in the shadows. It was the two targets, on time, and on schedule.

"I can see now why Emilio wants us to take out these two jokers." Ulysses Springfield was saying to Hector the Hunter whispering out of the side of his mouth. "They are as dumb as they are stupid."

"Whatever."

Hector the Hunter was not looking forward to what was about to happen while Ulysses Springfield was becoming excited, relishing the opportunity to shed blood.

"What's this?" Ulysses Springfield said to the two targets as they were coming close enough to notice Hector the Hunter and Ulysses Springfield standing in the shadows. "Going out for a fiesta without inviting us?"

The targets – Miguel Sanchez – a former Mexican Federales (Mexican Federal Police Agent), and Sergei Zalinski – a former Russia commando, were immediately surprised to see two of their other team members standing there in the alley.

"Vat… are you doing here?" Sergei said as he was trying to mentally ascertain if this informal encounter was an accident or not.

"You… want to have a little drink with us?" Miguel was as dumb as he looked while Sergei was suspiciously looking back and forth between Ulysses Springfield and Hector the Hunter.

"Vee ver just going out vor a little fresh air." Sergei was uselessly attempting to deflect the outcome of their unfortunate situation. "Being locked up in these cramped hotel rooms for so long is making us go stir crazy – as you Americano's like to say."

Ulysses Springfield put a friendly arm around Miguel's shoulder while telling him, "I have a bottle of tequila in our jeep parked right around the corner."

"Tequila?" Miguel was slovenly licking his lips. "Is good! Is very good."

Before Miguel could say another word, Ulysses Springfield had already pulled out, from the inside of his jacket, a seven-inch black steel Navy Seals dagger, which he instantly plunged into the side of Miguel's neck, so far into the side of Miguel's neck, the tip of the dagger was protruding out from the other side.

Hector the Hunter was watching from the side as he was walking along beside Sergei; close enough to be able to reach out at Sergei at any moment, but not close enough to attract any unnecessary attention. Hector the

Hunter already had his Japanese nightstick out the moment Sergei was fumbling to pull out a pistol he had tucked into the waistband of his pants. Before Sergei could raise the pistol, up, high enough to snap off a few shots, Hector the Hunter was already swinging the nightstick up and around, smashing and breaking Sergei's arm in two places between the elbow and wrist. Ulysses Springfield quickly pulled the knife out of the side of Miguel's neck and just as quickly slashed open Sergei's throat with one quick thrust. Hector the Hunter kicked away Sergei's pistol with the side of his boot the moment the pistol hit the ground as Sergei was falling back, gurgling, struggling, gurgling, unsuccessfully, to continue breathing.

"You don't have to thank me." Ulysses Springfield said to Hector the Hunter. "I knew you were going to wimp out."

"I got your back." Hector the Hunter angrily fired back at Ulysses Springfield.

"I know. That's why I did what I did. I know. When push comes to shove, you're the only one I'm going to be trusting to be watching my back."

"Yeah! Springfield! Okay! Just do me one favor!"

"What's that?"

"Just don't go all psycho on me!"

Ulysses Springfield merely sneered back at Hector the Hunter without saying anything more about their intimate, private, personal exchange.

Ulysses Springfield pulled out a penlight from his pocket and flicked the light on and off several times very quickly pointing the beam of light at the far end of the alley which was bathed in total darkness. There was the crunch of footsteps stepping towards them. Out from the darkness of the alley came Ramos, another team member who was clearly shocked as he was looking down at the

129

dead bodies of Miguel and Sergei. Miguel still had a puddle of blood forming around the front of his face and chest and Sergei had another puddle of blood forming over and around his head like an ever-expanding halo.

"Mamma Mia!" Ramos exclaimed. He was still unable to hide his shocked revulsion. He whistled one time very quickly as lowly as possible. From behind from where Ramos had come came the crunching sound of tires on the gravel and the slow, low, rumble of a vehicle engine. The driver did not turn on the headlights. He stopped the vehicle several feet away from where Ulysses Springfield, Hector the Hunter, and Ramos were standing. Team member Donny was driving the vehicle; he was one of the youngest of the team members hired for this assignment. Donny, Ramos, Hector, Ulysses, was all each other knew about each other; of course except for Hector the Hunter and Ulysses Springfield, who were more or less old acquaintances.

"Load the bodies onto the back of the jeep! Quickly now!" Ulysses Springfield immediately ordered Ramos and Donny. They were instructed to drive the bodies out into the swamps where the crocodiles, alligators, piranha, barracudas, and other carnivores in the deep jungle were going to make a quick meal of the carcasses. All that will be left of the bodies by the morning is a few scraps and bone splinters.

The next day the team received the intel that Hienrich Von Lichtenstein was going to be visiting the secret, hidden, underground laboratory in the next few days. The team of twenty-five, now twenty-three, minus two members, took turns sneaking out into the jungle to make their way down river to rendezvous with two stealth helicopters which took the team deep, deep, deep, into the jungle - flying so far into the jungle, for so long, until

130

an hour before the break of dawn. The team was deposited on the far side of a mountaintop, where they would rest during the day under the camouflaged of the dense foliage of the jungle, until before sunset, where the team would then hike down the side of the mountain on their way to the secret, hidden, underground laboratory. The secret, hidden, underground laboratory was so well hidden, at first, the team had thought that they had made a mistake. There was only a small bamboo hut by a small bamboo farmhouse. After a closer inspection and examination of the area, the team noticed a few trucks dropping off and picking up way too many supplies and equipment for the small bamboo hut and the small bamboo farmhouse to be able to hold. There had to be an underground structure a hundred times bigger, or more. The small bamboo hut had to be a walk-in foot entrance to the underground structure, while the small bamboo farmhouse had to be a vehicle entrance, complete with a two-way ramp and loading docks up above and down below.

Emilio and some of the other team members were studying a blueprint of the underground structure while Ulysses Springfield was quietly walking up behind Hector the Hunter, at first saying to Hector the Hunter, "Calm down! I'm not trying to sneak up on you!"

Hector the Hunter was watching Ulysses Springfield with one eye cocked to the side.

"I see that your knife is sheathed."

"While were inside, stay behind me, at all times, we're supposed to be going to take care of some special extra business, you and I. You can touch bases with Emilio, later, if you like, or before we bust in."

"I will."

"I knew you will. Emilio knew, too. He'll be coming by talking to us, when he gets a chance, a little later."

It was going to be your basic smash and grab job for the other team members, while the two Americano's, the two former Army Ranger snipers, and former C.I.A. espionage specialists, they were tasked with the duties of taking care of the more subtle and sensitive details of the operation.

The fun was about to begin... or the madness and mayhem.

Ten team members slowly eased their way towards the small bamboo farmhouse, while eight team members slowly eased their way towards the small bamboo hut, crouching and crawling on the ground, inch by inch (.03 meter by .03 meter), foot by foot (.3 meter by .3 meter). The ramp entrance in the small bamboo farmhouse was obviously bigger and would require more personnel to maintain and control. Despite the fact that they were supplied with a blueprint of the interior of the secret, hidden, underground laboratory, they still had no idea how accurate the blueprint may be and how many armed guards, or soldiers, or trained commandos may be inside, waiting.

The remaining five team members would remain outside guarding the entrances and exits.

Hector the Hunter and Ulysses Springfield went along with the eight team members assaulting the small bamboo hut, following behind while the others were going to be on-point breaching the entrance. There was nobody outside the exterior of the small bamboo hut. Just Before the first two team members in front were about to enter the small bamboo hut, Ulysses Springfield whispered to Hector the hunter, "Keep an eye on my back." As he was

132

skip, hopping, walk/running to the front, saying to the two in front, "I got this. Follow my lead and be ready."

The two team members in front seemed to be momentarily confused, but they stood back, following behind Ulysses Springfield as he entered the open entranceway at the small bamboo hut. There was one guard inside the small bamboo hut, he was sitting on a wooden crate with a submachine gun by his side and his head bowed down. At first Hector the Hunter thought the guard had been nodding off, but the second the guard spotted the team members entering he quickly lifted his head up. Not more so because he was surprised by the sudden appearance of the eight team members, but because he was afraid of being caught nodding off while on-duty.

The ultimate crime for a guard on duty was to either, abandon their post without being properly relieved, and falling asleep on post, or nodding out.

"Aye! ¡Que pasa! ¡Amigo! (Aye! What's happening! Friend!)" Ulysses Springfield immediately said to the confused guard.

"Como? (Huh?)" the guard said to Ulysses Springfield. "Quien errs? (Who are you?) De domed vienes? (Where did you come from?)"

Ulysses Springfield blew off the guard's head with an automatic pistol with a silencer attached to the barrel of the automatic pistol before the guard had a chance to react.

A spray of red blood as big and round as a grapefruit squirted out from the back of the guard's head as if his head were a spray bottle and someone had pressed the handle of the spray bottle.

Ulysses Springfield picked up the guard's submachine gun and unclipped the bullet cartridge from the bottom of the weapon. He flung the bullet cartridge across to one side of the small bamboo hut and ejected the one bullet inside the chamber of the submachine gun - basically, disarming the weapon. He tossed the submachine gun back away to the opposite side of the hut.

"That's one less toy we will have to worry about."

"You no play!" One of the eight team members said to Ulysses Springfield.

"I no play." Ulysses Springfield fired back.

The technical expert of the eight-member group, the designated techie, immediately began examining the control levers and the locking mechanisms to a steel door hidden behind a camouflaged tarp by where the now deceased guard was sitting.

After several minutes, the techie gave the team the thumbs up signal, meaning he was ready to unlock the steel door. Two or three of the team members nodded to the techie. Everyone braced themselves. The techie hesitated for one more moment, looking back at everyone and then he nodded one more time. The techie was tapping away on a few buttons of a handheld portable keypad that was connected by a wire the techie had connected to an open electrical panel on the side of the steel door. There were a few clicking sounds heard as the techie was tapping away on a few of the buttons of the handheld portable keypad. The door snapped open an inch (0.03 meters), revealing a sliver of light from a long hallway leading to a stairway going downward into the bowels of the secret, hidden, underground laboratory. The eight team members along with Hector the Hunter and Ulysses Springfield tiptoed down the long hallway and down the stairway until they heard someone yell, "Ernesto! Te dije tuvieras que mear! Mear afuera!" (Ernesto! I told you if you had to take a piss, piss outside!)

Ulysses Springfield had returned to the back and was now walking side by side with Hector the Hunter.

There was a psst, psst, psst, sound coming from the team members, on-point, at the front, firing their silencer muffled automatic rifles at whoever was calling out to Ernesto, which obviously must have been the name of the guard, posted, up top, on-duty, at the entrance.

The eight team members along with Hector the Hunter and Ulysses Springfield quietly stepped over the dead body of the guard inside and continued on their way. They came upon a large foyer, which was devoid of any guards, utility workers, laboratory technicians, or general personnel of any kind. There were several closed doors, a few locked and a few unlocked, and five other hallways leading to the main areas of the secret, hidden, underground laboratory; which was now not so secret, not so hidden, anymore.

It was then that the eight team members, Hector the Hunter, and Ulysses Springfield heard explosions and the sound of automatic rifles firing, faraway, somewhere inside, along with the loud, ear shattering, whine, of alarm sirens.

The other team members who had entered the secret, hidden, underground laboratory through the small bamboo farmhouse entrance were now engaging the armed guards/soldiers/commandos inside the facility in an all-out firefight.

The eight team members, Hector the Hunter, and Ulysses Springfield heard the rush of footsteps and the panic shrieks of several crowds of people running down the hallways towards the foyer where they were positioned.

"No mates al azar a todos – solo aquellos con armas y aquellos que se niegan a dejar sus armas!" (Do not randomly kill everyone – only those with weapons and those who refuse to lay their weapons down!)

One of the eight team members shouted out to the other team members and to Hector the Hunter and Ulysses Springfield.

"Did you hear what he said?" Hector the Hunter gently nudged Ulysses Springfield.

"Yeah! Okay! Just keep following behind me and keep watching my back and do me a favor and shut the fuck up!" Was Ulysses Springfield's response.

"I mean it!" Hector the Hunter angrily added. "This isn't a carnival shooting gallery and a lot of the people here aren't shooting gallery plastic ducks."

"Yeah! Yeah! Okay!"

"Only If they have guns!"

"Yeah! Yeah! Whatever you say!"

"And only if they refuse to put their guns down."

"Whatever! Whatever!"

Several, obviously unarmed, non-combatant civilians began rushing into the foyer, along with a few armed guards/soldiers/commandos. The team members were unable to identify, which was which, of the few armed guards/soldiers/commandos, rushing into the foyer, because the few armed guards/soldiers/commandos, rushing into the foyer, and also throughout the rest of the underground laboratory, they would soon learn, were all dressed in civilians' clothing's. The only similarities between the armed guards/soldiers/commandos, to identify them as security/soldiers/commandos, were their guns, pistols, submachine guns, and automatic rifles.

They were all immediately shot dead, on sight, by the eight team members, Hector the Hunter, and Ulysses Springfield who were strategically positioned throughout the foyer guarding the hallway and doorway entrances. There wasn't enough time in all the excitement for the team members to safely disarm the armed guards/soldiers/commandos.

The old adage applied here – He who lives by the sword – dies by the sword.

When the rush of civilian non-combatants had slowed to a small crawl, Ulysses Springfield said to Hector the Hunter,

"Shut-up! And just follow behind without complaining, preaching, and jibber-jabbing!"

And to the other two team members,

"Benga!" Which was bad Spanish for "Venga!" Which in English meant "Come!" Meaning for the other two team members to also follow behind, without Ulysses Springfield – colorfully – demanding that they remain silent and subservient as he had done to Hector the Hunter.

As Ulysses Springfield was glancing up and down and side to side and all around as he was walking along the hallways of the underground laboratory with Hector the Hunter and the other two team members, doing what they were told to do – follow behind – quietly.

"Aaaah!" Ulysses Springfield had guided them to a locked door. "There should be a certain amount of resistance on the other side of these doors." Meaning for Hector the Hunter and the other two team members to brace themselves for a fire fight once the lock on the door was blown open by a small Semtex plastic explosive charge.

It was one of the other of the two team members who set the explosive charge on the door lock. He set the explosive charge and stepped back.

Ulysses Springfield nodded. Everyone braced themselves.

"On the count of three!" Ulysses Springfield said to Hector the Hunter and the other two team members.

"One... two... three!"

BOOM!!!

The small Semtex charge blew out the door lock followed by the two team members who immediately kicked open the door and rushed through the doorway into the room with guns a-blazing, followed by Ulysses Springfield and Hector the Hunter, also rushing into the room with guns a-blazing. The smaller team of two, plus Ulysses Springfield and Hector the Hunter, more or less, had caught the armed guards/soldiers/commandos, off-guard, the armed guards/soldiers/commandos, who were by the doorway of what turned out to be a very large laboratory. The other armed guards/soldiers/commandos by the back areas of the large laboratory hunkered down behind the many laboratory tables, shelves, and cabinets spread out everywhere throughout the large laboratory. One magic bullet that the team members had that the armed guards/soldiers/commandos did not have were concussion grenades; specifically designed to be used in small, up-close and personal, conditions as in the situation the team members were currently engaged.

The powers-that-be would never allow their security contingent to explode grenades inside their newly-constructed multi-million-dollar laboratory complex. Being so – that even though the armed guards/soldiers/commandos were not outnumbered, they were outgunned. It was only after so many minutes until the armed guards/soldiers/commandos in the large laboratory were cut down into, more or less, shredded piles of pulp-like blobs of meat scattered about everywhere in the large laboratory.

The eight team members who had entered the secret, hidden, underground laboratory through the small bamboo hut had, so far, suffered only one fatal casualty. One of the team members by the name of Rafael was lying face down by the entrance of the large laboratory.

One of the team members was making the sign of the cross with his hand as he was stepping over the dead body of Rafael on his way to the back of the laboratory along to join the other team members.

Ulysses Springfield was looking up and down at a little piece of paper he was holding in his hand. He led the team further back inside the underground laboratory to another hallway with five locked doors on one side of the hallway and five more locked doors on the other, opposite, side of the hallway. Ulysses Springfield stopped at one of the ten locked doors and gestured for the team member who had set the Semtex charge on the other locked doors to set another Semtex charge on the door he had stopped in front of, all the while, still looking up and down at the little piece of paper in his hand.

The team member set the small Semtex charge on the lock of the locked door; everyone stood back, again, and braced themselves.

Ulysses Springfield gestured to all the team members, using hand and finger symbols, that he was to enter the room first, followed by two other team members, followed by two more other team members, with Hector the Hunter entering last.

It was because the other team members were obeying and following Ulysses Springfields orders and instructions without any hesitations, or any kind of discussions; further proved to Hector the Hunter that all that occurred had been pre-arranged by the team leader, Emilio Rodrigo, with Ulysses Springfield, beforehand, before they had left the ramshackle base in the warehouse back in the village. All of the team members were wearing their gas masks, as Ulysses Springfield was opening a pouch slung over his shoulder filled with smoke bomb cannisters.

Ulysses Springfield counted off to three, again, using only hand gestures.

First finger - up and down!

Second finger - up and down!

Third finger - up and down!

There was a smaller, more restrained, BOOM! Unlike what a regular explosive device would have made. Ulysses Springfield kicked open the door, simultaneously tossing into the room several smoke bomb cannisters. Ulysses Springfield immediately jumped through the doorway of the room into the room, as the room was being engulfed by the smoke from the smoke bomb cannisters.

Hector the Hunter was able to discern that whoever was inside the room did not fire any firearms at any of the incoming team members, and that none of the other team members were firing their weapons.

The only person firing a weapon in the room was Ulysses Springfield, and the weapon he was firing was his assault rifle.

The smoke was clearing as Hector the Hunter was entering the room. Much to the horror of Hector the Hunter, after the smoke had completely dissipated, lying dead in one corner of the room, riddled with bullets, were the bodies of Hienrich Von Lichtenstein – and two adolescent girls, who could not have been more than eight years of age. The two adolescent girls were obviously

Hienrich von Lichtenstein's daughters. The two adolescent girls did not need to die.

Hector the Hunter was shaking his head as he was becoming angrier and angrier.

"You son of a bitch! You dirty! Lowlife! Piece of shit! Son of a bitch!"

Ulysses Springfield was ignoring Hector the Hunter's oncoming fit of anger as he was ordering the other team members to pack up any intel that may be important, such as computer hard drives, computer disks, files, papers, samples, specimens; whatever may be relevant.

"You son of a bitch! You didn't need to butcher the children!"

"Collateral damage, old buddy."

"Collateral damage my ass!" Hector the Hunter punched Ulysses Springfield on the side of his jaw, knocking him to the floor. "And stop calling me old buddy!"

Ulysses Springfield just laid on the floor for a few moments, rubbing his sore cheek and rubbing a trickle of blood dripping from the side of his mouth. "We don't have the time to work this out now." One of the team members was helping Ulysses Springfield to stand. "We'll have to discuss... this... later."

"You son of a bitch! You son of a bitch!"

The team members, without any more drama, or infighting, packed up whatever intel they could carry on their backs and set explosive devices with timers on the detonators in the room they had just entered, the large laboratory, the foyer, and as many other rooms as they felt necessary to destroy, as they were making their way back out through the entrance/exit of the small bamboo hut as the other team who had entered through the small bamboo farmhouse were also doing – all the while allowing the non-combatants, unarmed civilians, to escape and run free into the jungle.

"Fucking baby killer!" "Fucking baby killer!" Hector the Hunter kept mumbling under his breath as the team members were leaving the secret, hidden, underground laboratory, making their way into the jungle.

The team members made it halfway up a rugged mountain slope when they heard the explosions going off from the explosive devices they had left everywhere throughout the secret, hidden, underground laboratory. Two fireballs appeared where the small bamboo hut and the small bamboo farmhouse had once been and was now no more.

The team members made it over the rugged mountain slope and were on their way to rendezvous with a few river boats waiting down below by the river, waiting to take them away to a safe location, where the team will essentially split up and disappear, as if they had never existed, when they heard the psst! psst! psst! sound of silencer muffled automatic rifle fire coming from somewhere inside the dense darkness of the jungle. Leaves and bush branches were breaking off flying everywhere as more than a few of the team members were being cut down. The team members did not know which way or where to fire back. It was too dark and the jungle too dense. They seem to be surrounded. Automatic rifle fire was striking out at them from everywhere. They were being attacked by reinforcements. Hector the Hunter felt as if he had been, suddenly, punched in the shoulder and kicked in the thigh. He collapsed to the ground. He had been shot in the shoulder and the thigh. The remaining team members began firing their weapons everywhere and in every different direction.

There! There! There! And there!

After taking on a few too many casualties and fatalities, the remaining team members, finally, figured out that they were being fired upon from two different directions and began concentrating their retaliatory rifle fire back at the two different areas of the jungle.

The team members with grenade launchers began lopping grenades at the two different directions.

Hector the Hunter must have been losing too much blood from the two gunshot wounds and was going in and out of consciousness, going in and out, back and forth, in and out, back and forth, from a sleep-like, dream-like state, to full wakefulness, to half-wakefulness, to a sleep-like, dream-like state, to full wakefulness, to half-wakefulness, imagining... dreaming... that Ulysses Springfield had lifted him up over his shoulders and was carrying him down the last stretch of the rugged mountain slope to the river boats waiting down below.

As the river boats were whisking away the remaining, last few, surviving, team members, Hector the Hunter was still imagining... still dreaming... that Ulysses Springfield was sitting beside him, in the river boat, tending to his wounds, all the while saying to him -

"You're never going to forgive me for saving your life... old buddy."

Hector the Hunter still imagining... still dreaming... remembering... remembering dreaming... trying to say back to Ulysses Springfield, mumbling, under his breath, under too much anesthesia, with his speech too slurred for anybody to understand -

"I told you not to call me... old buddy."

Several days later, when Hector the Hunter was in a private hospital recovering from his gunshot wounds, he realized that he did not imagine it, that he was not dreaming, that Ulysses Springfield, did indeed, save his life by carrying him on his back down the rugged mountain slope to the river boats waiting down below, and that Ulysses Springfield, did indeed, stay by his side on the river boat tending to his gunshot wounds.

It's hard to kill your worst enemy when your worst enemy keeps saving your life...

CHAPTER EIGHTEEN

Back to the wilderness hike.

No matter what Mira did, or wherever Mira went, she seemed to feel that Hector the Hunter and Security Expert Springfield were taking turns, following her, and watching her, as in spying on her; or was it all in her imagination? Dr. Lisa Wintergarden was noticing that too, but mostly with Hector the Hunter, who she was thinking was trying to seduce, harass, molest, and possibly rape, if he had the chance, her friend and fellow co-worker Dr. Mira Salinas.

"Is that creep still bothering you"" Lisa said to Mira, when they had a chance to speak together without being overheard.

"Who? Him? He's harmless, annoying, but harmless."

"At least as long as there's a crowd around, nearby, watching."

Mira was thinking about that for a quick New York minute. Lisa was probably right, but Mira did not say so out loud. Lisa knew Mira had agreed with her by the sideway glance Mira had given her.

>>>>><<<<<

After another day and night of hiking through the wilds of the Rocky Colorado forests and woodlands the research team and wilderness guides/hunters/mercenaries had seen not so much more as a hide or hair of any Bigfoots, Sasquatches, or Yetis. No footprints, no cave dwellings, no bones, no living habitat structures that could have been constructed by any possible Bigfoot, Sasquatch, or Yeti.

The research team and wilderness guides/hunters/mercenaries packed up and went home - home being the nameless, unmarked, unidentified Rand Biotech building in downtown Denver.

As Mira was turning into the driveway of her modest one-story rented cabin, all she could think about was taking off her soiled clothes and relaxing in a hot tub of perfumed water surrounded by the low glow of scented candles as the soothing sounds of violins and cellos from her stereo player filled the air.

It was going to take a while to clean off the muck, this time around, not just off of her precious skin and the flesh on her back, but also in her mind and soul.
A little meditation was going to do a lot of good.

As she was opening the door to her cabin, after parking her car, she immediately noticed that the furniture had been moved, ever so slightly, as to not be noticed – but Mira noticed. Upon a closer examination, Mira was able to discern that her cabin had been searched, but made to be unnoticeable, as if nothing had happened.

Nothing seemed to be missing. Why had her cabin been searched? And obviously by professionals. Regular burglars, or homeless, drug addicts, looking to make a quick buck would have completely torn apart the cabin.

There would be no point in contacting the police. There was probably going to be no fingerprints, and since nothing appeared to be missing – what would Mira have to report? The police would think she was paranoid and probably heckle her or treat her as if she were insane. They would probably think she was on drugs, or something.

Mira remembered the look Hector the Hunter and Security Expert Springfield had been giving her throughout their recent research hike together, which she had just returned from, and the other incidences of missing specimens and artifacts at the nameless Rand Biotech building in downtown Denver.

Mira tried to relax, the best that she was able to. Somehow, the hot tub of perfumed water, the low glow of scented candles, and the soothing sounds of violins and cellos from her stereo player filling the air were not as enticing and scintillating as they should have been.

After a few days of mandatory, rest and relaxation, or R&R, as all Rand Biotech employees were required to do after being out in the field for an extended period of time, that being the few days hike Mira and her colleagues have just returned from. Mira was finally back in the basement laboratory, or dungeon, of the nameless Rand Biotech building in downtown Denver.

The dungeon - was the nickname the staff members and general employees had given the basement laboratories, offices, and restricted storage areas of Lower Level II and III. Only those with 'high security clearances' were allowed to venture to Lower Level II and III. Lower Lever I was open to all the staff members and general employees. Staff members and general employees needed a special electronic key card to take the elevators down to Lower Level II and III, and then there were also other locked areas that could only be accessed by eye scanners. Cleaning crews and work crews were only allowed on Lower Levels II and III when escorted and monitored by security officers with 'high security clearances' themselves. Not all of the security officers working at the nameless Rand Biotech building were given 'high security clearances.' Those with 'high security clearances' were mostly ex-military and ex-law enforcement types; like Hector the Hunter and Security Expert Springfield.

Mira did not hear Lisa – Dr. Lisa Wintergarden – walking into the laboratory.

"What's that?" Lisa asked Mira, surprising and startling Mira. Mira almost fell out of her chair. Lisa was pointing to two vials of blood in the bulky computerized blood analyzer. "That looks different. I've never seen anything like that ever before." Lisa was squinting at the read-out on the side panel of the computerized blood analyzer.

"What?" Mira did not know what to say. "Oh, that?" Mira quickly switched-off the computerized blood analyzer. The read-out on the side panel of the computerized blood analyzer went blank. "It's a... it was a... umm..." Mira did not expect to be bothered, or interrupted, Lisa had every much of a right as any of the other staff members to be freely roaming the laboratory areas on Lower Levels II and III. "What-what-what is it that you wanted to know?" Mira finally said to Lisa.

"Those blood samples in the analyzer. They looked weird." Lisa was making a face as if she had just smelled something rotten or spoiled, like stale cheese or uncooked meat passed its due date.

"The blood samples?" Mira was still momentarily lost for words, and then she immediately recovered. "Oh! The blood samples!" Mira nervously chuckled to throw off any of Lisa's paranoid suspicions – or Mira was the one being paranoid. Lisa did not care either way about the weird looking blood samples. Lisa was just being friendly and trying to engage Mira in a harmless conversation about whatever and nothing in particular.

"Contaminated! Yes! Contaminated! The blood-blood-blood samples are contaminated. I forgot to take them out-out-out of the analyzer." Mira was fumbling with the two vials of blood as she was removing them from the

148

computerized blood analyzer. She quickly hid away the vials of blood by putting the vials of blood in the pocket of her pristine white lab coat.

"You okay?" Lisa asked Mira.

"Yes. I'm doing fine. I'm doing good."

"That creep isn't still bothering you?" Meaning Hector the Hunter.

"No. I haven't seen him since we got back."

"That's good. If he keeps bothering you, let me know. I'll personally punch him out, or we can gang up on him."

They both giggled at that. The tension had been broken. The conversation shifted to lighter, more benign and esoteric matters.

"I know what you need!" Lisa said to Mira.

"What's that?"

"You need a ladies night out! Just the two of us!"

"A ladies night... out?" It took a few moments for Mira to fully comprehend what Lisa was saying to her. The next day as Mira was finally opening her eyes to stare up at the ceiling of her rented cabin, she realized that it must be in the late afternoon and that she had purposely thrown her alarm clock across the room when it had rung earlier that morning. Thank God for her being a senior researcher at Rand Biotech. Senior staff members were only beholding to the top heads of certain departments. If Dr. Mira Salinas did not report to work at the nameless Rand Biotech building in downtown Denver, it would always be assumed that she was out in the field working. Lisa was probably functioning no better this morning, or this afternoon. She had left one of the last of the Denver nightclubs they both had visited? Assaulted? Attacked and conquered? On their ladies night out with a beefy hunk of a man who looked like he bench-pressed a thousand pounds a few hundred times a day. She must have had some fun; Mira was thinking as she was trying to lift herself out of bed. Eventually, after taking a hot shower and filling her belly with some good, nourishing, food, she decided to go to work for the evening. The nameless Rand Biotech building in downtown Denver was usually almost mostly empty in the evenings and late nights. Mira would practically have the whole building to herself; except for the security guards on-duty 24-hours a day and the maintenance staff which worked evenings and overnights. As Mira was re-entering the laboratory, after being interrupted by Lisa the day before, she was thinking - good - nobody's here. I can recheck those two vials of blood, the ones Lisa had seen Mira checking, which Mira was trying to secretly check. The moment Mira switched on the computerized blood analyzer she was immediately aware that someone had downloaded the internal memory of the blood analyzer and inadvertently rebooted the memory systems. Whoever, did this, did not intend for the memory systems to be rebooted. It was an automatic response when any of the computerized files are downloaded when a separate USB drive is inserted. Whoever had downloaded the internal memory did not know that. Whoever had downloaded the internal memory had done so with the false assumption that no one was going to know.

Curiouser, but not curiouser enough.

Mira reluctantly reinserted the two vials of blood into the computerized blood analyzer. There were other, official, and unofficial, duties Mira had to attend to. Before Mira switched off the lights to the laboratory on her way home after working until midnight, she couldn't help but to stop for a moment and listen to the silence of the building and the night. There were footsteps coming towards her from down the hallway in the dark. It was one of the late-night security guards patrolling the hallways of Lower Level I and II.

"Dr. Salinas... you're working very late tonight." The security guard said to Mira.

"I'm done for the day, or night, it's the nighttime. I almost forgot."

"It's hard to tell, sometimes, if you been inside all day. There's no windows in these basement offices."

"You have a nice night."

"Yes, sir, ma'am, I mean ma'am."

Mira merely smiled at the security guards unintentional indiscretions. He seemed more genial, honest, trustworthy, and warm, than his bosses were, his bosses being Hector the Hunter and Security Expert Springfield.

She was glad she didn't bump into them, while she was alone here, this late at night.

CHAPTER NINETEEN

Far, far, away on the other side of the Colorado Rockies, in a separate cave dwelling, separate from any of the many Heseetu cave dwellings, Tantoon and several of his fanatical followers were gathered together by a campfire, along with several other Rogues and Sawtooths. If any of the Rogues or Sawtooths should step out of line, the Rogues and Sawtooths would immediately be struck, very harshly, by any one or more than one of Tantoon's fanatical followers. The Rogues and Sawtooths would be struck by an open hand, or by a rope of vines braided into a whip, or by a wooden club; depending on how severe, or how frequent, the transgressions may be.

It was one of the many ways Tantoon and his fanatical followers have developed to quickly train the Rogues and Sawtooths into taking on certain, specific, duties, functions, and tasks. It was not necessary for the Rogues and Sawtooths to reach the level of those of the Citizenry, or Shadow-Walkers, or Healers who have abandoned their own Citizenries to become one of Tantoon's fanatical followers – which was now becoming and abstract, illegitimate, bizarro, Citizenry of its own. The Rogues and Sawtooths were mere pawns. They were expendable foot soldiers. All that was necessary was for the Rogues and Sawtooths to follow orders, to do as they were told, without thinking, or outright questioning why. Orgu, another of the Citizenry who had abandoned his own Citizenry, present, at the incognito, clandestine, campfire meeting, handed Tantoon an assault rifle, which were generally banned by the Citizenry on every continent of the world; ever since gunpowder and firearms had replaced the knife, blade, spear, and bow and arrow.

Will Tantoon's rebellion wither and die? Or survive and thrive? And ignite a firestorm?

Only time will tell.

The future is always being written and rewritten.

The barrel of the assault rifle was casting a shadow across Tantoon's face from the light of the campfire and against the cave wall from behind from where Tantoon was standing.

A Sawtooth handed Tantoon an ammunition cartridge to the assault rifle. Tantoon snapped the ammunition cartridge into place onto the bottom of the assault rifle.

"Well done, Neejat." Tantoon said to the Sawtooth. "You have learned much in such a short amount of time."

Neejat was the Rogue who had been pursued by Shantuu, Ringru, and Cazzii, several weeks ago in the woods. Orgu had rescued? or captured? The Rogue and instantly recruited the Rogue into the ranks of Tantoon's disgruntled, mad, crazy, insane, fanatical followers. Disgruntled if they were of the Citizenry – mad – if they were Sawtooth's, who were just beginning to learn to speak and read and use tools. Rogues did not know any better, either way, Rogues did not know how to speak or read or use tools. Neejat had gone from Rogue to Sawtooth in the shortest amount of time of any Rogue Tantoon and his fanatical followers have ever encountered.

Tantoon was so very much impressed with the Rogue, who was now a Sawtooth, that Tantoon had given the Rogue/Sawtooth the honorary name of his own father - Neejat - who Tantoon would always say his father Neejat had died too young from a broken heart after his mate-Tanara - Tantoon's mother - had been killed by human

154

Bigfoot hunters when Tantoon was barely a few years old. His father had quickly carried away his mother after the human Bigfoot hunters had shot her, before the human Bigfoot hunters had a chance to make a trophy of Tantoon's mother. When Tantoon's father arrived at the cave dwelling of the Citizenry of the Cororuru with the broken and bleeding body of his mother – Tanara – it was too late. She had died while Tantoon was still holding her in his arms trying to comfort her. A Healer had come shortly afterwards to attend to the wounds of Tantoon's mother, but the Healer had, unfortunately, arrived after she was gone.

The Citizenry of the Cororuru's territories have always been in the northwest between the United States of America and Canada. The Citizenry of the Cororuru were close cousins to the Citizenry of the Heseetu whose territories have always been in the southwest of the United States going all the way south to Mexico and the midwest and east of the United States.

Human bigfoot hunters were mostly professional and amateur academics and scholars only interested in photographing and documenting the existence of Bigfoots, Sasquatches, and Yetis, while the bigfoot hunters, with their guns and deadly traps, were only interested in killing and stuffing bigfoots, via the expertise and skill of taxidermists, to be kept as trophies.

Bigfoot Hunters were few and far between, but not few enough, and not far enough between.

Another Rogue/Sawtooth appeared from out of the shadows, clumsily, dressed in a badly tailored, human, military jungle camouflage uniform; which was badly altered to fit the 7-foot (2.13 meter) to 8-foot (2.44 meter) frame of a fully grown Bigfoot, Sasquatch, Yeti. The Rogue's/Sawtooth's feet were covered with tailored, black colored, leather pouches, which were designed to resemble from a distance - black, military styled, combat boots. The Rogue/Sawtooth had another tailored, black colored, leather pouch, which the Rogue/Sawtooth used to cover his entire head.

Tantoon was looking over, from head to toe, the Rogue/Sawtooth dressed in the badly tailored, human, military jungle camouflage uniform.

"We must fix the human coverings. The human coverings must appear authentic. Do we have more of the human coverings?" Tantoon was saying to no one in particular.

Orgu nodded answering Tantoon's question.

"We have all we will need of the human coverings."

"And of these mechanized weapons?" Meaning the assault rifles and ammunition cartridges.

Orgu nodded again.

Tantoon was satisfied with that and showed his satisfaction by yelping very loudly. The others of the Citizenry, and Sawtooths, and Rogues, present at the cave dwelling by the campfire began yelping along with Tantoon. It was as if a group of humans, as in a sports team, or at a large event, were all loudly chanting –

Hip-hip-hooray!

Hip-hip-hooray!

Hip-hip-hooray!

Hip-hip-hooray!

By the pricking of thy thumbs, something wicked this way comes.

The witches in Shakespeare's Macbeth couldn't have summed up the situation any better.

CHAPTER TWENTY

For the past couple of weeks Mira had been purposely leaving out vials filled with blood which were normally taken as samples for testing, randomly everywhere around her private office, laboratories, and medical and specimen storage compartments at the nameless Rand Biotech building. She had gotten these blood samples from patients when she was volunteering for the Red Cross on her personal days off. Mira was purposely doing this to distract and mislead anyone who may or may not have been surveilling and spying on her.

Mira was still wondering sometimes if it was all in her mind, if she was just imagining it all, as if she were experiencing mild paranoid delusions - or she was purposely appearing to be purposely appearing to be confused. That would be even more distracting and misleading.

You are only crazy when you don't know that you are crazy. If you know that you are crazy - then you are not crazy. Isn't that how the saying goes? Crazy is not a proper clinical term.

Mira and Lisa persisted in spending more and more time together until one day Hector the Hunter outright accused them of being lesbian lovers.

"What about you and Security Expert Springfield?" Lisa would joke with Hector the Hunter on the very few occasions when they were all in a good and playful mood.

"You two are always going off having private conversations and whispering in each other's ear all the time." Lisa would tease adding that Hector the Hunter and Security Expert Springfield were always locked up together behind closed doors and were always going off together on some field trip or workday.

Touché

Mira and Lisa's ladies night began to become a popular, but secretive, office activity, with other employees at the nameless Rand Biotech building joining the after work late night fun and festivities; including, not just some of Mira and Lisa's fellow researchers and academic associates, but also some of the custodial staff, as well as Red and Crystal – Hector the Hunter's subordinates – who after getting to know them personally in the more relaxed atmosphere of Denver's finest Discotheques and night clubs, were not so bad, mean, and grumpy as they first appeared to be.

It was on one weary Monday morning when Mira was metaphorically – limping into work – after one too many ladies night out that weekend that she discovered much to her dismay that CEO Rand had decided to make a surprise visit of the offices, laboratories, and facilities at the nameless Rand Biotech Building in downtown Denver. CEO Rand was short for Robert Montgomery Rand the 3rd – the grandson of Robert Fitzgerald Rand Sr. or Robert Fitzgerald Rand the 1st – founder and visionary creator of Rand Biotech – and son of Robert Wesley Rand Jr. or Robert Wesley Rand the 2nd.

Mira had that same paranoid feeling when she first locked eyes with CEO Rand that he was looking inside of her, as if he had X-Ray vision, and was seeing something different, something underneath the surface, something no one was telling her.

"Dr. Salinas." CEO Rand said to her as he was bowing slightly and gently taking her hand.

"Mr. Rand. It's so good of you to stop by." CEO Rand gently kissed the top of Mira's outstretched hand.

"Well, I own the place." CEO Rand jokingly said to Mira as he was releasing her hand. "Just checking up on everybody, making sure you all are not burning the building down."

Giggle! Giggle! Giggle!

Everybody was all smiles.

Smile for the big boss.

Everybody keep smiling.

"I've heard that you've been doing a fantastic job! Dr. Salinas! A Fantastic job!"

"Well..." Mira was slightly taken aback. "I've been doing the best that I can."

"Even though you and your colleagues still haven't found any evidence to prove or disprove the existence of Boogeymen." Meaning Bigfoots, Sasquatches, Yetis, and any other cryptozoological creatures.

"We're still double checking and double checking all the information we have. We still haven't come to any irrefutable conclusions."

"I'm sure you will, eventually."

Mira was surprised by CEO Rand's positive attitude, or was he being succinctly sarcastic? Sometimes it was hard to tell. These business moguls, tycoon, types were prodigies when it came to manipulating people and influencing events.

"So, still no miracle cures? No miracle medicines? No groundbreaking scientific discoveries?" CEO Rand continued as he was watching Mira much the same way a hungry lion will be watching a gazelle it had just captured and was about to devour.

Mira was negatively shaking her head from side to side. "No. Nothing. Not yet."

After what seemed like a lifetime, CEO Rand finally moved on to go bother the other members of the research

staff and employees at the nameless Rand Biotech
building; all the while licking his predatory lips while he
was speaking to whomever he was speaking to.

"What's he doing around here?" Dobie whispered
to Mira when CEO Rand was far enough away as to not be
overheard.

"Maybe they ran out of children to sacrifice where
he comes from?" Lisa sarcastically answered.

Mira and Dobie chuckled at that. Lisa was always
ready to share some twisted comment she had on her
mind.

The next day CEO Rand was escorted around the
nameless Rand Biotech building by Security Expert
Springfield and Hector the Hunter, who all three would
stand at the back of the offices and laboratories
whispering amongst themselves as if they were conspiring
to commit numerous, multiple, ungodly, seditious,
predatory, unholy, and venomous deeds, or at least it
appeared as if that was what they were doing.

Later that week on their regular ladies' night out,
which now included several of the guys, Mira, Lisa, Dobie,
Kasper, Red, and Crystal were enjoying a few Jello shots at
the Excelsiors Club when they were surprised to see CEO
Rand, Security Expert Springfield, and Hector the Hunter
walking in through the front door. Before Mira, Lisa,
Dobie, Kasper, Red, and Crystal had a chance to react, CEO
Rand, Security Expert Springfield, and Hector the Hunter
were walking towards their table to join them. As the new
arrivals were seating themselves, without asking for
permission, several of the drink servers had to put two
tables together and bring a few extra chairs to handle the
bigger party of guests.

After having so many Jello shots themselves and
whatever other alcoholic beverages and illegal illicit

substances that were being passed around amongst the crowd of partyers at the Excelsior Club, CEO Rand, Security Expert Springfield, and Hector the Hunter turned out to be, surprisingly, adept, and proficient at break dancing. It was especially surreal seeing someone as antiquated and dignified as CEO Rand spinning around on the dance floor. They all had over-done-it that night, over-done-it being an understatement. It was a surprise that any of the jubilant, celebratory, partiers at the Excelsiors Club that night made it to work the next day. What was even more miraculous, when Mira was driving by to give Lisa a ride to work, Lisa's car was in the repair shop that week, Lisa did not, immediately, come outside from her apartment when Mira pulled up at her front door and curtly honked the horn of her car three times, honk-honk-honk. Lisa was renting an apartment in separate two-story housing complexes with separate, individual apartments on the bottom floors and top floors. Lisa had one of the apartments on the bottom floors. Mira honked the horn of her car three more times, honk-honk-honk. When Lisa still did not come outside, Mira decided to go up to Lisa's front door and knock. Before Mira was about to knock on Lisa's front door, she saw Hector the Hunter through the window of Lisa's apartment having a panic attack running around Lisa's apartment looking for his pants, shirt, and shoes.

Oh my God! Was Mira's immediate reaction. Mira quietly back-stepped away from Lisa's front door and returned to her car, curtly, honk-honk-honking, three times more. When Lisa finally opened the passenger side door of Mira's car and plopped herself down in the passenger's seat, Mira at first refrained from commenting about what she had just seen through Lisa's window, only moments ago. After a while, Mira could not help herself.

"So, Hector the Hunter stopped hitting up on me and started hitting up on you?"

At first Lisa was taken aback, then she realized it would be futile to deny her scandalous, overnight, adulterous encounter.

"You're not jealous now?" Lisa asked jokingly, in an attempt to lighten up the mood.

Mira just laughed at that. "He's all yours. You can have him. I'm not interested. I've never been interested." Lisa was laughing too. "I'm going to throw him back and keep fishing." Giggle, giggle, giggle. "That was a one night, bad, very bad, drunken, very drunken, miscalculation." Lisa became somber and contemplative. "Never again. Never, never, never again."

They drove on in silence for the rest of the ride to the nameless Rand Biotech building in downtown Denver. Later that afternoon as Mira and Lisa were sitting together at the same table on the 1st floor cafeteria of the nameless Rand Biotech building, during a coffee break, Dobie, as in Dr. Dobie Doberson, suddenly stepped into the cafeteria. He immediately went over to join Mira and Lisa when he spotted them sitting together, without being asked, or without asking, if it was okay or not okay.

"Can you believe it?" Dobie said to Mira and Lisa after taking a seat at their table.

"Believe what?" Lisa asked Dobie.

"About who's sleeping with who?"

Lisa almost choked on her coffee and Mira couldn't help but to suddenly, temporarily, develop hiccups for a few seconds.

"Who... who... who is sleeping with who?" Lisa nervously asked Dobie.

Mira and Lisa braced themselves. As they were making eye contact with each other they both could tell what the other was thinking – and that would be – how did anybody else find out about Lisa and Hector the Hunter's recent, brief, tryst/encounter.

Okay who? Okay who? Okay who? Mira and Lisa were thinking in a panic, but more so Lisa than Mira. Mira did not transgress, Mira did not cross the invisible line between the researchers and the mercenaries/professional retired, reassigned, rehired professional spies/outdoor wilderness guides/Rand security officers. Lisa did. Lisa transgressed. Lisa had crossed that invisible line.

Dobie hesitated for a few moments. He was enjoying himself. He was enjoying the momentary state of suspense he was creating between himself and his fellow research staff members.

Dobie finally spilled the beans, much to the relief of Lisa and Mira.

"Weinberger and Red were seen in the parking lot in the back of the Excelsior club kissing and being generally touchy, feely, with each other and then…" Dobie paused for dramatic effect. "They left together in a cab!" That would be Weinberger – as in Dr. Kasper Weinberger – of the research staff and Red – Jason Redfield – of the security staff.

Mira and Lisa went from panicked to relieved in an instant. If they had been hooked-up to a blood pressure monitor, the needle on the monitor would've gone from one-hundred to zero from one second to the next second.

"You… you… don't say so." Lisa nervously replied with Mira nervously adding. "Isn't that something."

"That is something." Dobie added. "Not that it means anything and doesn't make a difference either way about anything but…" Dobie paused again, this time searching for words. "It's just that I never suspected, I never knew, not that it matters, to each his own."

"To each his own." Lisa and Mira agreed.

"Let them be. It's their own personal business, whatever anybody does in the privacy of their own homes, or bedrooms, or in the parking lot in the back of the Excelsior Club in downtown Denver." Mira added and everyone agreed on that, also.

People love to gossip, no matter who they may be, or whatever different worlds they may come from. Gossip was gossip. In the trenches at the front lines and the battlefields of war, in the halls of power, in the backrooms, corridors, alleyways and street corners, at the water coolers of every business, office, waiting rooms, and in every general public, social, civil facilities, from the nostalgic past to the present, modern, contemporary times - getting people to shut-up was something that very rarely, never happens.

Lisa was relieved. The only person, so far, who knew about her regretful, unfortunate night of passion with Hector the Hunter was Mira. Lisa felt that she could trust Mira. They already had a few scandalous secrets they were keeping hidden between them.
Life went on from there.

You couldn't say that CEO Rand was overstaying his welcome by remaining in Denver. He was the Big Kahuna. Besides the shareholders of Rand Biotech, CEO Rand was still the majority shareholder and grandson of the original owner who had created Rand Biotech and built up the company, from scratch, into the worldwide billion-dollar conglomerate Rand Biotech was today; he could do whatever he wanted to whenever he wanted to.

But all and all, it still made everyone nervous that CEO Rand was still poking his head around, and popping in and out, as if from out of nowhere, around all the laboratories and offices of the nameless Rand Biotech building when you least expected him to; that is, everyone, except for Hector The Hunter and Security Expert Springfield. They were both very buddy, buddy, and chummy, chummy with CEO Rand.

And then one day something happened where Hector the Hunter, Security Expert Springfield, and several others of the security staff were called out for some emergency as if they were firemen, paramedics, and emergency rescue workers, being called out to a hundred alarm fire – if there ever was such a thing as a hundred alarm fire.

An hour later, after originally being told to remain, on-site, on stand-by, at the nameless Rand Biotech building in downtown Denver, the research staff, which included Mira – Dr. Mira Salinas – Lisa – Dr. Lisa Wintergarden – Kasper – Dr. Kasper Weinberger – and Dobie – Dr. Dobie Doberson - were called in, also, to respond to whatever emergency, catastrophe, calamity, world shaking event, that had occurred; of which they were soon going to find out, more about, than they ever wanted to.

But that was partly what they were hired for.
It's in the fine print of their Rand Biotech employment contracts.

CHAPTER TWENTY-ONE

"Me no kill." Neejat was saying to Orgu. "We no kill." Neejat was a Rogue who until recently did not know how to speak. He was captured in the wild by Orgu, one of Tantoon's fanatical followers, and recruited into Tantoon's befuddled army of benign and inept rebels, where he now qualified as being a Sawtooth, after learning to speak, read, write, and to use tools.

"Yes, yes, no, no!" Orgu replied to Neejat. "We are not going to kill anyone or anything."

"Then why bring gun rifles?"

"We will be bringing along automatic rifles in case there is an emergency, and only, if there is an emergency. You know how the saying goes, or you don't know, because you are just learning about things like sayings. It's better to have automatic rifles and not need them, than it is to need automatic rifles and not have them." And then Orgu continued, jokingly. "I think Confucius said that, or Plato, or Socrates."

"I no kill." Neejat was saying again to Orgu.

"Yes, yes, I understand. It's okay. You no kill. No problem. Don't worry about it." And then to the others present in the cave dwelling. "Jeez! If he couldn't climb up the side of a building like a monkey climbing up a banana tree, we wouldn't need him!"

"You no like me?" Neejat asked Orgu with a hurtful look in his eyes, or as hurtful a look as Neejat was capable of making.

"I like you just fine! Neejat! I like you very, very, much!" Orgu was frantically shaking his head from side to side as he was walking away from Neejat. "Jeez!" Orgu repeated again. "Jeez!"

Tantoon was looking on at the whole absurd scene with as much of a smile on his face as any Bigfoot/Sasquatch/Yeti, was able to muster.

Tantoon had assembled a special team of Shadow-walkers for a special mission. The team consisted of Orgu, Ugat, Roku, and Neejat. Orgu and Ugat were seasoned, well-trained, experienced, professionals in the science and art of stealth and cunning, of making themselves appear invisible, like ghosts, like phantoms, like thieves in the night, moving through the forests, woods, deserts, swamps, mountains, and even the populated cities and streets of humans. This will be Roku's and Neejat's first time. Roku, a Sawtooth, had been recruited and trained much the same way as Neejat had been.

They left later that night at sunset - Orgu, Ugat, Roku, and Neejat. They were each carrying human made backpacks on their backs along with automatic rifles slung over their shoulders hanging by shoulder straps.

"We no kill! I no kill! We no kill! I no kill!" Orgu kept purposely mimicking Neejat, as a bad joke, purposely trying to irritate Ugat, who merely grunted and continued silently trudging along barely speaking.

After about two hours of hiking through the woods they finally came upon a secluded concrete and steel building complex completely surrounded by barbed wire fencing. There were security lights on the barbed wire fencing and on the perimeter of the building complex; no doubt so that the area could be monitored by well hidden, high tech, security cameras.

"Are you sure that there are no motion sensors on the ground?" Ugat asked Orgu.

"So I have been told." Orgu was impatiently waving Ugat away. "Motion sensors were invented a long, long, long time after this relic was originally built."

167

"They could have up-graduated"

"You mean up-graded, Ugat, it's up-graded, not up-graduated."

"Up-graded." Ugat corrected himself.

Orgu paused for a few moments contemplating Ugat's question.

"Anyway, we will soon find out, but... I do not think so." Orgu continued. "The humans do not realize the importance of this discarded dwelling, they no longer care to watch, the way they watch their dwellings of green bartering paper."

"You mean banks." It was Ugat's turn to correct Orgu. "Banks - where humans keep their money – their green bartering paper - and other valuable possessions." Orgu turned to Neejat. "Here is where your expertise is greatly needed and the main reason it was decided to bring you along."

"I help. I help you. I help Tantoon. I help." Neejat said to Orgu.

"Yes, yes, you help, but you no kill."

"I no kill. You no kill."

"Just stick to the plan, Neejat, just stick to the plan."

"I help. I plan stick. I help. I plan stick."

"Okay, okay, whatever, Neejat, whatever." Was that snorting coming from Orgu - Bigfoot laughter? Ugat merely grunted, as he has always been doing, at the exchange between Orgu and Neejat.

"Now here in your backpack." Orgu pulled out a wire cutter from Neejat's backpack. "Are wire cutters." Orgu demonstrated how the wire cutter was to be use by opening and closing the wire cutter, several times, all the while saying, "Snip! Snip! Snip! Snip!" Orgu pointed to the barb wire on top of the interlocking fence surrounding the concrete and steel building complex. "Those little pointed metal barbs and metal wirings circling around the top of the fence will tear the flesh off of your bones if you should accidently become stuck."

Ugat immediately pointed out. "Why do we not just cut a hole at the bottom of the fence instead of cutting the barb wire on top of the fence to climb over?" Orgu allowed Ugat to continue.

"Would that not be easier? With much less toil and trouble?"

"Yes, yes, it would be easier, but there are men with guns who walk along the outside of the human dwelling, back and forth, without warning, without announcing themselves. If they should see a hole in the fence and call for help on their handheld talking apparatuses (meaning radios, walkie-talkies, cellphones), many other men with guns will come before we have had time to complete our mission. Not only will there be the possibility that we will fail, but also the possibility that we could be captured and killed."

Orgu was referring to a separate security unit which periodically checked the outside perimeter of the building; sometimes by vehicle, sometimes on foot, before entering the concrete and steel building complex and patrolling the inside interior of the building; or vice versa, sometimes the separate security unit checked the interior of the building, first, before checking the perimeter.

"I go now. I do now?" Neejat asked Orgu.

"Wait a minute. One more thing. Everybody put on your camouflage gear." Meaning the 7-foot to 9-foot (2.13 meter to 2.74 meter) tailor-altered, human military uniforms, face coverings, and foot coverings resembling black commando boots, that the other members of

Tantoon's fanatical followers had borrowed/stolen/acquired.

When they were all finally, comfortably, attired in their camouflage gear Orgu said to Neejat. "You go now. You do now." And then Orgu brusquely grasped Neejat by the shoulder squeezing his shoulder as tightly as possible without doing any permanent damage. He was squeezing Neejat's shoulder to emphasize his next point. "Go now! Quickly! Very quickly." Orgu pointed to his eyes and then he pointed to Neejat's eyes and then back to his own eyes. "Very quickly so that no one will see!"

Neejat nodded. "I go, quick, kay, lee."

"That's the way to do it. I knew we could count on you."

Was Ugat just now grunting out of dissatisfaction? Or was he grunting as a way to express sarcasm at Orgu's own current unwarranted sarcastic witticisms.

"Go! Quick! Kay! Lee! Go! Neejat! Go!" Orgu said teasingly to Neejat and, then to the others. "Once more unto the breach!"

Neejat quickly climbed to the top of the barbed wire fence and then as gingerly and as carefully as possible – snip – snip – snipped – a 4-foot (1.22 meter) section of the barb wiring at the top of the fences, and then, just as quickly he was up and over the fence and running towards a back-alley area of the concrete and steel building complex which was out of view of the security cameras were the four Shadow-walkers could hunker down for a few moments.

Neejat was immediately followed by Ugat, who went up and over the fence, over the opened section at the top of the barbed wire fence, and then Roku, and then, finally, Ugat.

>>>>><<<<<

There were two armed security guards posted that night inside the concrete and steel building complex.

"What was that?" the one armed security guard in the in the CCTV (closed-circuit television) room said to the other armed security guard who was leaning back in a chair reading the newspaper.

"What was what?" The other armed security guard was saying as he was leaning forward to take a closer look at the CCTV screens.

"I think a big black bear just climbed over the barbed wire fence by the back freight entrances."

"Are you serious?"

"It could've been a bird flying on front of the camera or a leaf blowing in the wind."

The other armed security guard was now staring at the CCTV screen when three more figures resembling big, black, bears climbed over the barbed wire fence and run towards the back freight area out of view of the other CCTV cameras.

Both armed security guards were staring back and forth at each other.

"Those weren't black bears."

"And that definitely wasn't birds flying in front of the cameras or leaves blowing in the wind."

Both armed security guards simultaneously repeated, together, out loud, at the same time, "What the living hell was that?"

And then separately.

"We better call this in!"

"I'm calling it in! I'm calling it in! Right now! I'm calling it in!"

>>>>><<<<<

"Quickly now! Neejat! Quickly now!" Orgu was double-checking that Neejat had a climbing rope in his backpack. "Once you're on top (meaning the roof of the concrete and steel building complex), secure the rope and drop the longer end down to us, so that we can climb up behind you."

Neejat began climbing up a thick steel pipe on the side of the building to a barely three inch (0.08 meter) ledge, to another thick steel pipe on the side of the building, to a series of window ledges, to another small rooftop, to more window ledges, to another small rooftop, to more window ledges, until Neejat had finally made it to the uppermost topside roof of the concrete and steel building complex.

After so many minutes a rope was tossed over the side of the building from the roof to the others – Orgu, Ugat, and Roku – waiting down below. After Orgu, Ugat, and Roku had finally climbed up the rope to join Neejat, Orgu stepped away from the foursome and began mumbling to himself, counting off numbers with his fingers as he was simultaneously pointing at several different objects on the roof. After a quick minute or two, Orgu pointed to a nearby ventilation cover on the roof.

"There!" Orgu said to the others. "We will enter there!"

Ugat and Roku began disconnecting the ventilation cover and the ventilation unit from where it was connected to the roof, with the appropriate tools, they were carrying in their backpacks; even though as 7-foot to 9-foot (2.13 meter to 2.74 meter) Bigfoots, Sasquatches, and Yetis , they were strong enough to tear off the ventilation cover and ventilation unit with their bare hands

172

as if the ventilation cover and ventilation unit were made of cardboard. After the ventilation cover and ventilation unit was safely removed, Ugat tied another rope to a few sturdy pipes on the roof and dropped the rope through the exposed opening on the roof where the ventilation cover and ventilation unit once was.

Neejat stepped forward to climb down the rope first but was stopped by Orgu. "You are here to climb and jump over fences." Orgu gently nudged Neejat back away from the gaping hole where the ventilation cover and ventilation unit once was. "And to carry on your back what the others are unable to carry on their backs." Orgu called out to Ugat. "Are you ready?'

Without answering, Ugat immediately made his way down the rope, followed by Orgu, followed by Roku, and finally followed by Neejat.

Orgu seemed to know exactly where he was going with a little help from Ugat, it was as if they had been preparing in advance, for a very long time. Orgu stopped in front of one, specific, locked door. Ugat stopped Orgu, shaking his head, side to side, negatively. Ugat walked further down the hallway to another, specific, locked door. This time nodding his head, up and down, positively. Without hesitating any further and without bothering to use any of the tools they were carrying in their backpacks, Orgu, powerfully, struck the locked door with the side of his closed fist. The locked door, which was made of metal, shattered into three separate pieces with a small section of the door frame breaking off and falling to the floor. Neejat and Roku watched in silence as Orgu and Ugat began searching through the many drawers of the many metal filing cabinets that filled the entire room. The metal filing cabinets were special filing cabinets made to store table size blueprints of architectural, mechanical, and engineering layouts and schematics.

"Don't move or I'll shoot!" An armed security guard was standing in the doorway holding a .38 Caliber revolver pistol. And then as he was having a closer look at the foursome, he was saying, "What the hell... are you?" He was waving the .38 Caliber revolver pistol side to side at Orgu, Ugat, Roku, and Neejat. "Why are you all so big?"

The human security guard was stunned by the overly large Bigfoots disguised by the tailored altered camouflaged military uniforms, face coverings, and black foot coverings, made to resemble black commando boots. Nobody had ever seen 7-foot to 9-foot (2.13 meter to 2.74 meter) tall commandos in camouflage fatigues.

In an instant, Orgu, Ugat, and Roku, were immediately firing their automatic rifles at the armed security guard as they were simultaneously diving for cover behind the metal filing cabinets in the room, as Neejat looked on, dumbfounded, not knowing what to do. The armed security guard must have been just as dumbfounded, himself, never expecting to be in a life or death situation that day, or that he would have to be firing his firearm to kill or be killed. The armed security guard managed to squeeze off a shot or two from his .38 caliber revolver pistol, but he was no match for the barrage of bullets coming from the three automatic rifles simultaneously firing at him. The armed security guard was literally ripped to shreds by the three automatic rifles. Half of his head and face was blown off, as well as his left arm and right hand, and some of his intestines spilled out onto the floor before he collapsed, dead, onto the floor, as a bloody, bullet riddled, blob, of tattered flesh and bones.

"What have we done!" Neejat shouted out to Orgu, Ugat, and Roku. "You said we were not going to kill anyone! How is this not killing anyone?"

Orgu and Ugat were immediately somewhat confused, being educated members of the Citizenry, while Roku, being a Sawtooth, and who was only recently learning to speak properly, as well as to read and write, had no idea what Orgu and Ugat were confused about.

"Neejat, your sentencing structure has greatly improved. How is that?" Orgu looked back and forth from Neejat to Ugat.

"Maybe it is the fear and shock of what has just occurred that has affected Neejat's thought processes." Ugat added. "Some are more adept at retaining knowledge, while other take longer to memorize new ideas and concepts; either way, the knowledge is still always there inside their minds whether they can access the knowledge or not."

Neejat immediately returned to stumbling with his words as he had previously been doing. "You say we no kill! I say I no kill!"

"You did not kill, Neejat. You did nothing but stand there like a bump on a log." Orgu said to Neejat. "We have only killed to not be killed."

Ugat grabbed Orgu by the shoulder. "We do not have time for this."

Orgu and Ugat immediately returned to searching through the many metal filing cabinets in the room, but at a much faster pace than before, with Orgu saying to Ugat, over the filing cabinets as they continued frantically searching. "A silent alarm has to have been triggered. We have only so much little time left!"

After so much of a little while longer, Ugat exuberantly shouted, "I have it!"

Orgu immediately rushed to Ugat's side examining the large paper blueprints Ugat was holding in his hands. Orgu nodded in agreement. "We do not have the time to search for other documents. Quickly! Take the cannisters from your backpacks and begin pouring the chemicals from the cannisters throughout the room, being very careful not to spill any of the chemicals onto your clothing's and furs!"

Ugat and Roku were immediately doing as they were told while Orgu was rolling up the blueprints they had taken from the metal filing cabinet. After the blueprints were properly rolled up with a few rubber bands wrapped around them, Orgu stuffed the rolled up blueprints into his backpack. A reluctant Neejat finally joined Ugat and Roku and began dousing the room of metal filing cabinets with the cannisters of chemicals he had in his backpack; which were added to all four backpacks, as necessary supplies, before the start of their mission.

Before Orgu, Ugat, Roku, and Neejat exited the room with the metal filing cabinets, Orgu removed one more piece of equipment from his backpack. It was a small matchbox of wooden matches with a match striker on the side of the matchbox. Orgu took out a few of the wooden matches from the matchbox and lit the wooden matches by scraping the wooden matches along the match striker on the side of the matchbox. He only glanced sideways at the room with the metal filing cabinets for one moment before tossing the lit matches into the room.

The room with the metal filing cabinets instantly burst into flames.

Security supervisor Jim Sheridan was the first of the first responders to enter the CCTV room in the concrete and steel building complex.

"What the hell is going on here?" Jim Sheridan said to the armed security guard in the CCTV room as he was entering the room. "We have the building surrounded."

"They killed Billy Lainey!" The armed security guard in the CCTV room – Lester Mumford - who had remained behind while other armed security guard – Billy Lainey - went to investigate the possible security breaches, was saying to Jim Sheridan - the off-site, on-duty, security supervisor. "They killed Billy Lainey! He went to investigate! They just shot him dead! They filled him full of lead with AR-15's, or AK-47's, or M-16's. I'm not sure. I can't tell the exact make of the rifles!"

"Who killed Billy Lainey?"

The armed security guard inside the CCTV camera room replayed the security footage from the CCTV cameras.

"What is that? A commando squad? But... they must all be about 10-foot (3.05 meter) tall?" Security Supervisor Jim Sheridan was saying as he was watching the playback on the computer screens.
Security Supervisor Jim Sheridan was immediately barking off commands into his radio.

"We have four armed hostiles on-site! Do not hesitate to engage the intruders! I repeat! Do not hesitate to engage the intruders! Shoot first and ask questions later! You got that everybody? Shoot first and ask questions later!"

>>>>><<<<<

Orgu, Ugat, Roku, and Neejat were quickly running towards the nearest exit. They did not bother to use any tools to unlock the nearest exit door. Orgu tore off the doorknob while Ugat punched the top of the metal door outward. Orgu and Ugat proceeded to pull out and rip apart the metal door from the metal and concrete doorframe. They tossed the metal door to the side.

"Go! Neejat! Go!" Orgu ordered Neejat. Neejat hesitated for a moment.

Roku begrudgingly pushed Neejat aside and stepped through the dismantled open doorway - saying to Neejat. "You talk very much and say very nothing!"

Roku was instantly shot fifteen to twenty times by gunfire and fell back away from the dismantled open doorway back into the hallway of the building as Orgu, Ugat, and Neejat looked on in horror.

"More men with guns have arrived!" Orgu was saying. "Quickly! Neejat! Pick up Roku and carry him on your shoulders!"

Neejat immediately did as he was told. It was all part of their training. None of the others of the Citizenry, or Rogues, or Sawtooths, were to be left behind. That was always the most important rule of every mission.

Roku was barely breathing when Orgu, Ugat, and Neejat hoisted him up through the ventilation unit opening onto the roof of the concrete and steel building complex. They had tied a rope around his chest and underarms and pulled him up. By the time Roku reached the top of the building – he was breathing no more.

Orgu, Ugat, and Neejat were able to discern from peeking over the sides of the roof of the building that the building was surrounded by men with guns and several vehicles. They planned quickly. There was a gap in one corner of the building where the men with guns were not able to fully cover and a terrace and a detached shack by the terrace. The plan was to jump onto the terrace and then onto the detached shack to the ground and then on through the barbed wire fence and then into the forest where they will disappear as if they were never there. But they were there. Normally a team of Shadow-walkers would have cleaned up the blood from Roku's wounds and generally sterilized the area the best that they were able to. They did not have the time this time. They are going to be barely getting away with their lives... all except for Roku, so far, that is if they will be able to get away at all. Being that Neejat was the youngest and the strongest of the now threesome, he was tasked with the burden of carrying the corpse of Roku on his back. Orgu and Ugat quickly tied Roku to Neejat's back with several ropes they had stored in their backpacks. Ugat quickly went to the opposite side of the concrete and steel building complex and began randomly firing his automatic rifle at the men with guns surrounding the building down below – to distract them while Orgu jumped onto the nearby terrace and then onto the detached shack and then to the ground and then towards the barbed wire fence, followed by Neejat with the corpse of Roku tied to his back, and then followed by Ugat. By the time Ugat should have made it to the terrace, to the detached shack, to the ground, Orgu should have by then torn apart a small section of the barbed wire fence with his bare hands and flung the small section of the barbed wire fence to the side, so that Neejat and Ugat will be able to run up behind him, where they all will be able to escape together into the forest.

Surprisingly, there was a man with a gun outside the barbed wire fence, but his gun was not drawn, his gun was safely tucked inside his holster. The man with the holstered gun - armed security guard Pedro Serrano - did not expect to see Orgu running down the hill followed by Neejat with Roku tied to his back. He had thought that all the action was happening on the other side of the building. He had begun walking up the hill when he heard the sound of the barbed wire fence being ripped out from the ground and tossed to the side.

The man with the holstered gun was saying, "What? Who...?" Before the man with the holstered gun could say one more word, Orgu was right in front of him running past him. As Orgu was running past the man with the holstered gun, Orgu swung his massive Bigfoot arm up and around, instantly decapitating the man by the force of his one powerful blow. Neejat almost tripped over the man's decapitated head as it bounced up the hill for a few moments and then after the decapitated head lost its momentum, the decapitated head began rolling down the hill.

Orgu took one quick glance at Neejat following from behind. Orgu instantly saw the hate, disgust, and censure in Neejat's eyes.

I no kill? We no kill? Orgu was thinking. What's the big deal? They are not of us. They are not of the Citizenry, and they will never be of the Citizenry.

Several of the men with guns from the concrete and steel building complex chased after Orgu, Ugat, and Neejat as they escaped into the forest, but the men with guns were not as adept and experienced as the Bigfoots when it came to traversing the rough terrain. The men with guns were like *'a fish out of water'* compared to the natural expertise the Bigfoots exhibited when it came to hiding in the woodlands, forests, deserts, and wildernesses of the world. When Orgu, Ugat, and Neejat were far enough away from the men with guns they stopped to catch their breath, reorganize their thoughts, and revise

180

their plan of attack, or retreat; as their assault of the concrete and steel building was complete. Now all that mattered was getting away with their prize – that being the blueprints they had stolen.

Orgu and Ugat were well aware of Neejat's anger as they were all seating themselves on the plush fauna of the forest.

"We no kill!" Neejat shouted at Orgu and Ugat. "We no kill!"

"Calm down Neejat. We did what we had to do." Orgu was saying to Neejat.

"Was it necessary to decapitate the human by the fence? He did not even have his gun drawn!"

Orgu and Ugat were looking back and forth at each other again flabbergasted and befuddled by the sudden sophistication of Neejat's command of grammar – being that Neejat had only just recently been captured/rescued in the forest as a Rogue who had until now did not know how to speak.

"Where did you learn to speak as well as you are speaking? Do you also know how to read and write?" Ugat was inquiring.

"Never mind about where I have learned to speak. I have listened and I have learned. We are not unsophisticated nomads roaming the wastelands of the world. We are of the Citizenry. We are not utter barbarians!" Neejat was fervently shaking his head in frustration. "I have one question! It has just occurred to me! Why had it not occurred to you and you (meaning Orgu and Ugat) and Tantoon!"

"On with your question and then be silent!" Orgu warned Neejat.

"Why did we not use the wandererstones to enter and exit? We could have avoided all of this unnecessary carnage!"

"It is because we are only in possession of one wandererstone." Orgu said to Neejat with Ugat adding before he was instantly slapped on the side of the head by Orgu and ordered to refrain from speaking.

"And that is only because Tantoon had stolen the one wandererstone from his mentor and master - Threnatta - before slitting her throat with a boneknife."

"Silence!" Orgu shouted at Ugat for saying more than was needed to be said.

And then as if Neejat had suddenly devolved right before Orgu and Ugat's eye, he immediately reverted back to his simple and unsophisticated elocutions and mannerisms.

"I no wanted to kill. I no wanted to hurt any living, breathing being; human or not."

"Enough!" Orgu suddenly brusquely commanded. "We have, so far, outrun and outdistanced ourselves from the men with guns. Let us not permit our pursuers to regain their charge."

They quickly drank all the water they needed from the cannisters they were carrying in their backpacks and were soon back on their feet zigzagging through the dense brush of the forest back to the hidden cave dwelling where Tantoon and the others were waiting.

CHAPTER TWENTY-TWO

Shantuu was relaxing by the fire in the Heseetu cave dwelling hidden deep in the wilderness of the Colorado Rockies when Mimi ran into the cave enclave presently occupied by Shantuu.

"You have been summoned my Lord."

"Please, do not refer to me as 'Lord.' I am no more or no less better than you or any of the others."

"You have been summoned."

"Summoned? By whom? And for what? Summoned where?"

"You have been summoned by Zitmat of the Citizenry of the Magutiti in the Rain forests of the Amazonian jungles"

"Zitmat?" Shantuu was trying to remember the last time he had spoken to Zitmat. It was during a very cold and frigid winter in the Antarctic a long, long, time ago.

"I do not know why." Mimi seemed to be bowing her head out of respect. "But what I do know is that there are many others being summoned."

To the Amazon rain forest, Shantuu was thinking, it was always too hot and sticky, over there, at this time of the year. It will take two big and one small wandererstones to make the journey there.

"I will need to pack a bag." Shantuu said to Mimi. "Please, assist me. We must make haste. We are not being summoned out of idleness and folly."

"Yes..." Mimi immediately stopped herself from almost accidently calling Shantuu – 'Lord' – again, but instead just as quickly corrected herself. "Shantuu. Yes, Shantuu. It will be my pleasure."

Shantuu needed four wandererstones instead of three to make the long, very long, journey to the dwellings of the Citizenry of the Magutiti in the rain forests of the Amazon jungles. Not all of the dwellings of the Citizenry of the Magutiti in the rain forests were caves acquired for habitation, but a combination of caves and well camouflaged encampments hidden by the dense brush of the rain forest. Shantuu reappeared by a river in the Amazon jungle after disappearing – or teleporting - from a mountaintop in the Colorado Rockies all the while holding onto, tightly, the four wandererstones he had clasped in both hands – two wandererstones in one hand and two wandererstones in the other hand. Shantuu did not immediately recognize the river or the surrounding area. He had only visited here a long time ago in his younger days. His memory was not as clear and pristine as he had hoped it would be. Shantuu knelt down beside the side of the river to cool himself by pouring handfuls of water over his head and splashing water on his face. It was then that the scent of a large carnivorous beast filled his nostrils. Shantuu was able to discern that the beast was carnivorous by the stench of stale meat on its mouth, lips, teeth, and tongue. Shantuu did not immediately make any sudden movements. He did not want to alert the beast to the fact that he was aware of its presence. I must accurately pinpoint the location of the beast, Shantuu was thinking, before the beast was ready to strike. Shantuu was now, clearly, being stalked by a very, very large wild animal which was hiding nearby silently watching him. After so many moments, Shantuu heard the very, very slight sound of a twig snapping, which was instantly muffled, no doubt by the beast. Which meant that whatever was hiding in the brush stalking Shantuu was

184

definitely an experienced hunter - but Shantuu was also an experienced hunter himself. The twig snapping gave away the position of the beast. Shantuu's mind was racing in a multitude of different directions. Was the beast an alligator? Or a crocodile? Which had seen Shantuu replenishing himself by the river's edge and had crawled onto the land to circle back and sneak up behind Shantuu? Or was the beast a giant snake which was big enough to swallow a fully grown ox in a few big bites? Or a big cat? Like a leopard or a panther? Shantuu kept a watchful eye on the area where he had heard the twig snapping. The beast had washed itself in the rivers and streams so that it could not be identified by its smell, but it could not wash away its stale, rancid breath; especially as the beast was striving not to be overheard by inhaling and exhaling with long, slow, gasps as it slithered through the brush towards its intended prey. When the beast was close enough to strike, it crouched, and steadied itself before springing out from the brush to jump onto Shantuu and simultaneously ripping open Shantuu's throat with its powerful jaws.

Shantuu saw the beast breaking through the dense foliage as if it was flying through the air. It was a black panther, as black as the blackest night, maybe 14-foot to 15-foot (4.27 meter to 4.57 meter) long. Shantuu batted the black panther away with one powerful swoop of his arm, missing the black panthers neck, but making contact with the shoulder of the black panther. Shantuu had either broken the shoulder of the black panther or dislocated its shoulder. If Shantuu had struck the panther on the neck, Shantuu would have definitely broken its neck. That was not enough to deter the black panther. The black panther doubled back and ran towards Shantuu, roaring, flashing it's razor sharp fangs at Shantuu, and continuously striking at Shantuu with its outstretched razor sharp claws, but striking at Shantuu with only one hand. Shantuu had definitely hurt the black panther when he had struck the black panther the first time. The black panther jumped again, trying to get its mouth on Shantuu's neck again, to tear out his neck, but Shantuu was too fast and too strong. Shantuu grabbed hold of the black panther and flung the black panther against a nearby tree with as much force as possible. The tree almost seemed to wobble and shake as if the tree was going to fall over. The black panther must've broken a few ribs this time around. It growled a few more times at Shantuu before limping away and disappearing into the brush of the jungle. The scent of the black panther faded further and further away into the far reaches of the dense jungle.

It was then that Mintinka of the Citizenry of the Magutiti appeared running along the river's edge towards where Shantuu was huddled. Mintinka was one of the youngest Shadow-walker's Shantuu had ever seen, and a girl, none the less, barely old enough to birth a child.

"What was that?" Mintinka asked Shantuu.

"It was a black panther. It tried to make a meal of me. I am glad I did not have to fight the beast to the death to prevent becoming its dinner."

"That would be Panthera pardus. You are lucky. Others have not been so lucky." Mintinka picked up the leather pouch Shantuu had brought along and wrapped the shoulder strap over her shoulder. "We have been expecting you. The others have all arrived, already. They are waiting."

Shantuu followed Mintinka as she walked back along the river's edge towards the hidden dwellings of the Citizenry of the Magutiti.

The Magutiti dwelling that Shantuu was taken to, which was one of many, was indeed not a cave inside a mountain or beneath the surface of the terrain of the jungle, but a well-built, well-constructed, well-hidden series of interconnecting and interlocking huts; complete with straw, feathered, and fur beds, wooden and bamboo tables, chairs, benches, shelves, and an occasional window with flaps that can instantly shut, cover, and seal away the windows to avoid the rains, predators, and unwelcomed, prying eyes.

Sunni – an Elder of the Citizenry of the Xanunu and Krono - an Elder of the Citizenry of the Anatta greeted Shantuu.

"It is so good to finally meet with you again, Shantuu." Sunni said to Shantuu with Krono adding, "I wish it could have been under better circumstances."

The Citizenry of the Xanununu have always lived throughout the centuries further north and south, at the Artic and Antarctic regions of the world. Their fur was usually solid white – which made them what folklore legend have always referred to as – Yetis - and also, informally, as Abominable Snowmen. The Citizenry of the Anatta shared the rain forests of the Amazonian jungles with the Citizenry of the Magutiti, with the Citizenry of the Magutiti having always existed further north in what is now called Central America and the Citizenry of the Anatta have existed further south in what is now called South America.

Other Citizenries present were the Citizenry of the Bindubindu from the jungles of the African Congo, the Citizenry of the Tabunutabu from the lands of Europa, the Citizenry of the Chapupatta from the lands down under of Australia and New Zealand, the Citizenry of the Lititi from the Orient, what is now known as the Far East, the Citizenry of the Xuxu from the lands of Eastern Europa and Northern Asia, what is now known as Russia, the Citizenry of the Nayadeena from the deserts sands of Arabia and Persia, what is now known as the Middle-East.

There were many other Citizenries spread-out throughout the world, in the present and in the past, who have come and gone and where no more.

"You were attacked by a wild animal." Sunni continued politely conversing.

"I was very lucky. I managed to strike the beast once and then twice before the beast had a chance to take a bite out of me or to rip out a whole chunk of my hide."

"We must send out Shadow-walkers to watch for the others who will be also arriving shortly."

An Underling of the Citizenry of the Magutiti who was standing nearby by the entrance to the hut enclosure immediately stepped away saying to Sunni, "I will inform the others and arrange for Shadow-walkers to be out and about by the river's edge and the surrounding areas."

"Well done." Sunni said to the retreating Underling.

After all the other Elders had finally arrived from many of the other Citizenries from all around the world, a large feast was prepared. After relaxing and filling their bellies, the underlings of the Citizenry of the Magutiti removed the leftover food and corn husks, large, unfolded leaves, weaved grass mats, used as plates and hollowed out wooden tree branches, cut and shaped, used as cups. The Elders retired to a large hut, taking seats, making a large circle, around a brisk fire at the center of the large hut.

The topics of their first discussions revolved around the latest status of what they were referring to as the 'undivining' and whether a cure or vaccine had finally been developed. The disease which have plagued the Bigfoots, Sasquatches, and Yetis of the world, throughout history, was named the 'undivining' by ancient Seers and Prophets, long ago, who proclaimed that the 'undivining' was a curse caste upon the Bigfoots, Sasquatches, and Yetis, by the Devil or by God, because Bigfoots, Sasquatches, and Yetis were ungodly, half-animal, half-human, beasts, with no souls, and so were meant to be denied entrance into Heaven and the afterlife. The conversations went on and on like that for a while until the conversations turned to the dreadful deeds and horrific crimes being committed by Tantoon and his fanatical followers.

"Is this a new Citizenry evolving before our very eyes." One Elder was proclaiming while another Elder corrected that Elder.

"De-evolving! We have gone from enlightened to unenlightened!"

"Not you or I, but Tantoon and his followers!"

"They are a perversion!"

"We will finally become extinct!"

"If the 'undivining' is not enough, which we have so far, for so many centuries, been unable to control, we are now becoming our own worst enemy!"

"Not we! Not you or I! I repeat! It is Tantoon! Tantoon and Tantoon only! Tantoon is a malignant tumor worse than the 'undivining.'"

"Can he be redeemed?" All heads turned to look back and forth at each other.

It was Zitmat who spoke, before turning to Shantuu allowing for Shantuu to speak. "Tantoon is unredeemable, we must excise the malignant tumor, however, there may still be the possibility of saving some, but not all, of his fanatical followers. Tantoon was training to become a

Healer by the Citizenry he was born unto - the Citizenry of the Cororuru - and then was apprenticed to a Healer by the name of Threnatta of the Citizenry of the Heseetu, who Tantoon had murdered in cold blood before disappearing into the forests, woodlands, deserts and forming his own uncouth, illegitimate, immoral, ungodly Citizenry, so many seasons ago."

"The Citizenry of the blind leading the blind." Shantuu finally spoke up knowing that it was his moment to do so.

All eyes in the large chamber-like hut turned to Shantuu.

"We are still unsure as to Tantoon's motives and intentions, except for the fact that Tantoon is generally filled with hatred and rage and cannot be reasoned with, or bargained with, or satiated, or appeased."

"You have not heard, Shantuu?" Sunni said to Shantuu and to any of the others present at the meeting in the large chamber-like hut who have yet to be informed of the matters at hand. "Tantoon and his fanatical followers have attacked a human building structure and flagrantly taken the lives of two humans... that we know of, so far." An unrestrained murmur was followed by a harrowing hush echoing through the hollow emptiness of the chamber-like hut.

"It is the reason why we have been gathered together here now." Zitmat added.

"What human building structure?" Shantuu inquired.

"A human building structure not far from the many dwellings of the Citizenry of the Heseetu."

"I have no information regarding the incident you are referring too. I am sure I will be informed upon my return."

Maybe, Shantuu knew a little more than he was willing to divulge... at the moment... under the present circumstances.

CHAPTER TWENTY-THREE

The research team of Rand Biotech arrived at the concrete and steel building complex later that day. The concrete and steel building complex located on the back roads of the edge of Denver's city limits was also coincidentally nameless like the nameless Rand Biotech building in downtown Denver. The F.B.I (F.B.I - Federal Bureau of Investigation) and local police were already on-site, scurrying about everywhere, inside and outside the building.

"Are these the cryptozoological experts?" A Denver Police Sargent was asking another of his fellow police officers who had the perimeter of the building cordoned off by a combination of yellow caution/danger tape, police vehicles, and by the sheer force of their presence.

Indeed they are. Let them through. Let them through. They were greeted by F.B.I. Agent Brenda Caneo who escorted the Rand Biotech team into the interior of the concrete and steel building complex after being shown where a section of the barbed wire fence had been, literally, pulled up from out of the ground and tossed aside as if the fence was made of aluminum foil. Mira, Lisa, Dobie, and Kasper, or by their official, professional, scholarly, academic, snooty names – Dr. Mira Salinas, Dr. Lisa Wintergarden, Dr. Kasper Weinberger, and Dr. Dobie Doberson, quickly swept the area for fiber samples and swabbed the dismantled portion of the fence for DNA samples. Once inside the Interior of the concrete and steel building complex, Dobie was looking from side to side and up and down at the many hallways and many locked doors.

"What is this place?" Dobie asked F.B.I. Agent Caneo.

"High profile military and extremely sensitive public safety records are stored here." F.B.I. Agent Caneo stopped in front of a bullet riddled hallway. "They took something from the room at the end of this corridor. They set the room on fire to distract us. We have no idea what they took."

Lisa was sticking one of her fingers inside one of the bullet holes in the wall. "They certainly came with enough fire power to burn the whole place down to the ground. Why set fire to only the one room and possibly give away what they were obviously trying to keep secret?"

"They didn't have enough time." F.B.I. Agent Caneo answered Lisa. "They were fired upon by one of two armed security guards who were inside the building at the time." F.B.I. Agent Caneo began walking towards another hallway on the opposite side of the foyer away from the bullet riddled hallway followed by the Rand Biotech research team. "But that's not why we have invited you here." F.B.I. Agent Caneo stopped by the entrance to another room where the door had to have been, literally, ripped out from the hinges and pulled out from the door frame by sheer force and tossed aside like the barbed wire fence outside, but by what? Or by whom? It could only have been by the intruders. "Be careful where you are stepping." F.B.I. Agent Caneo said to the Rand Biotech research and security teams. "This is mainly why you are here." F.B.I. Agent Caneo was looking down at the ground. There were several puddles of dried blood, some smudged by what appeared to be footprints over 15-inches (4.57 meters) in length. Droplets of blood were leading from the door that was ripped open, across the foyer, to an open ventilation shaft in the ceiling.

"Are there more droplets of blood on the roof of the building?"

Kasper asked F.B.I. Agent Caneo.

"Yes, and leading from the roof, down the side of the building, across the yard to where the barbed wire fence was ripped apart, and into the forest." F.B.I. Agent Caneo continued after pausing for a moment. "We assumed the blood samples inside the building will be better preserved and have the least probability of having become contaminated."

After scraping up enough of the dried droplets of blood to do all the tests they needed to do, Mira, Kasper, Lisa, and Dobie, or Dr. Mira Salinas, Dr. Kasper Weinberger, Dr. Lisa Wintergarden, and Dr. Dobie Doberson, began scraping up dust particles off the floor with specifically designed plastic scoop strips and tape strips. They were interrupted by F.B.I. Agent Caneo who handed the research team several packets of plastic scoop strips and tape strips the F.B.I. evidence unit had already collected themselves.

"Is this what you are looking for?" F.B.I. Agent Caneo was holding up one specific tape strip sample inside a small clear plastic evidence envelope.

As the research team stepped closer, they all could clearly see a few strands of hair inside the small clear plastic evidence envelope.

"I'll take that." Kasper was saying to F.B.I. Agent Caneo as he was quickly snatching away the evidence envelope from her hand.

Before they were finally done and ready to leave, there was one more matter at hand that the F.B.I. wanted the Rand Biotech research team to be informed about. At this point the Rand Biotech research team were joined by the Rand Biotech security team, which consisted of

Security Expert Springfield and Hector the Hunter. What the F.B.I. – via F.B.I. Agent Caneo - wanted them to see was the security footage of the intruders, security footage showing what was clearly four individuals? Mutants? Cryptids? Aliens from another planet? Overgrown, overdosed, steroid addicted, fanatical, bodybuilding, muscle head, maniacs? Because the four individuals were all clearly at least 9-foot (2.74 meters) tall, dressed in jungle camouflage fatigues with their faces covered by black masks or hoods.

While Mira, Kasper, Lisa, and Dobie were left alone, inside the CCTV camera room to watch the security footage of the intruders, F.B.I. Agent Caneo, Security Expert Springfield, and Hector the Hunter had gone out into the hallway to have their own, private, personal conversation about what? Only God knows.

They rode back in silence later that night, either out of exhaustion, or because they were all each trying the mentally fathom what had occurred at the concrete and steel building complex.

CHAPTER TWENTY-FOUR

Orgu, Ugat, and Neejat, with the carcass of Roku, returned to the cave dwelling, which was a new, temporary home to Tantoon and his fanatical followers. After laying Roku down on a mat of furs, the trio were immediately escorted to a cave enclave where Tantoon was impatiently waiting.

"Do you have it?" Tantoon immediately inquired the moment Orgu, Ugat, and Neejat had stepped into the cave enclave. "Let me have it."

Orgu handed the blueprints they had stolen over to Tantoon, who immediately unrolled the blueprints and laid the blueprints onto the top of a bolder being used as a table. After perusing the blueprints for a few minutes Tantoon turned to Neejat and said, "Thank you for your assistance. You can go now. Nourish yourself. Rest by the fire. We will be speaking again together soon."

"As you wish, Tantoon." Neejat said to Tantoon.

Tantoon returned to perusing the blueprints as Neejat disappeared out into the natural rocky corridor of the cave dwelling, but Neejat did not walk all the way away, Neejat stepped back into the nearest shadows of the natural rocky corridor, out of sight, of Tantoon, Orgu, and Ugat, but not out of hearing range. Backed away in the shadows, Neejat was able to see and hear everything Tantoon, Orgu, and Ugat were doing. After conferring together over the blueprints for so long, Orgu asked Tantoon something about wandererstones. What about wandererstones? Neejat was wondering. His question was immediately answered. Tantoon dropped the two wandererstones he had stolen from Threnatta and the Citizenry of the Heseetu. One of the wandererstones was glowing, vibrating, and pulsating, as most wandererstones have been known to do. The other, second, wandererstone was dull and lifeless around the edges with only a small section of the middle, center of the second wandererstone glowing, vibrating, and pulsating.

"One of the wandererstones is dying." Tantoon said to Orgu and Ugat.

"Why is that?" Ugat was surprised. He had never seen a dying wandererstone before. Ugat had never seen too many wandererstones in his lifetime, ever, for that matter.

A rodent running along the natural rocky cave corridor ran past where Neejat was hiding in the shadows and accidently knocked over a few small rocks and pebbles. Tantoon, Orgu, and Ugat immediately looked up, out through the cave enclave opening, directly at where Neejat was standing, hidden by the shadows of the natural, rocky, cave corridor. Neejat was startled for a moment. They would have all been making eye contact except for the fact that Neejat was hidden in the shadows.

"See what that is about?" Tantoon ordered Orgu and Ugat. Being that Orgu was more so a Bigfoot of action and Ugat a Bigfoot of the mind, thinking, meditation, and contemplative introspection, Orgu responded and carefully began walking out of the cave enclave into the natural rocky cave corridor. Orgu walked to where Neejat was standing, hiding in the shadows, but Neejat was no longer there. Neejat was gone.

CHAPTER TWENTY-FIVE

The Lear jet was supplied with all the usual luxurious amenities afforded the rich and famous of the world, only the passengers currently jet setting on the Lear jet were not rich and famous, but ordinary, average, public servants of the Federal Bureau of Investigation and two guests from private industry - that being F.B.I Agent Caneo and Rand Biotech security officers – Security Expert Springfield and Hector the Hunter.

From the view through the window of the Lear jet the passengers were able to see, out in the near and far horizons, the Whitehouse, the Washington Monument, and the Pentagon.

"I'm so sorry that you've had to come all this way. We are not allowed to pass out files, documents, or photos of any sensitive materials, but we can show and tell, so to speak." F.B.I. Agent Caneo was saying to Security Expert Springfield and Hector the Hunter as the Lear jet was landing.

An unmarked, black, government van was waiting for them after the Lear jet had landed at the Ronald Reagan Washington Airport across the Potomac river in Virginia. F.B.I. Agent Caneo, Security Expert Springfield, and Hector the Hunter were quickly whisked away to their meeting at the Pentagon.

Hector the Hunter was shocked and awed at seeing the inside of the Pentagon for the first time in his lifetime - not so much so for Security Expert Springfield; he had been here several times before during his earlier days working with the C.I.A. (Central Intelligence Agency). F.B.I. Agent Caneo, after passing several security checkpoints, led the pair to a separate satellite surveillance room. There were several computer technicians there waiting. F.B.I. Agent Caneo did not introduce anyone to each other but merely ordered the computer techs to, "Pop it up on the screens!"

The room came alive from the bright lights of the computer screens taking up three of the four walls of the room.

"You see the heat signatures on the screens?" F.B.I. Agent Caneo asked Security Expert Springfield and Hector the Hunter.

They merely nodded.

"The military, for many years, with a little help from the private sector, have been developing satellite surveillance technologies where they can, more or less, accurately discern between different heat signatures to identify specific individuals. Much like facial recognition technology. Being that the distance between a corner of a room to another corner of a room or a few city streets compared to the distance from the atmosphere of the Earth to the surface of the Earth, facial recognition technology has been more accurate and dependable than identifying different heat signatures from space, but we have, or shall I say, they have, been improving more and more, over the past few years."

F.B.I. Agent Caneo paused for a moment.

"Go on." Security Expert Springfield urged F.B.I. Agent Caneo.

"So far the technology has been developed to the point where we can discern the difference between certain animals and humans, where before a heat signature could have been anything - an animal, or a human, or a campfire, or a large spotlight at an outdoor recreational event! The heat signatures can almost accurately identify anything as big as a dog, discerning between the differences in the size of a dog, or a deer, or a horse, or a bear, or a moose, etcetera, etcetera. Each heat signature has been given different computer codes or identification numbers. A fawn will have a heat signature and number designation of one-one-point-one-seven, or 11.17 sig. A deer will have a heat signature or number designation of one-one-point-two-four, or 11.24 sig. A moose, four-one-point-three-nine, or 41.39 sig. A bear, three-one-point-one-seven, or 31.17 sig. The average human male or female has a heat signature or number designation of two-four-point-two-six, or 24.26 sig. A thin male or female of, let's say, 120 pounds (54.43 kilograms), will have a heat signature or number designation of two-three-point-three-five, or 23.35 sig. While a heavier male or female of 300 pounds (136.08 kilograms) will have a heat signature or number designation of two-five-point-two-four, or 25.24 sig."

This time when F.B.I. Agent Caneo did pause, it was not to allow the others to follow her chain of thought, but out of sheer exhaustion.

F.B.I. Agent Caneo took a deep breath and continued.

"The cryptids that have, allegedly, attacked the record storage facility in Denver, have, almost the same heat signatures as grizzly bears in the warmer regions of the wilderness, forests, jungles, and deserts and polar bears in the colder regions of the Artic and Antarctic."

"And what would those heat signatures be?" Hector the Hunter was saying as he was taking out a pocket notepad and pen. "For the cryptids... uh, alleged cryptids."

"They will be of no use to you, or Rand Biotech, unless if you have access to surveillance satellites floating out in space." F.B.I. Agent Caneo said to Hector the Hunter.

"We do... Rand Biotech, that is."

"But nothing as sophisticated as the United States government." Security Expert Springfield added.

F.B.I. Agent Caneo pondered that for a moment. "Of course you do. Why not. Polar bears and grizzlies have a heat signature of three-one-point-one-seven, or 31.17 sig, and the, alleged, cryptids have heat signatures of three-one-point-two-five, or 31.25 sig."

Hector the Hunter was hurriedly jotting down what F.B.I. Agent Caneo was saying while mumbling to himself repeating what she was saying.

"We have noticed two different patterns between the two different heat signatures, one which appears to be natural, and the other, which appears to be unnatural." F.B.I. Agent Caneo gently tapped one of the computer techs on the shoulder. "Can you bring it up?" She asked the computer tech.

"Will do, ma'am, coming right up!" The computer tech was saying to F.B.I. Agent Caneo as he was tapping away on the computer keyboard on the table he was seated by.

"Now, Toby here (meaning the computer tech) is going to separate the two distinctive but similar heat signatures by color. The grizzly bear and polar bear heat signatures are going to be highlighted in red and the, alleged, cryptid heat signatures are going to be highlighted in blue."

Everyone leaned closer to the computer screen by where the computer tech Toby was sitting while red and blue sig dots filled up the computer screen as Toby was switching between different dates and times.

"Notice the patterns of the red heat signatures and the blue heat signatures?" F.B.I. Agent Caneo was saying. "Do you see the differences in the two patterns?"

Security Expert Springfield and Hector the Hunter were looking left and right and up and down and left and right and up and down again and again and again at the computer screen while F.B.I. Agent Caneo looked on with an amused smirk on her face.

"Do you see it? Do you see it? Do you see it?" F.B.I. Agent Caneo kept asking. "As CEO Rand had requested. He wanted us to pay extra attention in surveilling the Waywan Cliffs which were east of Little Bear Creek in Blue Valley of the Colorado Rockies."

"What am I looking at?" Security Expert Springfield was asking with a confused look on his face.
Hector the Hunter remained silent, but his eyes were darting left and right and up and down as he was staring at the computer screen.

"Do you see it?" F.B.I. Agent Caneo continued, "How the red 31.17 sig dots move back and forth, more or less, in straight and straight zigzagging patterns?"
F.B.I. Agent Caneo paused for a few moments while Security Expert Springfield and Hector the Hunter were mentally absorbing what she was saying.

"While the blue 31.25 sig dots seem to be jumping in and out of the brush covering, in and out of sight of the satellites? As if they were aware that they are being watched by satellites orbiting the atmosphere of the Earth."

A big, wide, brimming, smile began to spread across Hector the Hunter's face. "They, the blue dots, the 31.25 sigs, are hiding under the cover of the trees and using the mountain terrains and other natural obstacles in the forests to avoid being detected."

Security Expert Springfield still seemed to be confused. "I'm still not getting it."

Hector the Hunter was loudly chuckling out loud as he was repeatedly patting Security Expert Springfield on the back.

"I knew it! Now I know for sure!" It was as if Hector the Hunter had suddenly become obsessed.

"Ba-ha-ha-ha-ha!"

"What's so funny?" Security Expert Springfield was asking.

F.B.I. Agent Caneo spoke up. "The blue 31.25 sig dots are playing hide and seek with the satellites."

"Ba-ha-ha-ha-ha!" Hector the Hunter could not help himself.

"Look there!" Hector the Hunter was pointing to a spot on the map image on the computer screen. "Remember the other day? On our last hunting expedition?"

"Research trip! Research Trip!" Security Expert Springfield quickly corrected Hector the Hunter. "Never! Never! Never, publicly, refer to the hunting expeditions as hunting expeditions! Especially in front of any of the eggheads in the basement laboratories." Meaning the Rand Biotech research teams.

"That sasquatch we saw that jumped out of the bush and then disappeared back into the bush?" Hector the Hunter continued.

"I remember." Security Expert Springfield was nodding.

"It was playing with us! Just like the blue 31.25 sig dots are playing with the satellites!"

Security Expert Springfield was leaning in closer perusing the map image.

"It was leading us away from its lair. It was purposely leading us west when we should have continued going east!"

Security Expert Springfield was frowning.

The computer technician Toby kept switching from different dates and times downloaded from the surveillance satellites of the Waywan Cliffs which were east of Little Bear Creek in Blue Valley of the Colorado Rockies.

"Those are other dates and times of the movements of the blue sig dots."

F.B.I. Agent Caneo was nodding her head in the affirmative, repeating, "The 31.25 blue sig dots."

"Look at the movements of the blue sig dots on the other dates and times." Hector the Hunter was pointing at the blue 31.25 sig dots as the images on the computer screen changed with every different date and time displayed explaining to Security Expert Springfield what he had just become aware of. "All of the blue sig dots keep moving northeast from the Waywan cliffs and disappearing here!" Hector the hunter kept pointing at the images on the computer screen as each set of successive blue sig dots were displayed as the display kept switching back and forth and forth and back and back and forth from several different dates and times. "And here!" Hector the hunter pointed to the next computer screen display. "And here!" and to the next computer screen display and the next computer screen display and the next computer screen display. "And here! Here! Here! And here!" Finally, Security Expert Springfield was beginning to understand what Hector the Hunter was trying to explain to him. He whispered to Hector the Hunter, fearing that he would be overheard, but he was already being overheard by F.B.I. Agent Caneo.

"Their lair. Their hiding place. Their hole in the ground."

"We've found it!" Hector the Hunter surprisingly hugged Security Expert Springfield's in an unabashed act of comradery.

"You found it? You say?" F.B.I. Agent Caneo was curiously watching Hector the Hunter and Security Expert Springfield's sudden unexpected emotional exchange.

"The possible home of the cryptids responsible for the attack on the record storage facility?"

You didn't have to be a rocketship scientist to know that Hector the Hunter and Security Expert Springfield hated each other so much that they could easily kill each other, at any time, over any little thing, such as a squabble, spat, disagreement, or any other inconsequential misunderstanding.

F.B.I. Agent Caneo wasn't exactly a rocketship scientist, but she was still, definitely, no dummy.

CHAPTER TWENTY-SIX

Orgu was not wearing the tailored altered military camouflage fatigues, but he had an automatic rifle strapped to his back and in the palm of his hand the one good remaining wandererstone Tantoon had stolen from Threnatta of the Citizenry of the Heseetu, so many, many years ago; which was no bigger than an orange or an apple.

      As Neejat was entering the cave enclave where Tantoon, Orgu, Ugat, and about four to five of Tantoon's fanatical followers were huddled, conferring? conspiring? with each other, Neejat made his way around to stand at the back of one side of the small, intimate, crowd gathered there saying to whomever,

      "You have all gathered together and have not called Neejat?"

Tantoon looked up at Neejat.

      "Where have you been? Ugat was searching for you earlier today."

      "I was picking berries with Naydeena."

      "Naydeena?" Tantoon seemed to ponder that for a moment than turned to Orgu, ignoring Neejat.

      "I help. I help." Neejat said to Tantoon's back.

      "That will not be necessary at the moment."

      Tantoon tilted his head to the side to quickly reply to Neejat before returning his attention to the others present at the cave enclave.

      "We have only the one wandererstone at this time, but we hope to remedy that outcome before the day is done."

      Tantoon seemed to smirk.

      "I help. I help." Neejat repeated.

"Yes, yes, Neejat. Keep practicing the exercises Ugat, Orgu, and the others have been showing you. Have you been practicing dismantling and reassembling the automatic rifle we have given you?"

"Yes! Yes! I practice many, many, time." Neejat answered incorrectly saying 'time' – in the singular - instead of 'times' – in the plural.

"Keep practicing, Neejat, keep practicing!" Tantoon said to Neejat.

"I practice. I practice. Many, many, time."

As Tantoon was stepping back away from Orgu with the automatic rifle strapped to his back and the one good remaining wandererstone in his hand, the others in the cave enclave followed Tantoon's lead and began stepping back away from Orgu.

Orgu seemed to be meditating for a few moments as the wandererstone in his hand began to vibrate and glow, blue, red, green, orange, blue, red, green, and then Orgu vanished right before everyone's eyes.

Orgu could not have been traveling very far with the one wandererstone.

One wandererstone, no bigger than an orange or an apple, had only so much power.

>>>>><<<<<

Orgu reappeared, or teleported, via the magic, wonder, and mystery of the wandererstones, inside the Heseetu cave dwelling in the Waywan Cliffs in Blue Valley of the Colorado Rockies – which was one of the many cave dwellings of the Citizenry of the Heseetu spread-out throughout the Midwest and northern regions of the continent. Many of the cave dwellings were now mostly empty or inhabited by the very few barely thriving

Citizenry of the Heseetu that have survived through the ages. Once the Bigfoots, Sasquatches, and Yetis of the world were as plentiful as the green grass growing on the many fields, valleys, mountains, canyons, and plains; long ago, but no longer.

Orgu remained silent, sniffing the air, while slowly, very slowly, turning around in a full circle, all the while examining his surroundings. He was alone at the moment, but the scent of others, nearby, filled his nostrils.

Orgu took out an ion particle meter from a leather pouch Orgu also had slung over his shoulder, along with the automatic rifle, and extra ammunition cartridges for the automatic rifle. Orgu switched on the ion particle meter which was specifically designed to pick up tachyon wave emissions. Tantoon and his fanatical followers had stolen the ion particle meter from another research laboratory, other than a Rand Biotech research laboratory, associated with space exploration and communication. There was a faint ion reading coming from the cave tunnel to the right. Orgu proceeded down the long cave tunnel to the right all the while sniffing the air and listening for the slightest of sounds. The scent of two of the Citizenry of the Heseetu filled Orgu's nostrils. They were definitely of the Citizenry. Orgu was able to properly discern by their scents. Rogues and Sawtooths did not groom, bathe, and cleanse themselves as well as those of the Citizenry; who were more knowledgeable and accustomed to higher standards of manners and decorum.

The two others of the Citizenry of the Heseetu in the cave tunnel had also picked up the scent of Orgu, which was an unfamiliar scent. It was confusing. There was no one in the cave dwelling with that scent. A visitor? A Guest? An intruder? Their question will be answered much sooner than later, as the footsteps of the unfamiliar scent was coming upon them, immediately, from around the next turn in the cave tunnel.

As Orgu stepped around the next turn in the cave tunnel, he came upon Ringru and Cazzii sitting together on a comfortable looking bed of furs.

Lovers? Orgu was thinking. Never mind. To the task at hand.

"Hello there." Orgu said to Ringru and Cazzii. "I have lost my way. I have been told to collect a few wandererstones for an emergency visit to the Citizenry of the Cororuru."

Orgu was trying to hide the automatic rifle by hanging the automatic rifle over his shoulder and around his back, instead of in front or at his side, but Ringru and Cazzii could not help but notice the butt of the automatic rifle sticking up over Orgu's shoulder from behind his back.

"¿Quien eres tu?/Who are you?" Ringru in Spanish asked Orgu.

"We have never seen you before." Cazzii added.

"I am a friend. I am everybody's friend." Orgu was trying his best to appear as friendly and unthreatening as possible.

"¿Qus es eso, que tienes ahi, detras de tu espalda?/What is that, that you have there, behind your back." Ringru, speaking in Spanish, asked Orgu.

"What's all that gobbledygook you're talking?"

Orgu didn't understand Spanish and was immediately assuming that Ringru was a Rogue and didn't know how to speak or that Ringru was a Sawtooth and was beginning to learn how to speak.

Cazzii immediately intervened realizing the mysterious stranger did not understand Spanish and that he must be extremely dangerous considering the fact that he was trying to hide an assault rifle behind his back.

"He was asking, who are you, and what are you hiding behind your back?"

With only her eyes, Cazzii looked back and forth from Ringru to the assault rifle the mysterious stranger was hiding behind his back, trying her best to emphasis the danger, but Ringru was already aware.

"Speak English Ringru. Speak English."

"That?" Orgu reached up to tap the automatic rifle but stopped halfway. "What? Do you mean my bag? It is nothing."

"It is not nothing." Ringru said in English as he was standing up from the bed of furs and began slowly stepping forward towards where Orgu was standing. "That is..." Ringru was squinting for a moment. "That is... a human weapon."

"A human weapon? No! You are mistaken!" Ringru attempted to take a few quick steps forward to disarm Orgu, but Orgu was too quick, too fast, and immediately, forcibly, pushed Ringru back, away from where he was standing, as he was simultaneously swinging the automatic rifle away from his back, up over his shoulder, to his front. Orgu quickly lifted the automatic rifle up and pointed the rifle point blank at Ringru.

"Stand back!" Orgu demanded. "I do not want to hurt you, but I will, if I have to."

Ringru was unsure what to do, but he knew, human hunters roaming the forests and woodlands would kill deer, bear, rabbits, and birds, such as ducks and geese, flying in the air with the weapon the unknown stranger was threateningly holding in his hands.

"What do you want?" Ringru asked Orgu.

Tantoon had told Orgu, as Tantoon had been told, and discerned from his own experiences, even with the ion particle meter, wandererstones may still be hidden,

210

somewhere, inside the labyrinthian cave tunnels, or buried, so deep, in the ground or walls of the cave dwelling, that by the time anyone was able to get their hands on enough wandererstones to make a difference, they would be overrun and overtaken.

It will be better to coerce a Citizenry of the Heseetu in the cave dwelling to take whoever was tasked with the duty of acquiring wandererstones to wherever the wandererstones may be.

"As I have said, I have lost my way. I have been told to collect a few wandererstones for an emergency visit to the Citizenry of the Cororuru."

"Told by whom?" Cazzii asked Orgu.

"Shantuu. I was told by Shantuu."

Tantoon had told Orgu to use the name of Shantuu if he should encounter others of the Citizenry of the Heseetu who may be curious as to his presence and intentions.

"Shantuu?" Cazzii repeated. "Shantuu did not inform us that a visitor will be arriving and be in need of assistance."

"He did not? Did he?"

Enough! Orgu was suddenly thinking. He fired three shots from the automatic rifle at the cave wall over Ringru and Cazzii's head.

Ringru and Cazzii both ducked in shock and as an instant reflex action. They had never heard a firearm fire so close in front of them ever before.

"Enough!"

This time Orgu said it out loud.

"Enough! Take me to where the wandererstones are hidden or stored!"

Orgu menacingly waved the automatic rifle in front of Ringru and Cazzii's faces, inches (centimeters) away from their eyes.

"The next round of bullets fired from my weapon will be buried in your pelts!"

Ringru cautiously maneuvered himself to stand in front of Cazzii, protectively shielding her from the unknown stranger and his menacing weapon.

"We do not know." Ringru said to Orgu.

Orgu saw it.

As Tantoon had told him to look for.

Ringru and Cazzii's eyes flickered, ever so slightly, in the same direction down the tunnel that the ion particle meter had registered on.

"Walk this way." Orgu nudged Ringru and Cazzii with the barrel of the automatic rifle. "Be careful now. My weapon may accidently eject a projectile, if I should only stumble, ever so slightly, without my finger pressing on the firing mechanism. That is all it will take."

"But we do not know where the wandererstones are kept. Only the Elders know. We are still Underlings. We are still only Shadow-walkers still being trained."

"Keep walking." Orgu demanded.

The faint signal on the ion particle meter became unfainter and unfainter and unfainter, the further they walked along the cave tunnel and became unfainterer and unfainterer and unfainterer, after turning a few more corners and walking along a few more cave tunnels.

The main light signals on the ion particle meter were three yellow arrows that would flash from the first yellow arrow to the second yellow arrow to the third yellow arrow, pointing in the direction of any tachyon wave emissions.

The three yellow arrows, suddenly, stopped flashing, on and off, and remained on, while a red light on the side of the ion particle meter, suddenly, switched from red to green and began flashing, on and off, on and off, on and off, on and off.

"Where are they!" Orgu shouted at Ringru and Cazzii even louder than before. "The wandererstones."

It happened again. The slight flicker in Ringru and Cazzii's eyes. This time to the right, instead of the left. Orgu studied Ringru and Cazzie for a few moments longer and then he noticed a carved out hole on the right from where Ringru and Cazzii were standing, way up above their heads.

Orgu saw the slight flicker in Ringru and Cazzii's eyes again.

"Step back!" Orgu ordered Ringru and Cazzii, while still, menacingly, waving the automatic rifle in front of them. As they were reluctantly stepping back, Orgu reached up and stuck his other, free, hand, inside the hole and was feeling around for a few quick seconds.

"Hmmm!" Orgu sighed.

Orgu began pulling out from the hole and dropping onto the ground, first, one wandererstone, then, another wandererstone, then, another wandererstone, then, another wandererstone.

There were, all in all, four, healthy, glowing, vibrating, pulsating, wandererstones inside the hole in the wall.

Orgu carefully knelt down to the ground with one hand on the trigger of the automatic rifle, which was still pointed at Ringru and Cazzii, and proceeded with his other free hand, to, one by one, pick up and pack each of the four wandererstones into the leather pouch slung over his shoulder. After Orgu had all four of the wandererstones, safely packed away in the leather pouch, Orgu slowly stood and remained standing, staring, silently, at Ringru and Cazzii without saying anything.

Ringru did not like the look the unknown stranger had in his eyes.

"What are you going to do now?"

Orgu remained silent.

"You have four wandererstones. That should be more than enough for the emergency visit to the Citizenry of the Cororuru."

"Go. Please go now." Cazzii said to Orgu, sensing the same feelings Ringru was sensing. "Go. Please go."

"We have other matters to attend to." Ringru slowly grabbed Cazzii by the hand to lead her away down the cave tunnel, away from the unknown stranger and the automatic rifle.

"No. Stop." Orgu finally spoke. "You did not see me."

Ringru and Orgu were intensely staring into each other's eyes.

"We have not seen you."

They continued silently staring at each other.

"But you have." Orgu said. "But you have. I sincerely wish that you did not, even though you and your paramour have inadvertently assisted me with my task."

"What are you thinking?" Ringru asked, but he was already aware, even though he was not a mind reader, or gifted with telepathic powers, what the unknown stranger with the automatic rifle was thinking. The unknown Stranger had come with a weapon of death and destruction and was clearly lying about his reasons for needing to acquire the wandererstones he had now in his possession.

"Dead men tell no tales, so the saying of the human savages goes – so do also, Rogues, Sawtooths, and those of the Citizenry." It was an enigmatic statement for the unknown stranger to declare as he was raising the automatic rifle one more time at Ringru and Cazzii. Ringru did not think but react. Ringru turned quickly, turning his back on the unknown stranger with the automatic rifle and grabbed hold of Cazzii in a – bear hug? Bigfoot hug? Grabbing hold of Cazzii and completely covering Cazzii, from head to toe, with his entire body, with his arms and legs, pushing Cazzii tightly into the arc of his stomach and chest as the unknown stranger began firing the automatic rifle at both Ringru and Cazzii, firing the automatic rifle, repeatedly, over, and over, and over, and over, until the ammunition cartridge in the automatic rifle must have become empty.

The last sound Ringru ever heard, for all of the rest of existence, for all of the rest of eternity, was the others of the Citizenry of the Heseetu in the cave dwelling shouting and running towards where Ringru and Cazzii lay huddled together against the cave wall.

The unknown stranger - Orgu - had immediately run off down the cave tunnel the moment he heard the sound of the others shouting and running in their direction.

It was Mimi with several others of the Citizenry of the Heseetu residing in the cave dwelling who had come running the moment they had heard the sound of gunfire echoing through the walls and ceilings and floors and the many individual cave enclaves.

Ringru was dead.
Cazzii was holding Ringru in her arms, sobbing, uncontrollably.

They rummaged through the tunnels of the cave dwelling searching for the unknown stranger with the automatic rifle, but it was assumed that the unknown stranger with the automatic rifle had entered the cave dwelling, via, a wandererstone, and had exited, via, a wandererstone, or that the unknown stranger/murderer/thief with the automatic rifle had exited on foot and then used the one or all four of the wandererstones in his possession to further distance himself until chasing behind to capture him was the exemplification of a futile act.

It was later that night when Shantuu had finally returned from his meeting in the Amazon rain forests with the Elders of the other Citizenries of the world that he was told the sad and horrific news of the murder of Ringru and the theft of the four wandererstones.

Shantuu was clearly saddened and heartbroken.

CHAPTER TWENTY-SEVEN

Outside the cave dwelling of the Citizenry of the Heseetu in the Waywan Cliffs of Blue Valley in the Colorado Rockies, matters were proceeding much differently, but just as significantly.

F.B.I. Agent Caneo, Hector the Hunter, and Security Expert Springfield were huddled together along with a contingent of forty privately hired professional soldiers, or mercenaries, all armed with sub-machine guns, assault rifles, and pistols, hired by Rand Biotech, of what would have been a joint F.B.I. and private sector operation, except for the fact that the Federal Bureau of Investigations of the United States of America would have never authorized what the Rand Biotech security team and the forty professional soldiers/mercenaries were about to do.

Crystal – Crystal Gaines – and Red – Jason 'Red' Redfield of the security staff at the nameless Rand Biotech building were excluded from participated in this military-style operation. Hector the Hunter and Security Expert Springfield had decided to have Crystal and Red remain at the nameless Rand Biotech building, holding down the fort, working their regular security shifts.

F.B.I. Agent Caneo had become, an unofficial, off-the-books, under the table, Rand Biotech employee, advisor, and member of the Rand Biotech security team. She had gladly sold her soul to the Devil, the Devil being CEO Rand, for cash and for perks; like promotions possibly leading to the Directorship of the F.B.I. and a guaranteed high paying job with Rand Biotech, if or when she, eventually, resigns or retires from the F.B.I.

The Rand Biotech research team of Mira - Dr. Mira Salinas, Kasper - Dr. Kasper Weinberger, Lisa - Dr. Lisa

Wintergarden, and Dobie - Dr. Dobie Doberson were also here. They were ordered to come along for the ride; however, they were not informed as to the particulars of the operation.

The Rand Biotech research team had no idea what was about to happen.

"The Loon Platoon is here today, out, loud, and proud, flexing their muscles and polishing their shiny weapons of war." Dobie was saying to the other Rand Biotech researchers present at the mercenaries-for-hire jamboree.

"What are we doing here by the Waywan Cliffs?" Mira was nervously wondering out loud.

"We're here to start World War Three!" Lisa answered sarcastically.

Kasper was a little more serious. Kasper was always a little more serious about everything most of the time. "It must have something to do with the blood samples and the hair follicle samples we acquired the other day." Meaning the blood samples and hair follicle samples found at the concrete and steel building complex, now identified as a record storage facility.

"Cryptids! We're going cryptid hunting!" Dobie was giggling so much he could barely coherently finish saying what he was saying.

"What is wrong with these hillbilly, gun freak, maniacs? Did the forest run out of innocent deer to slaughter?"

"I don't like this. I don't like this one bit." Mira was definitely uncomfortable with the whole situation.

"Why are you taking it so personally, honey?" Lisa was tenderly rubbing Mira's back.

"I'm not taking it personally. I just don't like wasting my time, hiking out here in the middle of nowhere, riding back and forth in those cramped vans!"

"Take the money and run, honey, take the money and run!"

Dobie decided to come to Mira's defense. "There's a big deference between punching a time clock and going halfway around the world searching for the missing link and finding only a bunch of drunk, passed out, campers on a fishing trip."

Everyone suddenly stifled their derogatory and disrespectful chatter as Hector the Hunter, Security Expert Springfield, and their new best friend F.B.I. Agent Caneo were walking towards where the research team were gathered together.

They were dressed, from head to toe, in full camouflaged commando gear complete with bulletproof vests and infrared night vision goggles attached to their helmets.

It was Hector the Hunter who spoke first in his usual sarcastic, condescending manner. "We're on a very different, special, field trip today, kiddies."

"Somebody could've given us a heads up!" Kasper was immediately whining, but as respectful and intelligently as possible.

"This is your heads up!" Hector the Hunter had to chuckle at that. He was so much amused with himself. "We weren't too sure if any of you were going to be invited to the... party."

Security Expert Springfield was more circumspect and to the point. "We have located a possible entrance to a massive, labyrinthian cave structure where the cryptids that attacked the records storage facility may be hiding."

"You are all to remain a safe distance behind the strike team that will be breaching the entrance." F.B.I. Agent Caneo added.

"If we should encounter any cryptids or any evidence of cryptid activity." Security Expert Springfield continued. "We will call you to come in to examine the inside of the cave, or caves, as we are certain that there will most likely be many, many more than one cave structure inside the mountain."

"Which mountain?" Mira asked.

Hector the hunter pointed to the nearest clump of mountains to the northwest called the Waywan Cliffs.

"Are you sure? Why go there?" Mira was asking. "I think we have a better chance of encountering cryptids if we continued southeast away from the Waywan Cliff, towards the Riverview Swamps. There's all kinds of unknown, unexplored areas of the Riverview Swamps no one has ever documented."

"Don't you worry your pretty little head about where were going and why we're going there." Hector the hunter was saying to Mira. "We have it all planned out. We figured everything out in advance."

"You did now, did you?" Lisa couldn't help but to make a snide remark as she has always been known to do. "You didn't do that all by yourself?"

For a moment Hector the Hunter was going to answer Lisa, but then he thought better of it and just shrugged his shoulders and walked away to confer with the forty privately hired professional soldiers.

They did not waste any more time. After so long, the first of the forty privately hired soldiers were hiking down the grassy ridge and disappearing into the brush of the Colorado Rockies along with Security Expert

Springfield, Hector the Hunter, F.B.I. Agent Caneo, and the Rand Biotech research team.

They were hiking for no more than half-an-hour before they heard the rumble of gunfire.

The privately hired army had, coincidently, come to breach the entrance that Orgu had been exiting from after having stolen the four wandererstones and killing Ringru. Orgu was surprised to suddenly be confronted by so many men with guns, but he did not hesitate. Orgu was immediately firing his automatic rifle at the privately hired army, who were completely caught off-guard. The last thing the privately hired army expected was to be shot at before they even had a chance to breach the cave entrance. Orgu, in a shower of automatic rifle fire, had instantly killed ten of the forty privately hired soldiers and wounded five.

When Orgu was pinned down behind a large boulder with the remaining twenty-five privately hired soldiers firing at him with their sub-machine guns, automatic rifles, and pistols along with Security Expert Springfield, Hector the Hunter, and F.B.I. Agent Caneo, Orgu decided, and it was his only viable, possible, means of escaping being shot to death and/or captured dead or alive, he used the wandererstones he had to disappear and reappear, somewhere else, far, far, away. After all, Orgu had four new wandererstones he had stolen from the cave dwelling of the Citizenry of the Heseetu, plus the one wandererstone, he originally had, that made five wandererstones. Five wandererstones had the combined power to teleport Orgu across the ocean to another continent.

Security Expert Springfield, Hector the Hunter, F.B.I. Agent Caneo, and the remaining, surviving, twenty-five privately hired soldiers did not know, whomever, was firing at them was in possession of five wandererstones which, whomever, could use to vanish into thin air.

When they had finally made their way around the large boulder were their avenging angel or demon spawn was hiding, there was no one there.

Orgu had checked out – so to speak.

"Where did he go?" Security Expert Springfield was scratching his head, wondering.

"It was as if he had just disappeared?" F.B.I. Agent Caneo was saying.

"Not he! It! It!" Hector the Hunter vehemently repeated "That was no man! That was a cryptid! That was one of the cryptids that had attacked the record storge facility."

"My god!" Security Expert Springfield shockingly exclaimed. "They all have automatic rifles!"

"And they're not hesitating to kill!" Hector the Hunter exclaimed.

"And with ammo to burn!" F.B.I. Agent Caneo added.

Mira, Lisa, Dobie, and Kasper had come out of hiding behind a nearby rock outcropping and were immediately tending to the wounded privately hired soldiers the best that they were able to.

Alexie, one of the privately hired soldiers, was kneeling over another one of the privately hired soldiers, who was lying on the ground bleeding out, who was his younger brother, Lemmy.

Alexie was crying out. "Help! Help! He's bleeding! My brother! He's bleeding! Help! Somebody help!"

Dobie was nearest to were Alexie was crouched down on the ground over his wounded brother. By the time Dobie reached Alexie and his wounded brother Lemmy, Lemmy had just stopped breathing. He had at

222

least one bullet hole in his stomach and two more by his shoulder and upper arm.

Alexie was shaking his head from side to side.

"Who are these people? Who the hell are these people?"

In the background you could hear the other remaining privately hired soldiers shouting, "The one shooter disappeared!" "He disappeared?" "He went behind that big rock and then he was gone!" He?" "It looked like a bear with a gun!" "The others came from back here!" "They all have guns!" "Let's go get'em!" "Watch out!" "They all have guns!" "They're all shooting at us!" "Let's go!" "Okay!" "Let's go!" "Down here!" "This way!" Down here!" "Shoot'em first and ask'em question later!" "Let's go get'em!" "Let's go get'em!" "The bastards!" "Let's go get'em!" "kill them all!" "Kill them all!" "Kill them all!"

The remaining twenty-five privately hired soldiers began chanting, "kill them all!" "Kill them all!" "Kill them all!" With Alexie in the lead they began rushing down the grassy ridge towards the cave entrance of the Heseetu cave dwelling, which Orgu had just exited from.

"Stop! Everybody stop!" Security Expert Springfield, Hector the Hunter, and F.B.I. Agent Caneo were shouting at the backs of the rampaging remaining privately hired soldiers as they continued running down the grassy ridge towards the cave opening.

"We need to regroup!" "Stand down!" "Everybody stand down!" "We need to regroup!" Security Expert Springfield, Hector the Hunter, and F.B.I. Agent Caneo kept shouting at the remaining twenty-five hired soldiers, but they were not listening. The shock, anger, and bloodlust for revenge had overtaken them.

There were many uprooted bushels of trees and tree branches and other obstacles such as natural partitions made of weaved weeds, leaves, twigs, broken off tree branches, pine needles, hiding the entrance to the cave dwelling.

Orgu did not just only steal four wandererstones from the Heseetu cave dwelling, Orgu had inadvertently, but not purposely, given away the location to one of the cave dwellings entrances/exits; even though with the intel Rand Biotech had acquired from the C.I.A. via the help given to them by the F.B.I. they were already on their way to where they were assuming the cave entrance may be – they were still not 100% sure – now they were 100% sure – or the remaining twenty-five rampaging soldiers were 100% sure.

To quote William Shakespeare - Cry havoc and let slip the dogs of war!

The remaining rampaging twenty-five privately hired soldiers burst into the Heseetu cave dwelling with their guns a-blazing firing at everything and anything that moved and everything and anything that didn't move but looked like it could move.

It would've been an outright slaughter except for the fact that there were only no more than twenty to thirty Bigfoots, Sasquatches, and Yetis occupying any cave dwelling, at anytime, anywhere in the world today. The number of Bigfoots, Sasquatches, and Yetis were dwindling, year after year, decade after decade, century after century, because of the disease that has become to be known as the 'undivining,'

Bigfoots, Sasquatches, and Yetis have had centuries of practice evading and hiding from the world. Those bigfoots, Sasquatches, and Yetis, who were in the cave dwelling at that time were instantly maneuvering to

224

whatever safe hiding places may be available or exiting through other entrances/exits in the labyrinthian cave dwelling. Others had wandererstones hidden in other areas of the cave dwelling and used the wandererstones to disappear and reappear somewhere else were they will never be found.

Mimi rushed to the cave enclave where Cazzii was still crying over the dead body of Ringru. Cazzii was sitting beside Ringru crying while overhead was heard the muffled explosions of bullets reverberating everywhere throughout the cave dwelling.

"Cazzii! We must go! There are men with guns attacking us!" Mimi was shouted at Cazzii, but Cazzii was not listening. Cazzii did not want to leave Ringru, dead or alive.

"We must use the special oil which will incinerate the body and then we must go! We must go now! There is no time to doddle!"

Mimi was referring to a special oil the Bigfoots, Sasquatches, and Yetis of the world, throughout the centuries, have used to instantly incinerate the dead bodies of any of the Citizenry, or Rogues, or Sawtooths, who happened to die, to hide the truth of their existence. It was one of the many ways Bigfoots, sasquatches, and Yetis, have remained hidden from the world.

"No!" Cazzii was saying through a shower of tears. "I cannot leave him!"

"Ringru has already left us! He is no longer here! All that remains is the husk of what Ringru once was!"

"No!" Cazzii continued crying. "No! I cannot! I cannot!"

The gunfire was coming so close Mimi could see from way down at the end of the nearest cave tunnel the sparks flashing from the bullets exploding out of the barrel of the rifles and guns of the men with guns.

A couple of bullets ricocheted off the walls of the cave dwelling over where Mimi, Cazzii, and the dead body of Ringru were huddled.

"Run Cazzii! Run!" Was the last thing Mimi said to Cazzii as she was running herself, running for her dear life. Mimi had no alternative. She could not help Cazzii at the moment and it would be futile for her to sacrifice herself only to be butchered senselessly.

Their destiny's had diverged. It was the cold, hard, hand of fate, extending itself to be taken or not to be taken.

As Alexie and the other two privately hired soldiers entered the cave enclave where Cazzii was still sitting beside the dead body of Ringru, crying her eyes out, the three privately hired soldiers did not instantly fire upon Cazzii, out of sympathy, or because they had suddenly become overcome with a new found sense of morality, or because their unpent bloodlust had been satiated – they stopped firing their sub-machine guns, assault rifles, and pistols because they had never seen, ever before, a Bigfoot, Sasquatch, or Yetis, up close and personal; let alone two! Even though one of the two was dead, which they did not realize at their first sighting of the pair.

"What the hell is that?" Alexie was immediately saying. "That's... that's... that's... not... not... a bear!"

One of the other two privately hired soldiers was saying, "Def... def... definitely not a bear!"
And the other privately hired soldier was saying, "It's a Bigfoot!"

Alexie and the two other soldiers were staring at Cazzii and the dead body of Ringru for a few moments more when Alexie decided that he did not care. He wanted to avenge his brother's death. Alexie wanted blood for blood. He did not care about who or what blood - only that there was blood to spill like the blood of his brother that had been spilled.

"Let's kill it anyway!"

Alexie raised his firearm and aimed while the other two privately hired soldiers were raising their firearms and aiming, too, at Cazzii and the dead body of Ringru, which Alexie and the two other privately hired soldiers did not know was dead. They all thought that Ringru was sleeping.

"Stop! Don't shoot!"

A voice shouted out to Alexie and the two other privately hired soldiers from down the cave tunnel outside of the cave enclave.

Alexie and the other two privately hired soldiers immediately turned their firearms and began firing their firearms in the direction where the voice in the cave tunnel was shouting out to them.

Bang-Bang!

Boom-Boom-Bang!

Bang-Boom-Bang!

Bang-Bang-Bang!

Boom-Boom-Boom!

Bang-Boom-Bang!

"Don't do that! Stop shooting! Drop your weapons!"

Psst-Psst!

Psst-Psst-Psst!

Psst!

Psst-Psst-Psst-Psst!

Psst-Psst!

Before Security Expert Springfield, Hector the Hunter, and F.B.I. Agent Caneo had shouted out to Alexie and the two other privately hired soldiers, they had made sure that they were fully covered and protected by some boulders on the ground and a few rocky cave ledges on the sides of the cave tunnel while Alexie and the other two privately hired soldiers were out in the open, fully exposed, standing in the entrance of the cave enclave. Security Expert Springfield, Hector the Hunter, and F.B.I. Agent Caneo's automatic rifles had gone Psst! Instead of Bang! And Boom! Because they had state-of-the-art silencers on the barrels of their automatic rifles.

Security Expert Springfield, Hector the Hunter, and F.B.I. Agent Caneo had easily shot dead Alexie and the two other privately hired soldiers before they had a chance to turn and shoot dead Cazzii and shoot the already dead Ringru.

Maybe Cazzii wanted to die herself.

Maybe Cazzii wanted to go where Ringru had gone.

Cazzii did not care.

Cazzii did not care about anything anymore.

"Mother of God." Hector the Hunter was mumbling to himself as he was walking closer to where Cazzii was sitting beside the dead body of Ringru while carefully stepping over the dead bodies of Alexie and the two other privately hired soldiers.

"You mumbled the words right outta my mouth." Security Expert Springfield was solemnly commenting.

"I can't believe my eyes!" Was F.B.I. Agent Caneo's immediate reaction.

Security Expert Springfield, Hector the Hunter, and F.B.I. Agent Caneo slowly surrounded Cazzii and the dead body of Ringru with their automatic rifles drawn pointed point blank at Cazzii and the dead body of Ringru.

"The one lying on the piled up stacks of furs seems to be dead." Hector the Hunter was observing out loud.

"And the other one… seems to be crying." F.B.I. Agent Caneo was also observing out loud.

"It is mourning the death of the other one." Hector the Hunter replied while Security Expert Springfield was pulling out a dart pistol from out of his backpack loaded with tranquilizer darts.

Zip-Zip-Zip!
Security Expert Springfield shot Cazzii three times with three tranquilizer darts.

Zip-Zip-Zip!
Security Expert Springfield also shot Ringru three times with three tranquilizer darts, even though he was almost completely certain that Ringru, or the Bigfoot/Cryptid/whatever, lying on the piled up stack of furs was dead.

Normally it was better to shoot a target with one tranquilizer dart at a time, to avoid overdosing and accidently killing a target, but considering the size of the target they had encountered - it was better to be safe than sorry.

After Cazzii had fallen over, fully tranquilized, sleeping soundly, F.B.I. Agent Caneo turned and was looking down at Alexie and the other two privately hired soldiers lying dead at the entrance of the cave enclave.

"Damn! Damn! Damn!" F.B.I. Agent Caneo was regrettably gesticulating. "Did we have to kill the mercs?"

"We gave them a chance to stand down." Security Expert Springfield was quick to reply.

"I hate to say it." Hector the Hunter added. "But it was either them or us, or the cryptids"

"Which is the only reason we are here!" Security Expert Springfield exclaimed vehemently. "That one merc went berserk, crying about his dead brother, and the other mercs were running behind him like mindless zombies!" The sound of gunfire had stopped echoing through the tunnels of the cave dwelling.

"You hear that?" Hector the Hunter had his head craned to the side, listening. "The shooting has stopped."

"The other mercs have either killed off each other, or they already killed any other cryptid who may have been inside the caves!" Security Expert Springfield was saying. "They definitely didn't run out of ammo. They have all the ammo they need. They have enough ammo to fight a whole platoon of soldiers if there was a whole platoon of soldiers around to fight."

"We better keep these two out of sight." F.B.I Agent Caneo was pointing down at Cazzii and the dead body of Ringru.

The privately hired soldiers did not kill all the other Bigfoots – members of the Citizenry of the Heseetu - who were, present, in the cave dwelling.

They had all escaped.

All the other Bigfoots – members of the Citizenry of the Heseetu - had all safely gotten away; all except for Cazzii and the dead body of Ringru.

CHAPTER TWENTY-EIGHT

The attack on the San Onofre Nuclear Power Plant in Southern California was an unprecedented event. The perpetrators of the incident were just as equally unprecedented. What were the reasons and motivations of the perpetrators? Why did they do what they did? The question will always be debated behind closed doors in the halls of powers and in the hidden worlds of worlds within worlds. There was light and darkness and what is perceived to be light and darkness, reality and fantasy, truth and untruth, right and wrong, Heaven and Hell and Purgatory, in-between, and the spaces, in-between. Tantoon had taken the four wandererstones Orgu had stolen from the Heseetu cave dwelling in the Waywan Cliffs and the one wandererstone Tantoon had originally stolen, before that, to teleport, or in the vernacular of those of the esteemed, venerable, astute, refined, dignified, Citizenry, disappear and reappear, disappear and reappear, disappear and reappear, westward from Colorado, to further westward to Colorado, to further westward to Colorado, to further westward to Utah, to further westward to Utah, to further westward to Utah, to further westward to Nevada, to further westward to Nevada, to further westward to Nevada, to further westward to Southern California, until they were hunkered down, hidden, out of sight, in a wooded area in San Onofre in Southern California, nearby, the famous sight in the horizon of the two breasts and two nipples of the San Onofre Nuclear Power Plant.

Tantoon, Orgu, Ugat, Neejat, and a newcomer to the group, Cynad, who had replaced the deceased Roku, had taken the five wandererstones and painstakingly, one by one, one painstakingly step by one painstakingly step, traveled the distance from the Colorado Rockies to the sunny beach and surfing town of San Onofre in Southern California, along with backpacks packed with the tailored-altered camouflaged military fatigues, automatic rifles, ammo, several different explosives and explosive devices, and any other random items and equipment necessary to achieving the evil, demented, diabolical plan Tantoon had conceived.

They could have teleported, or disappeared and reappeared, directly, one time, from the Colorado Rockies to San Onofre in Southern California, if each of the five had three wandererstones instead of the one, or wandererstones that were bigger than the palm-sized wandererstones they were in possession of; bigger, by maybe the size of a cantaloupe, grapefruit, or coconut. If they had one wandererstone that was as big as a watermelon, all five could have teleported, or disappeared and reappeared, the long distance, together, directly, one time only.

The smaller palm-sized wandererstones had only so much power.

The bigger the wandererstone, the more powerful the wandererstone.

Neejat was staring at the two breasts and two nipples in the horizon from the wooded area where they were hiding.

"What is that?" Neejat asked the others.

"That!" Tantoon enlightened Neejat and the newcomer Cynad; Orgu and Ugat were already thoroughly informed. "Is the exterior of the interior, the outside of the inside, of the human dwelling which we have been training to overtake!" Tantoon waved his hand over the two breast-like structures, nearby, in the distance, of what was the San Onofre Nuclear Power Plant.

Neejat, being a former Rogue, who had just graduated to Sawtooth, was not supposed to know about such things, but he knew. Before Neejat had a chance to protest or react, Tantoon was already counting down for the group to take the next jump, or to disappear from the exterior, outside, to reappear in the interior, inside; inside being the inside of the San Onofre Nuclear Power Plant. They were all immediately suiting up, putting on their tailored-altered, camouflaged, military fatigues, complete with foot coverings which resembled black commando boots and black hoods to cover their faces and heads. "Have your automatic rifles drawn and ready to fire as we have been training." Tantoon tapped Orgu on the shoulder as he was holding the first of the five wandererstones in the palm of his hand. "Concentrate! Orgu! Concentrate! Five! Four! Three! Two! One!"

Orgu disappeared.

Tantoon tapped Ugat on the shoulder as he was holding the second of the five wandererstones in the palm of his hand. "Concentrate! Ugat! Concentrate! Five! Four! Three! Two! One!"

Ugat disappeared.

Tantoon tapped the newcomer, Cynad, on the shoulder as he was holding the third of the five wandererstones in the palm of his hand. "Concentrate! Cynad! Concentrate! Five! Four! Three! Two! One!" Cynad disappeared.

"Are You ready?" Tantoon said to Neejat. "We do not have any time to waste. Tantoon was immediately saying to Neejat after tapping Neejat on the shoulder.

"Concentrate! Neejat! Concentrate!" Neejat was holding the fourth of the five wandererstones in the palm of his hand. "Five! Four! Three! Two! One!" Neejat disappeared.

Tantoon, holding the fifth and last of the five wandererstones in the palm of his hand counted off to himself. "Five! Four! Three! Two! One!"
Tantoon disappeared.

They were all there for a few moments more and then they were all gone.

CHAPTER TWENTY-NINE

The expedition to the Waywan Cliffs in Blue Valley of the Colorado Rockies had been a success despite the nightmare tragedy of the deaths of ten privately hired soldiers/mercenaries and five others of the privately hired soldiers/mercenaries being severely wounded. Beside the two cryptids - Bigfoots - they had captured, one dead and one alive, the Rand Biotech research team and the Rand Biotech security team found a treasure trove of artifacts and relics inside the labyrinthian cave structures used by the cryptids as habitats or dwellings.

"What about glowing rocks?" CEO Rand had asked everyone involved. "You don't think any of the mercs may have found some glowing rocks and were keeping it secret?"

The Rand Biotech security team had thoroughly searched the privately hired soldiers as well as the Rand Biotech research team and each other.

No glowing rocks were found anywhere inside or outside the caves in the Waywan Cliffs, or near or around, the Waywan Cliffs in Blue Valley of the Colorado Rockies.

"Every time I'm seeing you now, you're like a million miles away." Lisa was saying to Mira as she was standing outside the magnetronic isolation chamber in the basement of the nameless Rand Biotech building in downtown Denver, Colorado.

Mira seemed to be so far away, at first, it was as if she didn't hear Lisa speaking to her or notice that Lisa was standing beside her in the hallway.
After a few moments Mira turned to Lisa. "What? What did you say?"

Lisa giggled. Mira was acting a little looney these days. Ever since they had returned from the expedition to the caves at the Waywan Cliffs. "Where did you go? Or where have you been going?"

"What do you mean by that?"

"You're here, but you're not here." Lisa was half smiling, half frowning at Mira. "Your body is here, but your mind is like a million miles away, lately, ever since we got back after we picked up the two Chewbacca's." Meaning the two - cryptids – Bigfoots.

"It's just... I just... what are they doing to the one living cryptid inside that room?" Meaning the magnetronic isolation chamber where the two cryptids have been hidden away

"We're going to be finding out soon enough." Lisa was saying. "They're gonna want our feedback before too long."

"Do you think they're hurting the cryptid?"

"When it comes to Rand Biotech, you never know. I mean, we just saw fifteen wannabe Rambo's getting gunned down and carted away like garbage left out on the curb."

And then Mira seemed to do it again. It seemed like her eyes were glazing over and she was no longer seeing what was right in front of her, but something else, faraway, far, far, far, away.

"Earth to Mira! Earth to Mira!" Lisa was joking playfully.
Mira seemed to suddenly snap out of her reluctant unintentional trance.

"I guess I did it again."

"You guessed right, girl! Whatsamatter with you? Have you been anesthetizing yourself or sniffing sleeping gas? Do we have sleeping gas here? We must have! We have everything here!"

"I'm alright. I'm okay." Mira said trying her best to reassure Lisa, who still seemed to be not too reassured. For Mira and Lisa, seeing the living cryptid happened much sooner than later, as one of the Rand Biotech security guards rushed out of the magnetronic isolation chamber into the hallway screaming, "Medic! Medic! We need a medic in here asap!"

Mira and Lisa ran through the opened door into the room the security guard had just rushed out of.

The magnetronic isolation chamber consisted of several rooms, the walls, floors, and ceilings of which were made of special materials which blocked and reflected several different kinds of electromagnetic waves and radiological emissions, which prevented the teleportation of matter, if there ever were such a science, technology, or devices capable of actually teleporting matter.

"This way!" it was Hector the Hunter waving for Mira and Lisa to follow him down a hallway into another room in the magnetronic isolation chamber. "I think she's having a heart attack or a seizure!"

Mira and Lisa followed Hector the Hunter into the room.

Cazzii was there, on the floor, or the one, living, cryptid – Bigfoot - they had captured. No one at the nameless Rand Biotech building knew that the cryptid's – Bigfoot's – name was Cazzii. She was gasping, struggling to breathe, shaking her arms and legs in an uncontrollable frenzied fit.

"Quickly!" Mira shouted to Lisa. "Load up a syringe with chlordiazepoxide, pentobarbital, diazepam, butalbital, whatever you can find!"

Lisa did not hesitate. There were several well-stocked standard medical cabinets nearby. Lisa was fervently ruffling through the medical cabinets searching for the sedatives Mira had asked for. She immediately filled a syringe and handed the syringe to Mira, who in the meantime, was doing her best to check Cazzii's vitals.

"Good!" Mira took the syringe from Lisa and immediately injected Cazzii in the thigh with the syringe. It only took a few seconds. Cazzii stopped shaking her arms and legs and her breathing returned to a normal, even, inhaling, and exhaling, gasp.

"What the hell is this!" Mira said to Security Expert Springfield, Hector the Hunter, and F.B.I. Agent Caneo, who were standing over Mira and the cryptid – Bigfoot – silently watching them.

Cazzii had her hands and legs chained together by her wrists and ankles and she also had a chain around her neck which resembled an oversized dog collar. One of her eyes was swollen completely shut and there was dried blood all over one side of her face that had, obviously, flowed out from her nose and mouth.

It was CEO Rand, himself, who answered Mira as he was, nonchalantly, strolling into the room as if he was taking a walk through the park on a sunny day and didn't have a care in the world.

"We want to know where they are hiding the magic glowing rocks. Especially the big one." CEO Rand seemed to be sneering, or was that his natural, normal, facial expression which he has been keeping hidden when he is in public, outside the privacy of his mansions, townhouses, and private islands? "We especially want to know where they are hiding the biggest of the big magic rocks. A magic rock rumored to be as big as a mountain!"

"Shouldn't we be trying to communicate and learn from these creatures?" Mira said to CEO Rand.

"These creatures! These creatures!" CEO Rand repeated. "These 'so-called' creatures are nothing more than oversized gorilla wannabe grizzly bears! A meteorite fell to Earth centuries ago! A meteorite from the other side of the cosmos that had been traveling in space for millions of years until it crashed into the Earth. A meteorite made up of subatomic particles capable of teleporting matter from one point in space to another point in space and back!"

CEO rand had to stop for a moment to catch his breath.

"They have it! Or they know where it is hidden under centuries of muck, soot, weeds, soil, sand, and dust!" CEO Rand made eye contact with Mira. "Your job, right now, is to stabilize the gimp so that we can inject it with amobarbital, and if that doesn't do the trick, we'll try sodium thiopental!"

You could clearly see that Mira was shocked at what CEO Rand was proposing. "Truth serums! The cryptid has barely survived whatever kinds of torture you have been subjecting her to! She won't survive a shot of amobarbital, let alone sodium thiopental afterwards. She'll die! She'll die! She'll definitely die!"

"She?" CEO Rand replied. "That is an 'it'! 'It' is not human!"

"She... it... is a living, breathing, and most of all – a creature of God!"

CEO Rand was not used to being disobeyed or arguing with subordinates.

"Do I need to find someone else who is capable of following simple instructions?"

Mira was immediately thinking it was better if she played along. They would replace her in a heartbeat! It was better if she stuck around. At the moment Mira was the only friend Cazzii had.

"Yes, sir! Sorry, sir!" Mira was suddenly as agreeable as she needed to be to remain on the premises. "I was only thinking of the wellbeing of the subject! The subject is barely holding on! You will not be able to interrogate the subject if the subject slipped away!" CEO Rand was eyeballing Mira, double checking to make sure he wasn't being played, which he was. Mira was smarter. Mira was better. You didn't need to be a fox to out fox a fox.

"Be quick about it then! The Feds are on their way here to take the gimp away!"

F.B.I Agent Caneo was on her cellphone talking to her superiors, when she heard CEO Rand say that, about the Feds being on their way here, she put her cellphone momentarily to the side to say to CEO Rand before returning to her cellphone call, "I'm so sorry Mr. Rand, but there's an incident at a nuclear power plant in Southern California, which I am forbidden to talk about. The presence of the cryptid has been requested, but they will not be arriving here until the morning... bright and early in the morning." F.B.I. Agent Caneo returned to her cellphone call.

"You here that! Everybody!" CEO Rand was saying out loud to everyone in the room at the magnetronic isolation chamber. "We have until the morning. It won't matter if there are two dead gimps, instead of one, when they pull up to pick them up!"

I have until the morning, Mira was thinking, after that, when the Feds finally arrive, they'll take away Cazzii to an unknown, hidden, secret, underground laboratory, somewhere, out in the middle of nowhere, where she will never be seen or heard from, ever, again.

CHAPTER THIRTY

When Neejat appeared/teleported, after disappearing/teleporting, from the wooded area, into the silo entrance/exit of the one of two nuclear reactors of the San Onofre Nuclear Power Plant. Orgu and Ugat were already there shooting, firing away, killing in cold blood, with their automatic rifles, any, and every, nuclear power plant employee they encountered, or were within firing distance.

Neejat knew better than to further incite the suspicions of Orgu and Ugat, and Tantoon, soon to be arriving/appearing/teleporting, into the nuclear reactor silo entrance/exit to join Orgu, Ugat, and Neejat. Orgu, Ugat, and Tantoon, will just as easily shoot Neejat – dead – on the spot, without any unduly provocations, if Neejat should show any resistance or disagree in any form or manner with their assault on the nuclear power plant. Neejat began firing his automatic rifle, but not at any living, breathing, souls. Neejat was firing his automatic rifle at the walls, ceilings, and floors, tricking Orgu and Nejat into believing that he was firing and killing the human workers at the nuclear power plant.

Tantoon was tricked, too, when he had finally arrived/appeared/teleported, into the silo entrance/exit of the nuclear reactor after Neejat.

After shooting and permanently rendering inoperable, any and all cameras, they were all then immediately placing bombs – C-4 explosives with detonators connected to gyroscopic sensors - on all of the doors to the entrances/exits of the nuclear reactor silo, with each of the five taking a predetermined section of the nuclear reactor silo, as they had planned in advance from the information they had acquired from the blueprints

242

they had stolen from the steel and concrete building complex/record storage facility.

When the gyroscopic sensors are switched on to the detonators connected to the C-4 explosives, any kind of movement, like opening any of the doors, will set off an explosion.

Neejat was doing his part, or appearing to be doing his part, to avoid alerting the others to his true intentions and motivations. He would have preferred to disconnect the gyroscopic sensors, or the detonators, to the C-4 explosives, and he would have gladly done so, except for the fact that he did not know, exactly, how to do that. He was afraid if he tampered with any of the bombs, in any way, that the bombs would go off and explode in his very face. The moment Neejat was out of sight of the other four, he slipped away behind several shelves of files inside the nuclear reactor silo and pulled out from his backpack, which he had been hiding and keeping secret from the others, a cellphone, which he immediately used to make a video call. Neejat was holding up the cellphone, showing whoever he was talking to, visuals of the nuclear reactor silo, via, the camera on the cellphone. After Neejat was done talking to whoever he was talking to, he quickly put the cellphone back into his backpack, hiding the cellphone, and continued to place the bombs they had been given on all the designated doors he was supposed to place the bombs on.

The bombs on all the doors to the entrances/exits of the nuclear reactor silo were supposed to hopefully, give Tantoon, Orgu, Ugat, Cynad, and Neejat enough time to place five whole bricks of C-4 explosives connected to timers on the nuclear reactor, itself, to blow-up the nuclear reactor and set-off a nuclear explosion which will incinerate and decimate Southern California and one/third of Nevada to the east and one/tenth of Mexico to the south.

No one had no idea as to the meltdown potentiality afterwards.

As far as Tantoon was concerned, he was hoping that the fires from the nuclear blast would keep burning all the way from the continent of North America, all the way through the planet, all the way down to China, on the opposite side of the planet.

Damn them all to Hell! Tantoon would keep muttering under his breath, barely audible to the others, but not to God.

God was hearing and listening and seeing – 7/24.

Tantoon picked up one of the discarded radios/walkie-talkies, certain nuclear power plant employees were carrying on their belts or that they had by their worktables and desks.

"Listen up!" Tantoon was saying into the radio/walkie-talkie. "We have placed bombs on all of the doors to the entrances and exits and in several other areas around the nuclear reactor silo! Do not attempt to open any of the doors! I repeat! Do not attempt to open any of the doors!"

The radio/walkie-talkie squeaked and fizzled and squeaked and rasped and fizzled a few times more. "Stand down and stand back! I Repeat! Stand down and stand back!"

Tantoon switched off the radio/walkie-talkie and tossed it aside, disregarding it and any other communication devices, altogether.

Tantoon was not interested in talking.

Tantoon did not come to talk, or rant, or to preach, or to make any speeches of any kind. He was here to complete a specific task, and no more, and that specific task consisted of setting off a nuclear blast to destroy Southern California and the surrounding areas.

Damn them all to Hell!

Where was God when you needed him?

Maybe it did not matter when it came to bare, barren, bereft, beasts who were vacant and devoid of eternal, everlasting souls.

CHAPTER THIRTY-ONE

Hector the Hunter rolled over to the side of the bed. He was completely naked and so was Lisa who was lying beside him on the other side of the bed.

"What are we doing?" Hector the Hunter was mumbling out loud. He was talking to himself. He had mistakenly thought that Lisa had fallen asleep.

"What do you mean?" Lisa propped her head up on the pillow. "We were just making love to each other. I would say what we were doing is having hot and heavy sex." Lisa giggled.

"No, I mean, what are we doing? What have we done? What are we going to be doing?" Hector the Hunter hesitated for a moment and then whispered, "About life…"

"Oh." Lisa said answering Hector the Hunter's question, which he more or less did not want or was expecting an answer, he was only asking the question to himself. "Oh. You're looking inside yourself. What do you see?" After she had said that, she immediately regretted that she had said that, or asked, it was a question as well as an off-hand statement.

"I see… someone… I do not recognize… sometimes. I see… someone… I never should have become." Hector the Hunter stood up from the bed.

"I have to go."

"Go where?"

"Don't worry about it. I have to take care of something."

"I'll come along, give you a hand."

"No. That won't be necessary. I'll be alright. This is something I have to do on my own."

"I'll make breakfast before you go"

"I don't have the time. Maybe next time."

Hector the Hunter quickly dressed and was out the door and driving along the boulevard before too long. What Hector the Hunter did not notice - while he was driving to go to wherever he was going - was Lisa in her own car following behind as far back away from him as she needed to be to remain unnoticed.

Meanwhile, Mira was fervently pacing back and forth in a vacant parking lot several blocks away from the nameless Rand Biotech building.

First one car pulled up into the vacant parking lot followed by another car. Dobie was in the first car and Kasper was in the second car.

Mira was seriously surprised to see them. She was completely caught off-guard.

"What are you doing here?" Mira asked them.

"Shouldn't we be asking you that?" Kasper said to Mira.

"We knew you were going to try to do something." Dobie added.

"Dobie called me." Kasper continued. "He told me to meet him downtown. He was driving by and saw you waiting in the vacant parking lot."

"We know what you're up to."

"We're here to help."

Mira didn't know whether to break down and cry or to hug the both of them.

Mira did both.

"Why are you here? Waiting here?" Both Dobie and Kasper asked Mira.

"I have to wait here for just a little bit longer." Mira was looking at the watch on her wrist to the road outside by the vacant parking lot to back at the watch on her wrist to back at the road outside by the vacant parking lot.

247

Dobie and Kasper kept looking at Mira looking up and down at the watch on her wrist to the road outside by the vacant parking lot and back and forth and back and forth again and again.

After not so much longer, headlights were spotted in the distance.

Another car slowly pulled into the vacant parking lot.

The other car remained, without moving, by the entrance of the vacant parking lot.

After a few short minutes, the other car slowly moved forward into the vacant parking lot to park beside where Mira, Dobie, and Kasper were waiting beside their own cars.

The door to the other car, slowly, opened. Hector the Hunter, slowly, stepped out of the car and slowly, walked towards where Mira, Dobie, and Kasper were standing together, waiting.

"For a moment there I was beginning to think that you weren't going to show up." Mira said to Hector the Hunter.

Hector the Hunter took a deep breath. "I'm here."

They didn't say anything anymore to each other. They all knew why they were there. They all began walking out of the vacant parking lot towards the nameless Rand Biotech building a few blocks away.

Finally Hector the Hunter spoke as they were crossing the street in front of the nameless Rand Biotech building. "We'll go around back, through the freight entrance. I have the keys." As they were walking towards the freight entrance in the back, Hector the Hunter pulled off his cap and was waving to the cameras surveilling the outside streets and perimeter of the building. He was waving to the cameras to let the on-duty security guards know that it was him entering the premises with a few guests through the back freight entrance. No need to panic. One of the big bosses was checking in at the middle of the night and he had some company with him. The on-duty security guards never questioned the big bosses when they were coming and going for whatever reasons, no matter whatever they happened to be doing. They didn't want to piss-off the big bosses. Hector the Hunter was hoping the night security supervisor wasn't in the CCTV (closed circuit television) room and that none of the other on-duty security guards would notify the night security supervisor. The on-duty security guards didn't want to piss-off the night security supervisor, too.

Sneaking into the magnetronic isolation chamber at the nameless Rand Biotech building to break out the cryptid - Cazzii – was easy, peasy, lemon, squeezy, considering that Hector the Hunter had a change of heart and had decided to help. They passed security checkpoint after security checkpoint with all the on-duty security guards waving the group on through, saying only, "Good evening Mr. Amaro." or "Working late, sir?" or "Let us know if you need anything, sir."

They finally made it to the basement without so much as a little fuss and unnecessary drama.

Good! Good! Good! Mira was thinking. When they finally reached the cryptid - Cazzii - she was still in a dazed trance after surviving being beaten, tortured, and injected with two separate, different truth serums.

Mira and Dobie quickly removed the chains from around her wrists, ankles, and neck.

Mira was gently shaking Cazzii by grabbing onto one of her shoulders.

"Wake up Cazzii! Wake up! Are you okay? Cazzii! We have to go! We have to go now! This is going to be your only chance to escape!"

Dobie and Kasper were looking back and forth at each other, shaking their heads.

Lisa, from since long ago, was no longer surprised by anything Mira said or did.

"What's a Cazzii?" Dobie was asking no one in particular.

It was Hector the Hunter who answered Dobie's question.

"Cazzii is the name of the cryptid. Dr. Salinas and the cryptid know each other. Dr. Salinas and the cryptid are friends."

"Friends?" Dobie parroted Hector the Hunter. "How is that?"

"It's a long story, better left unsaid, at the moment." Mira was saying as she was pulling a syringe out of her purse. "We don't have the time to reminisce and swap old war stories." Mira plunged the syringe directly into Cazzii's forearm. "I hope this doesn't kill her!"

"If the beatings and the torture and the truth serums haven't killed her already, a little amphetamines could only be no more than a little annoying." Hector the Hunter randomly commented.

"Okay Cazzii! Okay! Come alive! Come alive, girl! C'mon! C'mon!"

Cazzii began to stir a little, then she gasped and coughed, and gasped and coughed, again.

"Dr. Doberson! Dr. Weinberger!" Hector the Hunter was speaking directly to Dobie and Kasper. "Don't you think your time will be better spent if you two grabbed a gurney from the back and loaded the dead cryptid onto the gurney, while we see if we can revive the living cryptid! That is if the living cryptid doesn't also suddenly die. Then we will need two gurneys instead of one."

"Okay." Dobie said and then before Kasper or Dobie could say anything more, Hector the Hunter said to them. "Room B16! It's a cold storage room! The dead cryptid is inside there!"

"Okay." Dobie said again and was gone down the hallway followed by Kasper.

Cazzii struggled to stand but her knees were wobbling, and she fell back onto the floor, but her eyes were open, she was conscious, she tried to say to Mira, "Meee-raaa...." But Mira immediately stopped Cazzii from talking by squeezing her arm and slightly shaking her head from side to side, meaning – no – do not talk – do not say one single word - and flashing her eyes from side to side in the direction of Hector the Hunter, as a warning about Hector the Hunter, who was still in the room watching them.

"You need not worry Dr. Salinas. I wasn't born yesterday." Hector the Hunter playfully winked at Mira. "I know you and your friend – Cazzii – is that what you called her? I know the two of you can talk up a storm if you wanted to."

"I just want to get her out of here to safety. Do you know what's going to happen to Cazzii after the Feds take her away?"

Hector the Hunter casually sang the main passage from a popular song everybody had heard many times before – he sang - "Bye! Bye! Blackbird!"

"Exactly!"
Cazzii, very carefully and very painstakingly, was finally able to stand.

"Thank God!" Mira exclaimed excitedly.

When Dobie and Kasper entered the room wheeling in the gurney with the dead body of Ringru, Cazzii had immediately picked up Ringru's scent along with the stench of his decomposing corpse. Mira immediately saw the pain, hurt, agony, and sorrow, in Cazzii's eyes. Mira put a tender hand on Cazzii's shoulder. "Ringru will have wanted you to survive! You have to survive! For Ringru! For all the others! For the future of all the Citizenries of the world!"

Cazzii meekly nodded.

"Everybody! Follow behind me now this way quickly! Quickly now! Quickly!" Hector the Hunter said to everyone which was more of an order than a polite suggestion.

Everyone followed behind Hector the Hunter after quickly covering Cazzii's seven-foot (2.13 meter) frame with two to three hospital patient gowns.

As they were passing the several, few, security check points making their way to the back freight entrance/exit, each of the on-duty security guards couldn't help but notice the blanket covering the 'whatever,' 'something-something' on the gurney which was too big for the gurney by about a few feet (meters) and the other walking 'whatever,' 'something-something,' covered by two to three hospital patient gowns. Hector the Hunter would, nonchalantly, without any fanfare or fuss, wave on the group to keep walking, saying to the on-duty security guards at the security check points to stand down, stay alert, keep their eyes and their ears open, do not fall asleep on-post, do not abandon their post, and everything will be okay, everything will be fine. The on-duty security guards, especially, did not want to piss-off the security supervisor, so, they all were all staying off the radio and keeping their mouths shut.

Crystal – Crystal Gaines – and Red – Jason 'Red' Redfield of the security staff at the nameless Rand Biotech building had worked the day shift and were, either, home, sleeping soundly in their beds, or, out and about, having a good time, galivanting and revel rousing in the nightclubs and discotheques in downtown Denver and the surrounding areas; wherever a good party may be. Everything was going okay, everything was hunky dory, until they were about to load the dead cryptid onto one of the security vans parked inside the freight area.

"Is this why you left me all alone?" It was Lisa who was followed by Security Expert Springfield who was pointing a very lethal looking, very menacing looking, 9mm pistol at the – surprised – very surprised – group of reluctant conspirators and co-conspirators.

"Lisa!" Hector the Hunter and Mira, both, shouted out at the same time.

Dobie and Kasper were both looking a little, extra, dazed and confused themselves.

"What are you doing here, Kitten?" Hector the Hunter said to Lisa.

"Don't kitten me!" Lisa fired back at Hector the Hunter.

Security Expert Springfield took a few steps forwards towards where Hector the Hunter was standing and twirled the barrel of his 9mm pistol at Hector the Hunter while his 9mm pistol was still pointed directly at Hector the Hunter.

"You know what to do."

Hector the Hunter slowly lifted one hand and immediately stopped when Security Expert Springfield suddenly nudged his 9mm pistol, forward, at Hector the Hunter cautiously warning him.

"Ah! Ah! Ah! Carefully now old buddy! Very carefully now!" Meaning for Hector the Hunter to very slowly and very carefully disarm himself.

With his other hand, Hector the Hunter very slowly and very carefully opened one side of his jacket to reveal a firearm tucked inside a shoulder holster.

"I'm going to take out my gun now."

"Slowly... very slowly." Security Expert Springfield reminded Hector the Hunter.

With the tips of his pointer finger and thumb of his other hand, Hector the hunter slowly, very slowly lifted his 45 caliber revolver pistol out of the shoulder holster, then he slightly knelt down to the ground and dropped the 45 caliber revolver pistol onto the cement floor of the freight area.

"That's a good boy, now, Hector." Security Expert Springfield said to Hector the Hunter while smiling fiendishly. "You didn't fill out an itinerary for your unannounced field trip. Where are you going? Fishing? For a walk in the park?"

"We were just going out for a scenic drive." Hector the Hunter sarcastically replied. "We'll be right back in time for when the Feds arrive later this morning."

"I bet you will, old buddy. If your good friend Lisa here didn't give me a late night phone call I would never have been able to stop by to see you off to wherever it is you were going."

"We were going to come right back."

"Of course you were."

Mira whispered to Cazzii who was standing outside the open back door of the security van still covered by two to three hospital patient gowns. "If you hear a few loud bangs, Jump into the back of the security van as quickly as possible, the van is bulletproof, or when I say 'go'!"

Cazzii nodded slightly under the hospital patient gowns.

"And what do we have here?" Security Expert Springfield was saying meaning Cazzii covered by the two to three hospital patient gowns and the dead body of Ringru on the gurney covered by blankets.

Meanwhile, Kasper was slowly tiptoeing to the side, one tiptoe at a time, maneuvering himself to be standing at Security Experts Springfield's three o'clock while Security Expert Springfield was busy tormenting Hector the Hunter who was at his twelve o'clock.

"Taking our Bigfoot's for a walk in the park? Maybe, toss a frisbee back and forth, or a stick? Dogs and Bigfoots like sticks. The dead Bigfoot might not be so excited about going to the park and playing fetch."

Security Expert Springfield was amusing himself.

"What did the dead Bigfoot have to say about that?"

And then Kasper made his move. Kasper pulled out from inside his coat, which he had been keeping secret and hidden from the others, a 44 Magnum revolver pistol, the exact same type 44 Magnum revolver pistol Clint Eastwood used to have in all of his 'Dirty Harry' movies, and pointed the 44 Magnum revolver pistol, point blank, at Security Expert Springfield.

"Drop your weapon and put your hands up in the air!" Kasper spat on the ground to emphasize his point or just because he was feeling ornery. "And I've been dying to say this ever since your sorry, pathetic, psychotic ass showed up here!" Kasper snickered angrily at Security Expert Springfield. "Shut the fuck up! Asshole! You've been talking too much shit ever since the first minute you came from out of nowhere to harass and intimidate and generally break everybody's balls because you have no life! You're a loser! You have no balls!" Kasper was shaking his head, side to side. "Surprised that I have a pea shooter, too? Yeah! That's right! I used to be in the Marine corps! Once a Marine! Always a Marine!"

While Kasper was monolouging, F.B.I. Agent Caneo, suddenly, from outta nowhere, stepped out through from an open doorway, with her bureau-issued handgun, pointed, directly at Kasper.

"Freeze! Don't move!" Before F.B.I. Agent Caneo could shout out another command, Kasper had turned and fired off one shot – BOOM! - at F.B.I. Agent Caneo, hitting her in her right eye, instantly, blowing out her brains through the back of her head.

F.B.I. Agent Caneo fell back through the open doorway and was gone, in more ways than one. Gone - as in out of sight – and gone – as in dead.

Security Expert Springfield, immediately, very quickly, turned to the side and fired his 9mm pistol three times at Kasper before Kasper was able to react.

BANG-BANG-BANG!

In all of his bravado, Kasper forgot that Security Expert Springfield still had not dropped his weapon. The first bullet hit Kasper in the stomach, the second bullet hit Kasper in the throat, the third bullet hit Kasper in his left eye, blowing away the top upper left side of Kasper's face and head.

While Security Expert Springfield was shooting Kasper dead, Hector the Hunter was quickly crouching down on the ground to pick up his discarded 45 caliber revolver pistol to shoot Security Expert Springfield, but as Security Expert Springfield was shooting Kasper dead, he spotted the movements of Hector the Hunter crouching down to the ground from out of the corner of his eye.

Anyway, Security Expert Springfield was expecting Hector the Hunter to be trying to make a move like that.

BANG-BANG-BANG-BANG!

Security Expert Springfield shot Hector the Hunter four times as he had just gotten his hand on the 45 caliber revolver pistol and had just barely lifted up the gun a few inches (centimeters) from the ground. Security Expert Springfield also fired a few shots at Dobie, who he mistakenly thought might have had a gun of his own. Dobie was only trying to run for cover around to the front of the security van. Cazzii had done as Mira had told her to do and immediately jumped into the security van at the first BANG She had heard.

Mira remained where she was standing with her hands up through all of the mayhem, carnage, and madness.

The four bullets hit Hector the Hunter in the back of the head, the back shoulder, and the last two bullets hit him in the side of his lower chest and stomach.

Hector the Hunter dropped the 45 caliber revolver pistol to the cement ground again as he was falling over dead.

Dobie had been hit in the shoulder and was hiding, out of sight, under the front of the security van.

"Noooooooooo!" Lisa cried out. "Noooooooooo!" Lisa ran to where Hector the Hunter had fallen over dead on the ground and began hugging and cradling him in her arm as a puddle of blood was forming around where the dead body of Hector the Hunter had fallen.

"Noooooooooo! Why did you do that? I thought you two were old war buddies! I thought you two were like brothers!"

"We're here only for the money! That's the only reason he was here, too! For the money and only the money!"

Security Expert Springfield began to giggle and laugh. He enjoyed killing. He was having fun and he had just appeased his anger at the decades long grudge match he had been having with Hector the Hunter.

"He would've just as quickly and just as easily have shot me dead! Sweetie! I'm lucky to be alive! He's not so lucky!"

Before Security Expert Springfield could utter another word, Lisa had quickly grabbed Hector the Hunter's discarded 45 caliber revolver pistol from the ground and began firing it at Security Expert Springfield before he had even noticed or had time to react.

BOOM-BOOM-BOOM!

Lisa stood up from the ground and continued firing Hector the Hunter's discarded 45 caliber revolver pistol at Security Expert Springfield who had also fallen down to the ground from the impact of being hit by a few bullets.

BOOM-BOOM-BOOM!

Lisa kept firing even though the 45 caliber revolver pistol was now empty.

CLICK-CLICK-CLICK-CLICK-CLICK! CLICK-CLICK-CLICK-CLICK-CLICK! CLICK-CLICK-CLICK-CLICK-CLICK! CLICK-CLICK-CLICK-CLICK-CLICK! CLICK-CLICK-CLICK-CLICK-CLICK!

Lisa continued pulling the trigger of the empty 45 caliber revolver pistol until Mira, gently, very gently, took the 45 caliber revolver pistol from Lisa's hand saying to her, "Lisa... Lisa... please stop... please... Lisa... let it go... let it go..."

Lisa continued frantically sobbing as Mira helped Dobie onto the security van. Cazzii lifted the dead body of

Ringru and loaded him into the back of the security van. They quickly sped off in the security van as the other on-duty security guards at the nameless Rand Biotech building were running to the freight area responding to the sounds of gunfire.

Mira, Cazzii, a wounded Dobie, and the dead body of Ringru, sped off into the dark, cold, night.

CHAPTER THIRTY-TWO

Neejat and Cynad were standing back watching as Ugat was explaining to Tantoon and Orgu how to set the timers on the five timebombs they were going to attach to one of the two nuclear reactors at the San Onofre Nuclear Power Plant or attach to the outer perimeter of the radiation-proof wall surrounding the nuclear reactor. The nuclear reactor, itself, was lethal. The radiation levels were too high for anyone to be able to come near enough to stand several feet (meters) away, let alone touch with their hands; even with the most scientifically advanced radiation suits.

One timebomb would have been enough to do the job, to achieve the desired outcome, but as far as Tantoon was concerned; it was better to be safe than sorry.

Tantoon, Orgu, and Ugat had Neejat and Cynad standing back guarding the area with automatic rifles because they had only just recently graduated from being Rogues to becoming Sawtooths - newly learning how to speak, read, and write; in whatever language of whatever Citizenry they happened to have become part of.
Or so Tantoon, Orgu, Ugat, and even Cynad, were mistakenly thinking.

Neejat had examined and reexamined the scene and contemplated the proper course of action that was going to be necessary to be taken.

Cynad was standing beside Neejat, with his automatic rifle at the ready, watching in the opposite direction for any men with guns who will, beyond a question of a doubt, be soon arriving, to retake the taken nuclear reactor Silo while Neejat, with his automatic rifle, also at the ready, was supposed to be watching in the opposite direction for the soon to be coming men with guns.

They were not supposed to be there long enough for that to happen. After the five timebombs are attached to the outer perimeter of the radiation-proof protective wall surrounding the nuclear reactor, the plan was to disappear and reappear, teleport, outside the San Onofre Nuclear Power Plant and to keep disappearing and reappearing, teleporting, via, the magic, wonder, and mystery, of the wandererstones they had stolen, until they had disappeared and reappeared, teleported, so far away, they will be out of range of the nuclear blast.

That was the plan, but Neejat had, which will be much to the misgivings of the others, suddenly, on the spot, formulated, another, alternate, plan.

There was Cynad's automatic rifle, which he was holding in his hands, Neejat's automatic rifle, which he was also holding in his hands, and Tantoon, Orgu, and Ugat's automatic rifles, which were lying beside them, which they had, absent-mindedly, discarded while they were busy setting the timers on the five timebombs. Tantoon, Orgu, and Ugat had, finally, finished setting the timers on all five of the timebombs and had quickly finished attaching all five of the timebombs to the outer perimeter of the radiation-proof protective wall surrounding the nuclear reactor.

The combination of the five timebombs will cause the nuclear reactor to also explode, resulting in a nuclear explosion of such catastrophic and cataclysmic proportions, Southern California, including Los Angeles, San Diego, Baja California, two/thirds of southwest Nevada, and one/tenth of northern Mexico will be instantly obliterated.

They were almost nearly done with their evil deadly deed.

Neejat was looking back and forth and up and down and left and right at the automatic rifles and all around the room of the nuclear reactor silo.

Then Neejat had finally seen it!

The message!

The message Neejat had been waiting for ever since he had made the secret video call on the cellphone he had kept secretly hidden away from the others.

The message was a furry hand waving to him from around behind a corner in the room and another furry hand waving to him from around behind another corner of the room and a furry head or two peeking out from around behind a few other corners in the room.

The time had come to strike and for Neejat to show his hand; to use a card playing metaphor, so to speak. Without hesitating any further, Neejat grabbed away the automatic rifle from Cynad's hands, much to Cynad's surprise, shock, and horror, and in an instant, Neejat broke apart Cynad's automatic rifle into several many, little, pieces. Neejat, also, did so, to his own automatic rifle, and in the next instant, Neejat leaped across the room and jumped behind Tantoon, Orgu, and Ugat. Before Tantoon, Orgu, and Ugat had any time to react, Neejat, had also, just as quickly, grabbed up from the floor, Tantoon, Orgu, and Ugat's three remaining automatic rifles and smashed the three remaining automatic rifles, also, into several, many, little, pieces; just as he had done to Cynad's and his own automatic rifle.

Neejat had broken, bent, busted, and twisted, all of the automatic rifles the way Superman, could've and would've done, if Superman were real, or any other

Superhero with real superpowers, could've and would've done, if Superheroes were real.

"Neejat!" Tantoon shouted at Neejat. "What are you doing?"

Neejat stared directly into Tantoon's angry, fierce, hateful, wretched eyes and said to him.

"I am not Neejat. I am Cirroc, and I have never been a Rogue or Sawtooth. I was born into the Citizenry of the Heseetu. I was able to speak, read, and write, several months after I was born, many, many, years ago, and I have since, learned how to speak, read, and write, in several, different, other languages."

"I have thought as much!" Ugat was immediately commenting. "He has had too many slips of the tongue since he had first arrived and come into our confidence!"

"I have been trained by the best of the best Shadow-walkers to infiltrate and report on your activities and whereabouts and the activities and whereabouts of your fanatical followers."

Tantoon was gapped mouth. He was clearly in shock.

"By... by... by whom?" Tantoon asked Neejat, who had now revealed himself to being Cirroc of the Citizenry of the Heseetu.

"It was I who commanded Cirroc to infiltrate and expose your vile and decrepit schemes, unholy desires, and mad, insane, fixations!"

A voice from behind where Tantoon, Orgu, and Ugat were standing said to Tantoon, Orgu, and Ugat, as the furry foot from the voice kicked away and scattered across the room the pile of broken bits and pieces of Tantoon, Orgu, and Ugat's dismantled assault rifles.

Tantoon, Orgu, and Ugat turned to come face to face with Shantuu and twelve other Shadow-walkers, spread-out, throughout the room, who had along with Shantuu, appeared, teleported, into the nuclear reactor silo.

"Quickly now!" Shantuu commanded the twelve Shadow-walkers who had arrived with him. "Do not leave a single trace of our presence or existence behind to be scrutinized and catalogued." The twelve Shadow-walkers very quickly began putting away all of the equipment and supplies Tantoon, Orgu, Ugat, Cynad, and Neejat, now undisguised as Cirroc, had brought with them back the backpacks and into other separate bags and containers the twelve Shadow-walkers had also brought along with them. Ringru and Cazzii would have been part of Shantuu's twelve Shadow-walker team except for the fact that Ringru was deceased and Cazzii was currently recuperating from her recent ordeal.

Shantuu gestured for the one out of the twelve Shadow-walkers who had been specifically trained to handle explosives and explosive devices to remove the five timebombs from the outer perimeter of the radiation-proof wall surrounding the nuclear reactor.

"How dare you!" Tantoon roared at Shantuu.

"HOW DARE YOU!"

Tantoon pulled out a boneknife he had hidden inside a leather pouch strapped over his shoulder.

"HOW DARE YOU!" Tantoon leaped at Shantuu who was prepared to confront Tantoon.

Shantuu used the momentum of Tantoon lunging forward to bat him away to the side in another direction. Tantoon fell over away from Shantuu, but Tantoon was quickly back on his feet with the boneknife raised slashing side to side and stabbing forward and back at Shantuu who was blocking and side stepping each side to side slash and forward and back stab. Shantuu and Tantoon were circling each other and circling and circling and circling. Shantuu held up one hand, saying to the other Shadow-walkers in the room, "Not yet! Not yet!

"Not yet – what?" Tantoon said to Shantuu. "What do you mean by that? Not yet to kill me? Not yet to kill Orgu, Ugat, and Cynad?"

"We do not kill, Tantoon, we have never killed until now, and it was you, who has done the killing, after so many centuries, and centuries, and centuries gone by." Shantuu was shaking his head from side to side. "We have only killed when we have had to hunt to feed ourselves. We have never killed out of selfishness or folly."

"Humans kill! Humans kill each other's and others who are not of their kind. Humans kill out of anger and for fun and they kill making games of killing! They practice killing and invent more and more and more ways of killing until they have come to be able to kill the whole, entire, planet in one, swift, clean, swoop!"

Shantuu, in a lightning quick flash, leaped forward and slapped the boneknife out of Tantoon's hand. Shantuu grabbed Tantoon with both hands and picked him up, holding him up over his head. Shantuu spun Tantoon around, then he dropped Tantoon back down on the ground with a loud, hard, thud.

"Enough!"
Shantuu roared back at Tantoon.

"Do not ever compare us to them!"

"We are not savages like the humans!"

"Human hunters killed my mother." Tantoon cried, whimpering, as he was lying there on the floor. "Why did the human hunters have to kill my mother? Why? Why? Why? She never hurt anyone."

Tantoon reluctantly picked himself up from the floor. Everyone could clearly see that Tantoon was banged up a little more than he was willing to allow anyone to witness.

"Blood will only bring more blood." Shantuu replied. "You are dishonoring your mother. How many more mothers will die if you succeeded in doing what you were attempting to do here! How many more fathers and sisters and brothers will die if we had not come to stop you?"

Shantuu waved one of his hands, up and down, in the air, signaling the other Shadow-walkers to do what he had stopped them from doing the first time he had held up his hand in the air.

Tantoon noticed Shantuu signaling.

Zip!

Zip!

Zip!

Zip!

Tantoon felt a stinging sensation in his neck. He put his hand up to his neck and pulled out from the side of his neck a dart fired at him from a blowstick.

Darts from blowsticks had also been fired at Orgu, Ugat, and Cynad.

"A foreversleep dart? So, you are going to kill me, after all." Tantoon said to Shantuu.

Before Tantoon lost consciousness, Shantuu said to Tantoon.

"No. You are not going to be killed. We are not going to kill you. We do not kill. You have been hit by a dreamsleep dart. You, Orgu, Ugat, and Cynad will awaken in a cold, dark, icy, cave enclave in the Antarctic, where you, Orgu, Ugat, and Cynad will be held prisoner by the Citizenry of the Xanununu for the rest of your lives."

The Citizenry of the Xanununu have always lived throughout the centuries further north and south, at the Artic and Antarctic regions of the world. Their fur was usually solid white – which made them what folklore legend have always referred to as – Yetis
- and also, informally, as Abominable Snowmen.

Tantoon's eyes began to droop, he was still conscious, but not for much longer.

"It will be determined if your fanatical followers are indeed fanatics. Those who can be reeducated and renounce their wicked and evil aspirations will be forgiven and pardoned. Those who are determined to be indeed fanatical and incorrigible, will join you, Orgu, Ugat, and Cynad in your cold, dark, icy, cave enclaves, which are not so much cave enclaves, but cold, dark, icy, prison cells." Tantoon was going to be passed out cold, sleeping like a baby, in the next second or two.

Before Tantoon became completely unconscious, Shantuu said to him.

"Good-bye and farewell, Tantoon, and sweet dreams, even though I know your dreams will never be dreams, but nightmares, and your nightmares will never be sweet."

>>>>><<<<<

When the S.W.A.T. team of the San Onofre Police Department, in a joint venture with an F.B.I Emergency Response team and a National Security Anti-Terrorism team had finally, successfully, retaken the one of two nuclear reactor silos that had been breached at the San Onofre Nuclear Power Plant – they found nothing there. There was no one there. No terrorists. No bombs. No guns. No evil doers. No blue Meanies.

Nothing.
It was as if ghosts had come and gone, or,
appeared and disappeared/teleported?
But nobody would ever believe that.

EPILOGUE

A few months later, in a cave enclave in another cave dwelling of the Citizenry of the Heseetu in a canyon in Pine Valley in the Colorado Rockies, which was a long way, far away, east of the Heseetu cave dwelling in Blue Valley, that had been discovered and overtaken by a group of hired professional soldiers hired by Rand Biotech, or heartless mercenaries, a few months ago. Cazzii had just given birth to Ringru's child. She named the child Ringru, after the child's father, who was no longer with us. "Congratulations Cazzii!" Shantuu said to Cazzii. "Do we call the new addition to the Citizenry of the Heseetu – Ringru Jr.? or Ringru the 2nd? Shantuu teased Cazzii.

Mimi entered the cave enclave. "We have a guest with us who has come to see the newborn child and congratulate the mother."

Mira stepped through the opening of the cave enclave.

"Congratulations Cazzii!" They all kissed and hugged each other; Mira and Cazzii, and Mira and Shantuu.

Cazzii held up the baby for Mira to see.

"Do you want to hold him?" Cazzii asked Mira. Being that the baby was a Bigfoot, he was a little over 2-foots (0.61 meters) tall and had to have weighed at least 80 to 100 pounds (36.29 kg to 45.36 kilograms) even though the baby was only one day old.

"I'm sorry, Cazzii." Mira politely confessed to Cazzii. "I'm only a weak, meek and mild-mannered human. Maybe, if I was into weightlifting then maybe I would be strong enough to be able to hold up the child in my arms. I don't want to break my back."

They all chuckled at that.

Mira and Dobie, after Dobie had recovered from his gunshot wound, had only just recently returned to working in the medical research field after being in hiding for a few months. CEO Rand had put out a contract on Mira and Dobie's lives. For a short while, there were a few hitmen and professional hired killers, out there, searching everywhere for Mira and Dobie, including, Crystal – Crystal Gaines – and Red – Jason 'Red' Redfield of the security staff at the nameless Rand Biotech building who especially wanted to personally avenge the death of their fallen Brother-in-Arms, comrade, and confidant, Hector the Hunter, but through friends of friends, namely, Lisa being one of the friends of friends, Mira had come into possession of a dossier compiled by Hector the Hunter. It was part of Hector the Hunter's retirement plan, containing documents, photos, videos and audio recordings detailing CEO Rand and Rand Biotech's illicit deeds and unscrupulous business practices, which if made public, would result in criminal charges being filed against CEO Rand and Rand Biotech. CEO Rand would have spent the rest of his natural life behind bars.

The lawyer who handled the negotiations, between Mira, Dobie, and CEO Rand and Rand Biotech, had connections in the underworld and the dog-eat-dog world of big business. He was an expert at dealing with cutthroat businessmen and psychotic gangsters. He was very expensive to hire, too expensive for Mira and Dobie to hire.

It was Shantuu, with a little help from other Citizenries from the past, who had come to Mira and Dobie's rescue, after finding out about their unfortunate predicament. Where do you think Mira and Dobie were hiding while all those hitmen and hired killers were out gunning for them? At one of the many cave dwellings of the Citizenry of the Heseetu in the Midwest of America. When Shantuu had found out, as a gift, he had given Mira a sack filled with nuggets of pure gold the Citizenry of the Heseetu had acquired going back from the California goldrush days to the Native Americans when the Spanish explorers had come to the New World on the Nina, the Pinta, and the Santa Maria, and further back to the Aztec Empire in the 15th and 16th centuries, to even further back to the Inca Empire from the years 1438 to 1533, who had built entire cities made of pure gold and decorated and adorned by other precious gems like rubies, diamonds, sapphires, and emeralds, long, long, ago.

And there were plenty more sacks filled with nuggets of gold, gold coins, precious gems, and artifacts made of gold and precious gems, available, if that was not enough to do the trick.

The Citizenries of the world had gold and precious gems like buried pirates treasure chests, and also the wandererstones, which made them the Gods of the Speed of Light, but they did not desire to be Gods, nor lust for wealth and greatness – they were always content with only a warm fire, the rising and setting of the sun, God, Mother Nature, and the beauty of the four seasons – winter, fall, spring, and summer.

The civilized beasts of the primeval worlds had long ago witnessed for far too long the depravity, hypocrisy, deceitfulness, and narcissism of civilized savage humankind and kept their backs turned, forever, looking away towards other near, not so near, and distant far away horizons.

Mira and Shantuu bid goodnight to Cazzii and Ringru Jr.? Ringru the 2nd? And stepped away to a separate cave enclave in the cave dwelling to discuss other important, crucial, serious, matters.

From a leather pouch, the same leather pouches Shantuu and Mira had been, secretly, exchanging with each other over the years during Mira's occasional hikes out into the woodlands, deserts, and forests. Shantuu produced a few vials of blood which he handed to Mira in exchange for certain experimental drugs, that, so far, have had no effect in curing or curtailing the progression of the disease unofficially designated, the 'undivining,' that has been plaguing the Bigfoot, Sasquatches, and Yetis of the world for these past few centuries.

Shantuu and Mira had both agreed on a day and time a couple of months from now where Mira and Shantuu will again, secretly, exchange leather pouches containing blood samples of those afflicted and those who have been taking the experimental drugs Mira and her fellow researchers have been developing to help find a cure, remedy, or vaccine, for the 'undivining.'

"We must be even more careful now. I'm being watched even more now by Bigfoot hunters, The F.B.I., other unknown, unidentified, scary, agents of other unknown, unidentified, scary, governmental agencies, and news reporters. There are news reporters out and about everywhere now these days. Dobie and I and a few other associates of ours have vowed to keep working on finding a cure, remedy, or vaccine.

So far, in the past few centuries nine/tenths of nine/tenths of the Bigfoots, Sasquatches, and Yetis, throughout the world, have died off from the disease of the 'undivining.'

The population of Bigfoots, Sasquatches, and Yetis over the centuries have gone from Citizenries of thousands, to Citizenries of hundreds, to Citizenries of less than hundreds. Where there used to be thousands in a cave dwelling and then hundreds in a cave dwelling, there were now only twenty to thirty, to maybe forty, sometimes fifty, but fifty is very rare now.

"I'm so sorry, Shantuu."

Mira said to Shantuu.

"We're never, never, never, going to give up. We're never, never, never, going to stop trying to find a cure for the 'undivining,' but at this point..."

It was hard for Mira to say what she was about to say to Shantuu, but he deserved to know the truth, it was his right to know the truth.

"At this point... the next generation, or the generation after the next generation, will be your last. After that, your species, your kind, will become extinct."

THE END

Made in the USA
Middletown, DE
14 March 2023

26728015R00163